Giuseppe Garibaldi

Autobiography of Giuseppe Garibaldi

Vol. II

Giuseppe Garibaldi

Autobiography of Giuseppe Garibaldi
Vol. II

ISBN/EAN: 9783741126475

Manufactured in Europe, USA, Canada, Australia, Japa

Cover: Foto ©Raphael Reischuk / pixelio.de

Manufactured and distributed by brebook publishing software
(www.brebook.com)

Giuseppe Garibaldi

Autobiography of Giuseppe Garibaldi

AUTOBIOGRAPHY

OF

GIUSEPPE GARIBALDI.

AUTHORIZED TRANSLATION

BY

A. WERNER.

WITH A SUPPLEMENT BY
JESSIE WHITE MARIO.

IN THREE VOLUMES.
VOL. II.

1849–1872.

London:
WALTER SMITH AND INNES,
(LATE MOZLEY),
31 & 32, BEDFORD STREET, STRAND, W.C.
1889.

CONTENTS OF VOL. II.

FOURTH PERIOD.

1860-1870.

FIFTH PERIOD.

AUTOBIOGRAPHY

OF

GIUSEPPE GARIBALDI.

SECOND PERIOD.

(*Continued.*)

CHAPTER VIII.

THE DEFENCE OF ROME.

THE legion's stay at San Silvestro was of short duration, as on the following day we received orders to encamp on the square of the Vatican, and then to garrison the walls from Porta San Pancrazio to Porta Portese. The approach of the French being imminent, it was necessary to prepare at once for their reception. The sun of April 30, 1849, was to shine upon the glory of the young and inexperienced defenders of Rome, and the shameful flight of the clerical and reactionary forces. General Avezzana's system of defence was quite worthy of that veteran of liberty, who, with unwearied activity, had provided for everything, and was to be found at all points where his presence was likely to be required.

Being charged with the defence between Porta San

Pancrazio and Porta Portese, I had established strong advanced posts outside these two gates, utilizing for this purpose the commanding situation of the palaces of Villa Corsini (Quattro Venti), Vascelli, and other points suitable for defence.

Observing the dominant position of these buildings, it was easy to conclude that they must not be allowed to fall into the enemy's hands, as, once lost, the defence of Rome would be difficult or impossible. During the night preceding the 30th, besides the scouts sent along the two roads leading to the gates guarded by us, two small detachments had orders to ambuscade themselves by the side of the road, at such a distance as to be able to pick up at least a few of the enemy's scouts.

At break of day I had a French cavalry-soldier on his knees before me, asking for his life. However insignificant this acquisition of a prisoner might be, I confess that it rejoiced me ; and I drew from it a happy augury for the day. It was France on her knees, making the *amende honorable* for the disgraceful and unworthy conduct of her rulers.

This prisoner was captured by the detachment under young Ricchieri, of Nice, with great courage and coolness. A squadron of French scouts was put to flight by our own, and the fugitives, though superior in numbers, even abandoned some of their weapons.

When one knows of the approach of an enemy, it is always a good thing to place some ambuscades on the roads he will have to pass over. Two advantages are in this case almost certain—that of knowing how far the head of the enemy's column has advanced, and that of making some prisoners.

Meanwhile, from the highest points in Rome, the hostile army was seen advancing slowly and with precaution, marching in column along the road from Civita Vecchia to Porta Cavalleggieri. Having come within cannon-shot, they placed some of their artillery in commanding positions, and deployed several corps, which resolutely marched up to attack the walls.

The French general's mode of attack showed an utter scorn of us; it was a case of Don Quixote and the windmills. He attacked us just as if we had had no ramparts, or as if our walls had been garrisoned with children. In truth, General Oudinot, the son of a marshal of the First Empire, had not thought it necessary, in order to crush " four *brigands d'Italiens*," to provide himself with a map of Rome.

He soon perceived that we were men defending our city against hirelings who were republicans in name only. Those gallant sons of Italy, after having calmly allowed the enemy to approach, poured into them a volley of cannon and musket-shots, which killed a great many of the most advanced.

From the height of Quattro Venti, I had seen the attack of the enemy, and the reception he met with from our men at Porta Cavalleggieri and the wall on either side. An attack on the enemy's right flank seemed to me a thing not to be despised; and I pushed forward two companies, who threw the French into great confusion. Being, however, greatly outnumbered by the enemy, they were obliged to fall back on their base of operations—that is, on the small houses outside the walls in that part of Rome.

In the first encounter, we had to deplore the loss of the gallant Captain Montaldi. Any one who knew Goffredo Mameli and Captain De Cristoforis can form an idea of Montaldi; he resembled them physically and morally. Montaldi in a battle, at the head of his men, was as cool and calm as when on the parade-ground, or conversing with a group of his friends. He had not, perhaps, as much education as the two brave champions of Italian liberty mentioned above, but the same intrepidity, the same courage, and the same genius. What a general he would have made! Italy has not lost the pattern of such men as he, and to such she ought to entrust her sons in the day of judgment for the tyrants, when all stains of outrage are to be washed away.

Montaldi had joined the Italian legion at Montevideo when it was first raised, and, though then very young, took part with his usual courage in innumerable engagements; and his was one of the earliest names entered on the roll of those about to cross the sea from Montevideo to serve their country's cause. Genoa may with pride carve Luigi Montaldi's name beside that of her warrior-poet, Goffredo Mameli.

The French, reaching our positions in the suburban houses, were received with a cross-fire from our posts, and halted, sheltering themselves behind the inequalities of the ground and the walls of the numerous villas in the neighbourhood, and firing thence as fast as they could load. In this way the fight lasted for some time; but when we received reinforcements from within, we charged the enemy with so much vigour that they gradually lost ground, and were at last driven into a precipitate retreat, while the cannon from the walls and a sally from Porta Cavalleggieri completed the victory. The French had a few men killed, and retired in confusion, leaving in our hands several hundred prisoners, and never stopping till they reached Castel Guido.

The principal honour of the day is due to the gallant General Avezzana, who had organized the defence. He showed himself indefatigable during the fight, wherever it raged most fiercely, and cheered on our young soldiers with his voice and his manly presence. General Bartolommeo Galletti, with his Roman legion, accompanied us during the action, and contributed greatly to the victory. So also General Arcioni, with the corps under his command, who, though he arrived late, had a hand in the enemy's discomfiture, and also made a large number of prisoners.

A battalion of young students at the university, and other fractional corps associated with the legion during the battle, also behaved exceedingly well. A Prussian colonel, Haug—the same who was general with us in 1866—served under me as staff-officer, through the whole action, with great courage and coolness.

Marrocchetti, Ramorino, Franchi, Coccelli, Brusco (Minuto), Peralta, and all my Montevideo comrades, maintained their just reputation for bravery. Musina,

Daverio, Nino Bonnet, and other gallant fellows whose names I wish I could remember, also behaved brilliantly.

This first engagement with regular troops greatly raised the *morale* of our legion, as they subsequently proved.

The day following the attack, I had orders to reconnoitre the enemy, and marched with the legion and a small number of cavalry towards Castel Guido, where we remained part of the day in sight of them. Towards afternoon, a French surgeon came to open a parley, and I sent him to the Government. General Oudinot, feeling himself too weak to attack Rome, was trying to temporize by means of negotiations, while waiting for reinforcements from France. We could easily have taken advantage of his weakness and his fears to drive him back into the sea; we might have settled accounts afterwards.

In May took place the two affairs at Palestrina and Velletri, in both of which the legion covered itself with glory. Arrived at Palestrina, the Neapolitan troops of the Bourbon, who some time before had invaded the Roman territory in conjunction with French, Austrians, and Spaniards, attacked us, and were completely repulsed. Among those who distinguished themselves then were Manara with his gallant Bersaglieri, Zambianchi, Marrocchetti, Masina, Bixio, Daverio, Sacchi, Coccelli, and others. At Velletri, where Rosselli, the general-in-chief, was in command, the fighting was the more serious that the King of Naples was present in person with the whole force of his army, while we had in all about 8000 men. Leaving Rome in order to get into the rear of the Neapolitan army, we followed the Zagarolo road as far as Monte Fortino. I had been selected by General Rosselli to command the main body; but, as Colonel Marrocchetti was in the van with the Italian legion, specially attached to me from its first formation, and principally composed of my old comrades, I marched with the vanguard, picking up information as to the enemy's movements from the inhabitants, and sending it to head-quarters.

I inferred, from the answers to my careful inquiries, that the enemy were retreating, and soon found this impression to be correct. Having arrived with the van at the heights which overlook Velletri, in the direction of Monte Fortino, I halted my troops, and, after reconnoitring, made them deploy to right and left of the road to Velletri. The third line regiment, which also belonged to the vanguard, remained in part on the road, as a reserve column, while some companies were écheloned in the vineyards which commanded it on either side, the road being formed by a cutting.

Two guns placed in a commanding position behind the third regiment covered the road, and Masina's cavalry were partly sent on as scouts, partly kept in reserve. The enemy had sent on the baggage and heavy artillery towards Naples, by the Via Appia; but, still having the greater part of his forces at Velletri, and being informed of the small numbers opposed to him, wished at least to attempt a reconnaissance. He therefore advanced a column along the road in our direction, assisted and supported by strong lines of sharpshooters on his flanks, in the vineyards; and attacked our outposts with great fury, driving them back on our main body.

Part of the vanguard of the Neapolitan cavalry had charged a few of our horse, who were out along the road as scouts; and, to support the latter, I had the enemy's cavalry charged by our small reserve of horse, who gallantly beat them off. But when the reserve reached the top of a rise in the road, they met the van of the principal column marching towards us, and naturally retreated, charged a second time by the Bourbon cavalry. Our horses, mostly young and untrained, rushed back at full gallop; and as this seemed to me scarcely decent in the presence of so many friends and enemies, I was imprudent enough to throw my horse across the path to check their flight, which was also done by some of my staff, and my brave black assistant, Andrea Aguiar. In an instant the spot where I stood was a heap of prostrate men and horses. Unable to hold in their horses, our cavalry had rushed upon us with such fury that they knocked us over and fell themselves, thus forming a shapeless heap in the narrow cutting, which was so blocked up that not a single foot-soldier could have passed. The enemy's horsemen rode up to sabre us, but we were saved by the confusion; and immediately after, our legionaries drawn up in the vineyards on either side of the road, at the word of their officers, energetically charged the Neapolitans, drove them back, and relieved us from a distressing embarrassment. A company of young lads on my right, seeing that I had fallen, rushed like furies on the enemy; and I believe that my safety was chiefly due to those gallant boys, since, with men and horses passing over my body, I was so bruised that I could not move. I rose at last, with great difficulty, and felt all my limbs to see if there was anything broken. The charge of our men on the right—the dominant position, and therefore the key of the whole—led by Masina and Daverio, was made with such headlong impetus that our men almost entered Velletri, swept away among the flying enemy.

Having got somewhat nearer to the city, I was able to assure myself still further that the enemy's arrangements were all with a view to retreat. Besides the information I had received as to the march of the baggage and heavy artillery, I could clearly see the Neapolitan cavalry, arranged *en échelon*, on the other side of Velletri, parallel to the Via Appia—that is, on the road by which they were to retreat.

Meanwhile I sent a full report to the commander-in-chief, but, unhappily, our main body was detained in the rear, near Zagarolo, waiting for the provisions, which were long in coming from Rome. I, on the other hand, had rationed my men as we went along, by killing some of the cattle which we found in abundance in the rich estates close at hand, belonging to cardinals.*

* I mean to write calmly about Mazzini, but I will not lie to my own conscience; and when I say Mazzini, I mean the Roman

At last the commander-in-chief and the heads of our columns arrived, about 4 p.m.—the battle had been fought during the forenoon.

I was a long time trying to convince General Rosselli of the enemy's retreat, but in vain; and, notwithstanding my representations, he ordered a feigned attack immediately on his arrival, and afterwards made the troops take up a position suitable for an attack on the following morning. But the enemy did not find that it suited him to await our convenience, and evacuated Velletri in the night, making the soldiers march barefoot, and bandaging the wheels of the cannon, so as to retire more silently. At dawn we knew that the town was clear of the Neapolitans, who could be seen, from its highest points, swiftly retreating along the Via Appia, toward Terracina and Naples.

From Velletri, our main army, with the commander-in-chief, retired to Rome, while I had orders from the latter to invade the state of Naples, by way of Anagni, Frosinone, Ceprano, and Rocca d'Arce, where I arrived with Manara's Bersaglieri, who formed the vanguard.

Government, since he was virtually Dictator of Rome—a title of which, though he would not assume the responsibility, it is well known that he had the power—knowing the modest and pliant character of the triumvirs, Saffi and Armellini. The Dictator Mazzini, then, who took umbrage at the position of Avezzana and myself, sent the former to Ancona, while I was left to defend Porta San Pancrazio, and Colonel Rosselli was appointed commander-in-chief—a man who, I believe, would have done his duty excellently well at the head of his regiment, but who had not sufficient experience to take the supreme command of the republican army.

The Masi regiment, the Italian legion, and a few cavalry followed our movements. The gallant Colonel Manara, in the van with his Bersaglieri, was in pursuit of a Neapolitan corps under General Viale, who did not stop for a single moment to see who was pursuing them. At Rocca d'Arce we were met by several deputations from the neighbouring villages, who came to greet us as their deliverers, and request our entrance into the kingdom, where they assured us of general sympathy and adhesion.

There are critical moments in the life of nations as well as of individuals, and this was a solemn and decisive occasion—one, indeed, that required positive genius to meet it.

I had my own opinion, and was preparing to march on San Germano, which we could have reached with little trouble and no opposition. We were in the heart of the Bourbon states, on the slopes of the Abruzzi, whose stalwart mountaineers were quite ready to pronounce for us. The good-will of the population; the demoralized state of the Neapolitan army, which had been beaten in two engagements, and which I knew to be on the point of dissolution, as the soldiers were anxious to return to their homes; the ardour of my young soldiers, victorious in all battles so far, and therefore ready to fight like lions without inquiring the number of the enemy; the still unconquered state of Sicily, encouraged by the defeats inflicted on her oppressors;—all these considerations inclined me to think our success exceedingly probable, if we only pushed on boldly. And yet, in spite of all this, an order of the Government recalled me to Rome, which was again threatened by the French! To palliate such an act of untimely weakness, such a fatal error, they left me the choice of marching along the Abruzzi or not, as I liked, on my return route.

If this man—who had called on me to repass the Ticino, in 1848, after the capitulation of Milan, and not only kept my volunteers back in Switzerland, but got them to desert from me, even after the victory of Luino, sending Medici to tell me that he and his would have done better; who, yielding to my own opinion, had let me march to l'alestrina and succeed there, but afterwards, I know not for what motive, sent me to Velletri, under General Rosselli's orders; —if Mazzini, in short, who had the casting vote in the Triumvirate, had been willing to understand that I might possibly know something about war as well as he—he would have been able to leave Rosselli at Rome, entrust the second enterprise, as he had done the first, to me alone, and let me invade the kingdom of Naples (whose defeated army was disordered beyond recovery, while the populace were awaiting us with open arms). If, I say, he had acted thus, how differently would things have turned out! What a future just then presented itself before an Italy not yet disheartened by foreign invasion!

Instead of this, he summons all the troops of the state from the Bourbon frontier to Bologna, and then reconcentrates them at Rome, thus allowing the tyrant of the Seine—who, if his 40,000 men had not been enough, would have sent 100,000—to annihilate us at a single blow.

Any one who knows Rome and its eighteen miles' circuit of walls, is well aware of the impossibility of defending it with a small force against an army which, like that of the French in 1849, is superior in numbers and in every kind of munition of war.

It is therefore obvious that the whole force of the Roman army ought not to have been employed in the defence of the capital, but the greater part should have occupied the impregnable positions with which the territory abounds, and the whole population have been called to arms; while I should have been permitted to continue my victorious march into the heart of the Neapolitan kingdom; and, finally, after having sent out as many means of defence as possible, the Government itself should have left Rome, and established itself in some central and defensible situation.

It is true that at the same time some measures ought to have been taken to secure the public safety against the machinations of the clerical element. This was not done, and the priests were left, with an ill-judged toleration, to plot and intrigue, and, in the end, contribute to the fall of the Republic and the misfortunes of Italy.

Who knows what results might have followed the salutary measures detailed above? Our fall—if we were destined to fall in any case—would at least have taken place after we had done our very utmost, and certainly not till after that of Hungary and Venice.

On arriving at Rome after my return from Rocca d'Arce, and seeing the way in which the national cause was being managed, I claimed the dictatorship—as sometimes during my previous life I had demanded and seized the helm of a vessel which was being driven on the breakers. Mazzini and his partisans were scandalized. However, a few days after, on June 3, when the enemy, who had deluded them, had made himself master of the positions commanding the city, which we vainly attempted to retake at the cost of many precious lives,—then, I say, the head of the Triumvirate wrote to me, offering me the post of commander-in-chief. Being employed in the post of honour, I thought it as well to thank him, and go on with the bloody work of those ill-omened days. Oudinot, having received all the reinforcements he needed, thanks to the negotiations with which he had lulled to sleep the suspicions of the Republican Government, prepared for action, announcing that he would recommence hostilities on June 4, and the Government trusted to the word of the faithless soldier of Bonaparte.

From April to June, as long as the danger lasted, not a single defensive work had been thought of—not even on those important and commanding positions outside the walls which form the key to Rome. I remember that on April 30, after the victory, General Avezzana and I, in a conference at the Quattro Venti, had determined to fortify this eminence and some other lateral positions of almost equal importance. But Avezzana was sent to Ancona, and I was occupied with other business. There were a few men on outpost duty outside Porta San Pancrazio and Porta Cavalleggieri, the enemy being on that side, in the direction of Castel Guido and Civita Vecchia. I returned from Velletri, I confess, grieved to the heart at the ruinous course taken by my country's affairs. The legion then occupied San Silvestro, and no one seemed to think of anything but letting the soldiers rest after the toils of the campaign.

Oudinot, who had given us warning for June 4, found it better to take us by surprise in the night between the 2nd and 3rd. In the early hours of the morning, we were awakened by the sound of firing near Porta San Pancrazio. The alarm was sounded, and the legionaries, though worn out with fatigue, were under arms in a moment, and marching towards the spot where we heard the fighting going on. Our men who garrisoned the posts outside the walls had been surprised in a cowardly way, massacred or made prisoners, and the enemy was already in possession of Quattro Venti and other important points when, in all haste, we reached Porta San Pancrazio. In the hope that it was not yet occupied by a great number, I ordered an attack on the Casino of Quattro Venti, feeling that on our possession of this point depended the safety of Rome. It was attacked, I do not say bravely, but heroically ; first by the Italian legion, then by Manara's Bersaglieri, and lastly by several other corps in succession, supported by the artillery from the walls, till night had fallen.

The enemy, knowing the importance of the position I have mentioned, had occupied it with a strong body of their best troops; and we vainly attempted to regain possession by attacking it repeatedly with our bravest men.

The Italians, led by the gallant Masina, actually entered the building, and there fought the French man to man, several times even driving back the hardy soldiers of Africa. A tremendous struggle at close quarters began; but the enemy was too far superior in numbers, and several fresh reinforcements arriving in succession rendered our men's heroic efforts useless.

I sent Manara's corps, which had shared our glory in all previous battles, and, though small, was of perfect bravery and the best disciplined one in Rome, to the assistance of the Italian legion. The struggle lasted for a time within the walls of the building, but at last, overpowered by the still-increasing numbers of the enemy, our men were forced to retreat.

This action of June 3, 1849—one of the most glorious for the Italian arms—lasted from dawn till night. Various attempts were made to retake the Casino dei Quattro Venti, but all resulted in a terrible loss of life. In the evening, after dark, I had the assault tried once more by some fresh companies of the *Unione* regiment, supported by others. They marched up to the Casino with great daring, and then engaged in a fearful struggle, but were too hard pressed by the enemy, and, after losing their commander and a great number of the men, were obliged to draw back. Masina, Daverio, Peralta, Mameli, Dandolo, Ramorino, Morosini, Panizzi, Davide, Melara, Minuto—what names!—and many other heroes whom I cannot recall by name, on that day fell victims to the priests, and to the soldiers of a fratricide Republic.

Rome, freed from the unholy arts of these plunderers, will one day build a monument to those noble sons of Italy, on the ruins of the mausoleum erected by the priests to the foreign robber and murderer.

The original Italian legion, consisting of barely 1000 men, lost twenty-three officers, nearly all killed. Manara's corps, and the *Unione* regiment, which had fought with equal valour, also suffered heavy losses; not to mention the officers of other corps, whom I do not remember.

The 3rd of June decided the fate of Rome. The best officers had been killed or wounded; the French remained masters of the key to all the dominant positions, and, with their great strength in numbers and artillery, had firmly established themselves there. In the lateral positions carried by surprise and treachery they began regular siege-works, as though they had to deal with a fortress of the first order, which proves that they had met with Italians who did fight.

I will pass over the siege-works, parallels, breaches, bombardment with mortars, etc. All this, I think, has been related in detail by many others; and I should not be able to do it with great accuracy, being at the moment without the necessary data and documents. What I can assert, however, is that from April to July our raw levies fought creditably enough against a veteran army, far superior in numbers, better organized, and possessed of immense resources. At each position the ground was disputed foot by foot, and there is not a single example of flight before so formidable an enemy, or of a battle in which they yielded to force of numbers without Homeric fighting.

As I said above, the corps were robbed of the best officers and men. In the corps of the line, those which had formerly constituted the papal army, some who had behaved well at first, now, seeing the hazardous position of affairs, presented that inactive and ill-humoured aspect which precedes disaffection or treason. This they showed in a Jesuitical fashion, quite in accordance with their clerical training, by refusing to perform the services demanded of them.

Some of the superior officers in particular, who lived in hopes of a papal restoration, and whom the Republican Government had been either unable or unwilling to get rid of, not only refused to obey orders, but attempted to stir up disaffection among all ranks of their subordinates—a course of conduct which caused endless annoyance to the good and gallant Manara, my chief of staff, and was at the same time an undoubted presage of our ruin.

We tried a night-sortie, but a panic among the front ranks, which spread to the whole column, completely nullified the enterprise. We had no longer sufficient forces to garrison all the posts outside the walls, and therefore had to abandon some of them. Villa Vascello alone was held to the end by Medici and his men; and when at last it was evacuated, nothing remained of the spacious building but a heap of ruins.

The situation grew more difficult every day. Our brave Manara found it less and less easy to find men for outpost and line duty, indispensable as this was for the public safety. The weakness of this part of the defence was certainly a potent cause of the easy entrance effected by the mercenaries of Bonaparte through the breaches their cannon had already made.

If Mazzini (and the blame rests on no one else) had had as much practical capacity as fertility of imagination in planning movements and enterprises, and if he had possessed—what he always claimed to have—the genius for directing warlike affairs; if, moreover, he had been willing to listen to some of his friends, who, from their antecedents, might be supposed to know something; —he would have made fewer mistakes, and, in the crisis I am describing, might, if he could not have saved Italy, at least have indefinitely retarded the Roman catastrophe; and, I repeat, have left Rome the honour of having been the last to fall, instead of succumbing sooner than Venice and Hungary.

I had sent Manara—the very day before his glorious death—to Mazzini, with a message suggesting that we should leave Rome, and march with all available men and supplies, of which we possessed a considerable amount, to some stronghold in the Apennines. To this day I do not know why it was not done. History does not lack precedents. Of one such salutary resolution I myself witnessed an instance in the Republic of Rio Grande. The United States furnish another, also of comparatively recent date. It is not true that such a measure was impossible, for when I left Rome a few days later, with about four thousand men, I met with no obstacles. The representatives of the people, mostly young and energetic patriots, much beloved in their native districts, might have been sent thither to kindle the enthusiasm of the populace, and so tempt fortune once more.

Instead of this, it was said that defence was becoming impossible, and the representatives remained at their posts—a courageous resolve, honourable to them as individuals, but not greatly tending to promote either the glory or the interests of their country. Nor were they to be praised for adopting it, while our resources were yet abundant, and Hungary and Venice were still in arms against the enemies of Italy.

Meanwhile we were awaiting the entrance of the French, to hand over to them the arms by whose means a painful and shameful period of slavery was to be prolonged. I myself, having a handful of comrades that I could count on, was resolved not to surrender, but take to the country and try our fate again.

Mr. Cass, the American ambassador, knowing how matters stood, sent to me on July 3, saying he wished to speak with me. I started for his house, but met him before reaching it; when he told me, with great kindness, that an American corvette at Civita Vecchia was at my disposal, if I wished to embark, with any of my friends who might be compromised. I thanked the generous representative of the great republic, but stated that I intended to leave Rome with all who might be willing to follow me, as I would not believe that my country's cause was lost, without striking one more blow to retrieve it. I then turned towards Porta San Giovanni, where I was to meet my followers, who had orders to prepare for leaving the city. On reaching the square, I found most of them awaiting me; the rest were gradually arriving. Many men belonging to other corps, who had guessed or been informed of our project, also came to join us, rather than submit to the degradation of laying down their arms before the priest-ridden soldiers of Bonaparte.

CHAPTER IX.

RETREAT.

My dear Anita, in spite of my entreaties that she would remain behind, had resolved on accompanying me. In vain I reminded her that she was again about to become a mother, and that I should be exposed to a life of tremendous hardships, privations, and dangers, surrounded by enemies on every side; this consideration seemed only to confirm her resolution. At the first house we came to, having asked a woman to cut off her hair, she put on men's clothes, and mounted a horse.

After having made sure, by observations from the top of the ramparts, that none of the enemy's troops were visible on our route, I gave orders to march along the Tivoli road, ready to fight in case any attempt should be made to obstruct our progress. The march took place without opposition, and on the morning of July 3 we reached Tivoli, where I intended as far as possible to organize the miscellaneous elements which formed my small brigade.

Up to this time, things did not look quite desperate. The majority of my best officers were missing, dead or wounded—Masina, Daverio, Manara, Mameli, Bixio, Peralta, Montaldi, Ramorino, and so many others. But some still remained—Marrocchetti, Sacchi, Cenni, Coccelli, Isnardi; and had it not been for a general depression of spirits, on the part of both soldiers and civilians, I could have carried on a glorious war for some time longer, and given the Italian nation—once recovered from their surprise and dejection—an opportunity of shaking off the yoke of foreign plunderers. But, alas! this was not to be.

I soon perceived that there was no inclination to continue the glorious enterprise placed before us by fate. When I marched northward from Tivoli, to throw myself into the midst of an energetic population, and kindle the flames of their patriotism, not only was it impossible for me to enlist one man, but night after night, as if they had felt the need of committing the shameful act under cover of darkness, some of those who had followed me from Rome deserted.

In my own heart I often recalled the steadfast endurance and self-abnegation of those Americans among whom I had lived, who, deprived of every comfort of life, content with any kind of food, and often with none at all, kept up a war of extermination for many years in deserts and forests, rather than bow the knee to a tyrant or a foreign invader. When I compared those brave sons of Columbus with my unwarlike and effeminate countrymen, I was ashamed to belong to these degenerate descendants of the greatest of nations, who were incapable of keeping the field a month without their three meals a day.

At Terni we were joined by the gallant Colonel

Forbes, an Englishman, who loved the Italian cause as well as the best of us could have done. He was a most brave and honest soldier, and brought with him several hundred well-drilled men.

From Terni we proceeded northward, twice crossing the Apennines, but none of the inhabitants responded to our appeals. The muskets abandoned in these wholesale desertions were carried with us on mule-back; but their excessive number and the difficulty of transport at last forced us to leave them, with the ammunition, at the disposal of those inhabitants who were thought most trustworthy, that they might keep them hidden against the day when they should be weary of disgrace and defeat.

Though our situation was not a prosperous one, yet we might well congratulate ourselves on having, in quitting the neighbourhood of Rome, distanced the French corps which had vainly followed us for a time; and also escaped the Austrian, Spanish, and Neapolitan troops among whom we had afterwards found ourselves entangled.

The Austrians were seeking us everywhere—aware, no doubt, of our far from flourishing condition, desirous of increasing the glory so cheaply acquired in the north, and also jealous of the French successes. They knew perfectly well from their numerous spies (priests, indefatigable traitors to the land which, to her sorrow, still tolerates them) that our column was melting away day by day. Besides, the priests, being absolute masters of the peasantry, and all residents in the district (one peculiarly adapted for night-marches), kept our enemies minutely informed of all our affairs—of the positions we occupied, and every movement we undertook. I, on the other hand, could hear little about the enemy, as the friendly part of the population were thoroughly demoralized, and afraid of compromising themselves, so that, even for money, it was impossible to obtain guides.

Guided, then, by experts (I have seen the priests themselves, crucifix in hand, leading our country's enemies against us), the Austrians always found us at a certain hour of the day, all our movements being undertaken at night; but they usually found us in strong positions, where they durst not attack us. This kind of thing though very wearisome, and a fruitful source of desertion, continued for some time, our little column sustaining neither attack nor defeat. This proves how much we might have done in our country's service had the priests —and consequently the peasants—instead of being, as they always were, hostile to the national cause, been favourable to it, and used their influence against foreign oppressors.

We kept at bay such bodies of troops as the Austrians —who were then fresh from the victory of Novara, and had reconquered all the northern part of the Peninsula by mere marching—without their daring to attack us, though they were far more numerous than ourselves.

Our fellow-citizens should indulge in no illusions with regard to the country population. As long as they are under the domination of the clergy, supported by an immoral government, both peasants and priests will always be ready to betray the national cause. The Italian Government, which is in fault—being more positive than any doctrinaire—feels the unstable condition of the country, and, rather than trust to the masses (which it robs and misgoverns, but which might, if properly treated, furnish it with a superabundance of men and means to oppose any hostile power whatever), humbles itself to seek outside alliances, which are never disinterested.

Between the depressed state of the towns, as I have said, and the hostile condition of the priest-ridden country districts, our condition became exceedingly precarious, and we soon began to feel the effects of the reaction taking place in all the Italian provinces.

During the night I was obliged to change my position, as it was only to be expected that, if I remained more than one day in the same place, the enemy, possessed of exact information, would at once overwhelm us with their numbers; so that my movements became still more difficult than before. I could not obtain a single guide in Italy, while the Austrians had as many as they wanted! I leave this fact to the consideration of those Italians who continue to go to mass, and to confess themselves to those black-robed cockroaches.

In consequence, few incidents of importance took place till we reached San Marino, save a few unimportant skirmishes with the Austrians.

Two of our horsemen, sent out as scouts, were made

prisoners by the Bishop of Chiusi's peasants—a bishop, be it understood; and, if I am not mistaken, Chiusi has still a bishop at the present day (1872). I demanded my men—whom I certainly thought in danger, in the clutch of Torquemada's descendants— and they were refused me. I then, by way of reprisals, made a whole convent of monks march at the head of my troops, threatening to have them shot; but the archbishop was hard-hearted enough to give me to understand that there was plenty of raw material for monks left in Italy, and declined to restore the prisoners. I think, moreover, he was quite desirous of the massacre of his subordinates, intending to hold them up to the populace as holy martyrs; and, suspecting this, I let the monks go.

The most trying part, to me, of this retreat were the continued desertions, especially those of the officers. Even some of my old comrades were guilty of this baseness. Bands of deserters spread uncontrolled over the country, committing every species of violence. They were Garibaldi's soldiers! Being cowardly enough to abandon the sacred cause of their country, it was quite natural that they should descend to foul and cruel acts against the inhabitants. This distressed me more than anything else, and greatly heightened the misery and humiliation of our position. How could I follow up those lawless bands of ruffians, surrounded as I was by enemies? A few, caught in the act, were shot, but this was little use, as long as the greater number went unpunished.

The situation having become desperate, I tried to reach San Marino. The excellent republicans of this city, hearing of my approach, sent a deputation to meet me. While I was engaged in conference with them, an Austrian corps overtook our rearguard, and threw it into such confusion that all—or, at least, the majority—took to flight, almost without seeing the enemy. Warned of this disaster, I returned to find the men flying, and my brave Anita, with Colonel Forbes, making every effort to stop them. Incapable of fear herself, her face expressed the bitterest scorn, and she could not control her disgust at such an exhibition of terror in men who, a short time before, had been fighting bravely.

Here I must mention a small cannon, which a few of our brave Roman gunners, who had so greatly distinguished themselves in the siege, had brought along with them since the beginning of our retreat. With matchless patience and perseverance, without horses or appliances, they had dragged it along, with the greatest labour, over the rugged mountain-paths. On this day of flight, being deserted by the others, they for a time defended it alone; and only abandoned it after a desperate fight, resulting in the loss of some of their number.

These Austrians, accustomed to frighten Italians, also made use of those famous squibs—their favourite weapon—which they flung at us in marvellous profusion, and by which I have never yet seen a man injured. I hope my young countrymen will be able to treat these toys with the contempt they deserve, on the day—perhaps not so far distant, after all—when we shall teach those masters of the Tyrol that the air south of the Alps is fatal to them.

Arrived at San Marino, I wrote, standing on the steps of a church outside the city, the order for the day, which was expressed somewhat in the following terms :—" Soldiers, I release you from the obligation of accompanying me. Return to your homes ; but remember that Italy must not be left in slavery and shame ! "

The Austrian Government had communicated with that of the San Marino Republic, offering to make terms with us, on conditions we could not possibly accept. This occasioned a favourable reaction in the feelings of the soldiers, who resolved to fight to the last, rather than stoop to terms so ignominious.

Our agreement with the Government of the Republic was to the effect that we should lay down our arms within that neutral territory, and that then all should be freely allowed to return to their homes. Such was the treaty concluded with this Government ; we would make no terms with the enemies of Italy.

For my part, I had no idea of laying down my arms. With a handful of comrades, I knew that it was not impossible to cut our way through to Venice. A dear but painful hindrance was my Anita, now near her confinement, and very ill. I entreated her to remain in that city of refuge, where we were justified in thinking that she at least might find a secure asylum, and where the inhabitants had shown us much kindness. In vain ; that resolute and noble heart, indignant at all my remonstrances on this subject, silenced me at last with the words, " You want to leave me ! "

I determined to leave San Marino about midnight, and try to reach some Adriatic port, where we might embark for Venice.

As many of my companions were resolved to risk all for the sake of following me, especially some gallant Lombards and Venetians who had deserted from the Austrians, I left the town with a few men, awaiting the rest at a spot previously agreed upon. This arrangement caused some delay, and I was obliged to wait some time before I had got them all together.

During the day I wandered about the country, getting information as to the most accessible points on the coast. Fortune—in which I have never entirely lost faith—sent me a man who was of the greatest service in these difficult circumstances. Galopini, a courageous young man from Forlì, drove up in a cart to find me, and proved invaluable as a guide and scout, hastening with lightning speed to any place where the Austrians were to be found, making inquiries of the inhabitants, and keeping our men informed of the latest news. The intelligence brought by him decided me to proceed by way of Cesenatico. Galopini found some guides to take me thither, and we arrived about midnight. The Austrian guard we found at the entrance to the village were thunderstruck by our sudden appearance, and I took advantage of the momentary hesitation on their part, to order the men riding next me to get down and disarm them. It was the work of an instant; we entered the village and remained in sole possession, arresting a few gendarmes, who certainly had not expected us that night. One of our first steps was to requisition from the municipal authorities a sufficient number of boats for the transport of the men. Fortune, however, had ceased to favour us that night. There had been a violent squall from the sea, and the breakers were so heavy in the mouth of the bay, that it was almost impossible for vessels to put out.

Here I found the advantage of my seamanship. It was absolutely necessary that we should leave the port; day was at hand, so were the Austrians, and no retreat was open to us except by sea.

I went on board each of the *bragozzi* (fishing-boats), had a hawser fastened to two kedge-anchors lashed together, and tried to get out of the harbour in a small boat, in order to drop the anchors and warp the boats out. Our first attempts were fruitless. In vain we sprang into the sea, to push the boat by force of arm through the breakers; in vain we encouraged the rowers with cheering words and many promises. Only after repeated and laborious attempts did we succeed in carrying the anchors to the proper distance and sinking them. As, having let down the kedges, we returned to the harbour, gradually slackening the hawsers as we went, the last one, being thin and made of inferior hemp, parted and we had to do the whole of the work over again. Such mishaps were enough to drive a man crazy. At last I was obliged to return to the fishing-boats, and get fresh hawsers and fresh kedges; and all this with a sleepy and unwilling crew, who could be made to move at all—not to speak of doing the necessary work—only by means of blows with the flat of our swords. At last we tried once more, and this time succeeded in taking out the kedges as far as was needful.

My men embarked in thirteen fishing-boats.* Colonel Forbes was the last to go on board, having remained, as long as our preparations lasted, at the land-entrance to the village, constructing barricades to repulse the enemy in case they should arrive.

Having, by kedging, got out all the fishing-boats one after the other, with all the men on board, we distributed to each a share of the rations requisitioned from the municipal authorities. Some verbal instructions were then given to all, recommending them to keep as close together as possible, and we got under way for Venice.

The day was already somewhat advanced when we left Cesenatico; the weather had turned fine, and the wind was favourable. If I had not been so distressed by the situation of my Anita, who was in a deplorable state of suffering, I might have said that our condition—having overcome so many difficulties, and being on the way to safety—could be called fortunate. But my dear

* It will be seen that those willing to accompany me were still numerous—about two hundred. They fared none the worse for doing so. Many of those who remained behind fell into the hands of the Austrians, and were flogged—not to mention those shot. Let Italians remember this.

wife's sufferings were too great; and greater still was the misery caused by my own inability to relieve them.

What with the stress of weather, and the difficulties encountered in getting out of Cesenatico, I had not been able to turn my attention to the provisioning of the boats. I had entrusted it to an officer, who had collected all he could; but at night, in a strange village, where we had taken the inhabitants by surprise, he had procured but a small quantity of supplies, which were distributed among the different boats.

The chief thing wanting was water, and my poor suffering wife was tormented by a feverish thirst—no doubt one of the symptoms of her illness. I too was thirsty, worn out as I was by the night's work; and we had very little drinking-water. All the rest of that day we coasted along the Italian side of the Adriatic, at a certain distance off shore, with a favourable wind. The night, when it came, was most beautiful. The moon was full, and it was with a terrible misgiving that I watched the rising of the mariner's companion, contemplated by me so often with the reverence of a worshipper. Lovelier than I had ever seen her before, but for us, unhappily, too lovely,—the moon was fatal to us that night.

East of the point of Goro lay the Austrian squadron, left intact, and in undisturbed possession of the Adriatic, by the patriotic Sardinian and Bourbon Governments. I had heard from the fishermen of the existence of this squadron—anchored, perhaps, behind this very point— but all the information I had received was vague and uncertain. Pursuing our course for Venice, the first ship we discovered was a brigantine, the *Oriente*, I think, which sighted us to the north. As soon as she had sighted us, she put about to approach us.

I contrived to make the other boats understand that they were to alter their course to port, so as to approach the coast and get out of the line of the moonlight, in which it was easier for the enemy to discover our small craft.

This precaution was of no avail, the night being the clearest I had ever seen; and the enemy not only kept us in sight, but began, while we were still at a considerable distance, to signal our approach to the rest of the squadron with guns and rockets. I tried to pass between the Austrian vessels and the shore, turning a deaf ear to the shots aimed at us; but the crews of the other boats, terrified by the din of the firing and the increasing numbers of the enemy, retreated, and, as I did not wish to leave them, I went with them. When day broke, we were in the bay formed by the curve of the Punta di Goro, surrounded by hostile vessels, which continued to fire on us. I saw with great grief that several boats had already surrendered. It had become impossible either to advance or retreat, the enemy's craft carrying much more sail than ours; so that there was nothing for it but to run for the shore, which we reached under fire from the fleet, and pursued by their boats. Only four of the fishing-vessels remained, all the rest having fallen into the hands of the enemy.

I leave it to be imagined what was my position at

that unhappy moment. My poor wife dying, the enemy pursuing us inshore with the confidence gained by an easy victory, and the prospect of landing on a coast where, in all probability, we should find more enemies,—not only Austrians, but papal partisans, then in full swing of reaction.

There was no help for it—we had to land. I took Anita in my arms, stepped ashore, and laid her down on the beach. I told my comrades, whose looks asked me what they were to do, to set out by ones and twos, and seek refuge wherever they could find it; but, whatever they did, to leave the point where we then were, as the enemy's boats might arrive at any moment. For myself, it was impossible to proceed, as my wife was dying, and I could not leave her.

The men whom I addressed were also very dear to me—Ugo Bassi, and Ciceruacchio with his two sons. Bassi said to me, " I shall go and try to find some hut where I can get another pair of trousers; these are certainly too conspicuous." He was wearing red ones, which, I think, had been taken by one of our men from the corpse of a French soldier at Rome, and given to Ugo Bassi, whose own were quite worn out, some days ago. Ciceruacchio bade me an affectionate farewell, and left me with his sons. We parted from those true-hearted Italians, never to meet again. The ferocity of priests and Austrians satisfied its thirst for blood by shooting them, and thus, a few days later, wreaked its vengeance for all past fears. With Ciceruacchio were, besides his two sons, a Captain Parodi, one of my brave comrades

at Montevideo, and one Ramorino, a Genoese priest.
I do not recollect the rest.

"Dig nine graves," said an Austrian captain under
the orders of an Austrian prince, who commanded in
that part of Italy, and who had arrested my nine fellow-
soldiers—"dig nine graves!" was his imperious order
to a crowd of peasants, who, thanks to the priests, were
afraid of the Italian liberals, whom they had been taught
to look on as murderers, and not of the Austrian soldiers.
The graves were dug in a few minutes in that light
sandy soil.

Poor old Ciceruacchio! true type of the honest
man of the people,—standing there before the graves
which were to hold himself, his comrades, and his sons
—one of them a boy of thirteen! The graves having
been tried and found large enough, they were all shot
and buried—of course, by Italian hands. The foreign
soldier was master. He gave orders to his slaves, and
obedience had to be instantaneous, if not—the scourge.
Ugo Bassi was also arrested and shot, together with
Levré, one of my comrades at Montevideo, a brave
and lovable Milanese. Ugo Bassi was tortured by the
priests before being shot; he had been a priest himself,
and therefore their rage against him was all the greater.

I remained in a maize-field near the sea, with my
Anita and Lieutenant Leggiero, my inseparable companion, who had also remained with me in Switzerland,
after the affair at Morazzone in 1848. My beloved
wife's last words referred to her children, whom she had
a presentiment she would never see again.

We remained for a time in the maize-field, rather undecided what to do. At last I told Leggiero to advance a little inland, in order to discover some house in the neighbourhood. With his accustomed daring, he started at once. I waited a short time; but after a while I heard people approaching, and, coming out of our hiding-place, saw Leggiero accompanied by a man whom I recognized at once, and the sight of whom was a great consolation to me. It was Colonel Nino Bonnet, one of my most distinguished officers, who, after being wounded at the siege of Rome, where he had also lost a brother, had gone home to recover. Nothing more fortunate could have happened to me than a meeting with this true comrade. Residing in the neighbourhood, where he was a proprietor, he had heard the cannonading, and, concluding therefrom that we had landed, had hastened to the sea-shore to find and help us. Brave and intelligent, Bonnet, at great peril to himself, searched for us, and found what he sought. Having once found such an ally, I placed myself entirely under his directions, which was, of course, our only chance of escape. He immediately proposed that we should make our way to a small hut not far off, where we might find some help for my unfortunate companion. We went on, supporting Anita between us, and with difficulty reached the house, where the poor people supplied us with water, the first requirement of the suffering woman, and some other things. Thence we passed on to the house of Bonnet's sister, who was most kind. Leaving her, we crossed the valley of Comacchio and approached La

Mandriola, where we hoped to find a physician. When we reached La Mandriola, Anita was lying on a mattress in the cart which had brought her, and I said to Dr. Zannini, who arrived almost immediately, "Try and save her." The doctor said to me, "We must try to get her to bed." The four of us then each took a corner of the mattress, and carried her into the house, to a room at the head of the stairs. In laying her down on the bed, I thought I saw the death-look in her face. I felt her wrist—there was no pulse. The mother of my children, the woman I loved, was lying before me a corpse. When I first meet them again, they will ask me for their mother!

I mourned bitterly for the loss of my Anita, my inseparable companion in the most adventurous passages of my life. I directed the good people about me to bury the body, and left, yielding to their entreaties, and knowing that I should compromise them by remaining longer. I staggered along, scarcely able to walk, to Sant' Alberto, accompanied by a guide, who took me to the house of a tailor, a poor man, but honest and generous.

With Bonnet—to whom I must acknowledge that I owe my life—begins the list of my protectors, without whose help I should never have been able to perform my thirty-seven days' journey, from the mouths of the Po to the Gulf of Sterbino, where I embarked for Liguria.

From the window of the house I stayed in at Sant' Alberto, I could see the Austrian soldiers walking about, with their usual insolent air of mastery. I lived in two houses in this worthy little village, and in both

I was guarded, hidden, and treated with a generosity which was scarcely to be expected from these good people's miserable way of living. From Sant' Alberto my friends decided to transfer me to the neighbouring pine forest, where I remained for some time, moving about from place to place for greater security.

Several people were in the secret of the concealment which saved me from the researches not only of the Austrians, but of the Papalini, who were worse still. These courageous Romagnoles—most of them young men—were untiring in their care for my safety. When they thought me in danger in one place, I used to see them coming up at night with a cart, to remove me to a safer situation, many miles distant. The Austrians, for their part, and the priests, spared no efforts to discover me. The former had divided a battalion into sections, which marched in every direction through the pine woods. The latter, from pulpit and confessional, exhorted the ignorant peasant women to act as spies— "to the greater glory of God."

My young protectors had arranged their night-signals with admirable skill, so as to transfer me from one point to another, and to give the alarm in case of danger. When all was known to be safe, a fire was lit in an appointed place, and we passed on; if, on the contrary, no fire was seen, we turned back or took another direction. Sometimes, fearing some mistake, the driver stopped the cart, got down, and himself went on to reconnoitre—or else, without getting down, found some one to give him directions at once.

These arrangements were made 'with admirable precision. Be it noted that, if anything had transpired—if my persecutors had had the slightest hint of what was happening—they would have shot even the very children of the people who showed me such devotion, without trial and without mercy.

It is a grief to me that I cannot put on record the names of those generous Romagnoles, to whom certainly I owe my life. Had I not been already consecrated to the sacred cause of my country, this fact would certainly impose the obligation on me.

In this way I passed several days in the beautiful pine forest of Ravenna, sheltered for a time in the cabin of a noble, honest, and generous man called Savini; at others hidden in the thickets which abound. On one of these occasions it happened that, while I lay stretched out beside my comrade Leggiero, on one side of a clump of bushes, the Austrians passed on the other—their voices, anything but welcome, somewhat disturbing the quiet of the forest and our peaceful reflections. They passed very near us, and we probably formed the subject of their rather animated conversation. From the pine forest we were passed on to Ravenna, finding shelter in a house outside one of the city gates—I do not remember which—where we were welcomed with the same care and loving-kindness as everywhere else. From Ravenna we went on to Cervia, to the farm of another good man, whose kindly face I remember perfectly, but not his name. We remained there a couple of days, and then started off for Forlì, where we passed the night, sheltered by an honest family; and then went on across the Apennines, accompanied by guides.

It is worthy of remark, in passing, that none among that noble population is capable of stooping to the baseness of an informer, and that, meeting with an outlaw, they regard him as sacred, rescue him, feed him, guide him with unequalled kindness.

The long sway of the most perverse and corrupting of governments has failed to enervate or deprave the characters of those manly and generous folk. The Government of thieves (1872) which has succeeded the Government of the priests, does not know these people, whose unhappy lot is cast under its administration, and tortures them heedless of consequences. It will become aware of their quality on the day when the whole country, from the land of the Vespers and from Romagna to the Alps, will call on it to give an account of its stewardship.

Crossing the frontier of Romagna into Tuscany, we met with the same interest and kindness in this part of Italy—that country so divided by clerical influence and her long misfortunes, yet destined to form but a single people. One Anastasio, among others, welcomed and sheltered us in his house among the mountains. Then a priest! A true guardian angel to the proscribed, he sought us, found us, and took us to his own house at Modigliana. I repeat here what I have often said already—that I hate the false and perverse priestly character; but when the individual is shorn of his factitious qualities, and returns to simple human nature, I look upon him as a man among other men. '

Padre Giovanni Verità, of Modigliana, was the true priest of Christ; and by Christ I understand the virtuous man and legislator, not that being deified by the priests, who make use of his name to cover the foulness and futility of their own existence. Padre Giovanni Verità, as soon as a man persecuted by the priests for the love of Italy approached his part of the country, made it his business to shelter, feed, and guide him, or have him guided, to a place of safety. He had thus saved, by hundreds, the proscribed Romagnoles, who, condemned by the inexorable rage of the clergy, had sought refuge in Tuscany—a country whose government, though not good, was at least less atrocious than that of the priests. Proscriptions were frequent among the unfortunate and courageous people, and whenever, in my wanderings, I met with banished Romagnoles, I always heard them bless the name of this truly pious priest.

We remained a couple of days in Don Giovanni's house, in his own village of Modigliana, where the universal affection and esteem in which he was held served as a protection to his hospitable home. We were then guided by him across the Apennines, with the intention of passing along the ridge of these mountains, so as to get into the Sardinian states.

One evening, when we had reached the neighbourhood of Filigari, our generous conductor left us in a retired spot, while he pushed on to the village to find a guide. A mistake arose on this occasion, which, greatly to my regret, separated me from him. A guide he sent—perhaps overcome by sleep, as the night was already far advanced—lost his way, and was late in reaching us. When we entered the village, Don Giovanni had already left it by a different road to join us, impatient at the delay, which was not ours, but the guide's. It was already growing light,—we were on the high-road from Bologna to Florence, and could remain no longer in so exposed a position. We then resolved to get a cart, and go along the road to Florence, feeling great regret at parting from the generous man who had so far guided and protected us.

Following the road leading to the Tuscan capital, we came, when it was already broad daylight, upon an Austrian corps marching to Bologna. We had, perforce, to put a good face on the matter, and in this way proceeded for some time towards the western slope of the Apennines.

Having reached an inn on the left-hand side of the road, the driver stopped, and we found it convenient to halt there for a time. We entered the house, discharged the driver, and asked the host for a cup of coffee. While we were waiting for it, I had sat down on a bench beside a long table, of the kind usually found in such establishments, on the left side of the door, and, being rather tired, fell into an uneasy doze, my head resting on my arms. Leggiero awakened me by touching me on the shoulder with his finger, and as I looked up, my eyes fell on the unprepossessing

countenances of some Croats who had invaded the inn.
I laid my head down again on my arms without
appearing to have seen any one. As soon as the inn
was cleared, and we had taken some refreshment—our
masters having been duly served first—we crossed the
road, and sought and found shelter in a peasant's
house to the right of it.

Having rested for a time, and made the necessary
inquiries, we started for Prato, with the intention of
reaching the Ligurian frontier. After marching through
the greater part of the day, we reached a valley, where
we found a kind of rustic inn, and asked for a night's
lodging.

At this inn we saw a young sportsman from Prato,
who seemed to know the country well, and be intimate
with the people of the house. This young fellow was
respectable in appearance and frank in manner, with
one of those honest, open faces which seldom deceive
one. I watched him for some time, in such a way as
to express a desire to speak to him, and at last
approached him. After a little conversation, I told
him my name, and saw at once that I had not been
mistaken. The young Pratese was visibly touched by
my name, and I could see his eyes light up with the
pleasure of doing a kindness. He said to me, " I will
go at once to Prato—it is only a few miles ; I will speak
to my friends, and come back to you in a short time."

He was as good as his word, returning before long ;
and we followed him to Prato, where his friends—the
advocate Martini at their head—had got ready a carriage

to take us by way of Empoli and Colle, to the Tuscan Maremma, where, having recommendations to other honest Italians, we thought it probable we should find a vessel to cross to some point in the Ligurian territory.

The resolution taken by the good patriots of Prato, to send us on towards the Maremma, was occasioned by the rigorous examination to which travellers were subjected by the Ducal Government, on the Sardinian frontier, in order to prevent the escape of those politically compromised—then very numerous—who were likely to seek safety beyond the western frontier, on that part of Italian soil where Austrian arrogance was never more to find scope for its lust of murder and plunder.

The advocate Martini, of Prato, among the rest of our benefactors and deliverers, deserves unbounded gratitude. He not only went out of his way to facilitate our journey, but recommended us warmly to his friends and connections in the Maremma, who were of the greatest service to us. It grieves me much that I cannot remember the name of the young man who had so conspicuous a share in our rescue, and with whom I left a little ring, of trifling value, as a souvenir and token of affection.

Our journey from Prato to the Maremma was indeed singular. We passed over a great extent of country in a closed carriage, stopping every now and then to change horses. Our halts in some places were rather longer than was absolutely necessary, some of our drivers being much less careful of us than others. In this way time was given to the curious to surround the carriage; sometimes, too, we were obliged to leave it for meals, instead of having them brought to us, to conceal in some degree our exceptional situation. In small villages, our vehicle was, of course, turned into a species of pillory by the idlers of the place, who offered aloud a thousand conjectures as to who we were, and were naturally disposed to gossip about people whom they did not know, and who, therefore, in those difficult and terrible times of reaction, seemed doubtful or even dangerous characters. At Colle, in particular, nowadays quite a patriotic and advanced place, we were surrounded by a crowd, from whom our faces, certainly not those of peaceful and indifferent travellers, drew manifest tokens of suspicion and dislike. However, nothing took place beyond a few abusive epithets, which, as was to be expected under the circumstances, we pretended not to hear.

We were, unhappily, still in the times when the priests used to tell people that the Liberals were a set of murderers (1849). A few years later, however, I was received in the same village with the most enthusiastic kindness, which I shall certainly remember all my life.

We passed under the walls of Volterra, where Guerrazzi was at that time in confinement, with some of the political "suspects" of Tuscany; and were forced to content ourselves with pulling our hats down over our eyes as we drove by. The first safe place of refuge we came to was San Dalmazio, where we were already in the neighbourhood of the Maremma. We stayed in the house of Dr. Camillo Serafino, a generous man and true Italian patriot, of uncommon courage and firmness. As Tuscan deputy to the parliament of 1859, after the emancipation of his country, I know that he, like the honest Giovanni Verità, participated in every courageous deliberation of that assembly; and I imagine that he, like many others, must have retired in disgust at finding himself associated with men unworthy to represent Italy.

We remained several days at Serafino's house, and were afterwards taken to a bathing-establishment belonging to another Martini, a relative of the first, and as kind-hearted as he. Thence we went on to the house of one Guelfi, nearer the sea—in each place meeting with a hospitality worthy of the greatest gratitude.

In the mean time, these generous friends were negotiating our passage to Liguria with a Genoese fisherman. One day, several young men of the district, armed like Ravenna hunters, with their double-barrelled fowling-pieces, and, like them, active, strong, and fearless, came to fetch us at honest Guelfi's house, gave each of us a weapon similar to their own, and guided us through the woods to the shore, which we reached at a spot a few miles east of Follonica, a coaling-station in the Gulf of Sterbino. Here we found the fishing-boat waiting for us, and embarked, deeply touched by the kindness of our young deliverers.

How proud I felt then of my Italian birth, of my

connection with this land of the dead, and with the people who, according to our neighbours, do not fight! Though we were fallen from the high estate of our world-ruling forefathers, yet these insolent neighbours, unable to forget our former greatness, endeavoured to subject us, humiliated, depraved, and corrupted in body and soul, to the power of a debased sacerdotalism, so that, reduced to the miserable condition of political *crétins*, we might kiss the rod, no longer even conscious of the degradation to which they had doomed us to all eternity. They seemed to think their pigmy sway would endure for ever, even while Time with the chill blast of his wing sweeps away the gigantic structures of human greatness, past, present, and future—structures whose ruins this day stand on the Seven Hills. Proud, I say, of my birth in Italy, where yet, in spite of the sway of priests and robbers, a young generation is growing up, which, scorning torture and death, is marching straight to the goal—the fulfilment of duty, the emancipation of the slave.

Having embarked in the Gulf of Sterbino, on board a Ligurian fishing-vessel, we sailed towards the island of Elba, where we were to take some necessaries on board. After passing part of the day and one night at Porto Longone, we coasted along the Tuscan shore, and reached the roadstead of Livorno, whence we continued our course westward without stopping.

I had no expectation of a favourable reception from the Sardinian Government, and this induced me to entertain the idea of asking for an asylum on board an

English vessel which was at anchor there. However, the desire of seeing my children before leaving Italy—where I knew that I could not remain—was too strong for me; and we landed in safety at Porto Venere about the month of September.

Between Porto Venere and Chiavari, nothing worth mentioning happened to us. At this last town we were hospitably received at the house of my cousin, Bartolommeo Pucci, of whom I entertained an affectionate recollection. We were quite fêted by my relatives, as well as by the good people of Chiavari, and the numerous Lombards who had taken refuge there after the battle of Novara. But General La Marmora, then royal commissioner at Genoa, hearing of my arrival, ordered me to be transferred to that city, under the escort of a captain of carbineers in plain clothes. I was not surprised at the general's proceedings; he was merely an instrument of the policy then prevalent in our country, and connected with the most secret workings of the same—therefore on his own account an enemy to every man who, like myself, bore the brand of republicanism.

I was imprisoned in a secret room of the ducal palace at Genoa, and then at night placed on board the frigate *San Michele*. I was treated with courtesy, both by La Marmora at Genoa, and on board the *San Michele* by the chivalrous commander, Persano.

I only asked for twenty-four hours, in which to land at Nice, embrace my children, and return to take my place as a prisoner. General La Marmora allowed me to go, on parole.

Whether or not there were other disguised Government agents on board the *San Giorgio* (the steamer which took me to Nice), I cannot say, but certain it is that, on my arrival, the alarm had been given, and the carbineers were on the alert. They kept me waiting for several hours—after the usual custom of the royal authorities—before allowing me to land, so that I had barely time to get to Cavas, where my children were, pass the night there, and return again immediately.

The sight of my children, whom I was forced to leave for I could not tell how long, was unspeakable pain to me. It is true that I was leaving them in friendly hands, the two boys with my cousin, Augusto Garibaldi, and my Teresa with the Deiderys, who acted the part of parents to her. But it was clear that I had to leave them for an indefinite period, since one of the propositions made to me was, that I should choose a place of exile. Here I must not pass by in silence the manly defence of my cause undertaken by the deputies of the Left, in the Piedmontese Parliament. Baralis, Borella, Valerio, Brofferio, raised their voices earnestly in my behalf, and, if they failed to save me from exile, certainly saved me from some worse fate. The Austro-clerical party had, as usual, an insatiable thirst for blood, and had been victorious everywhere in the Peninsula.

Being requested to name a place of exile, I chose Tunis. My hopes of better destinies for my country made me prefer a spot not too distant; where, moreover, I knew I should find Castelli, of Nice, a friend of my childhood, and Pedriani, a devoted comrade who shared my first proscription in 1834.

I therefore embarked for Tunis on board the war-steamer *Tripoli.* At Tunis, the Government, which was subject to the dictation of France, did not want me, and I was sent back and landed in the island of Maddalena, where I remained about twenty days.

Ridiculous as it seems, there were persons foolish enough to accuse me to the Sardinian Government—or, at least, so the Government pretended—of plotting a revolution in that island, where a good half of the population were at that time either actually in the royal service, or in receipt of royal pensions;—good people, for the rest, who treated me very kindly.

From Maddalena I was sent to Gibraltar, in the war-brigantine *Colombo.* The English governor of the place gave me six days in which to leave it. The affection and just gratitude which I have always felt towards that generous nation, made this proceeding seem all the more discourteous, futile, and unworthy.

CHAPTER X.

EXILE.

IF that kick to the fallen had been given by a base or weak nation, one could have borne it. But from a representative of England, the universal haven of refuge, it cut me to the heart.

Forced to leave—even though, to do so, I had been obliged to throw myself into the sea—I resolved, under the advice of some friends, to cross the strait and seek refuge in Africa, with Signor G. B. Carpeneto, Sardinian consul at Tangier. This gentleman received and entertained me in his house for six months, with my two companions, Leggiero and Coccelli. At Modigliana I had found a beneficent priest; at Tangier I met with a consul in the royal service, who was a generous and honest man: to both I owe the deepest gratitude. These facts prove the justice of the old proverb, " The cowl does not make the monk;" and show that the exclusiveness professed by some people is a mistake, while it is very difficult to find perfection in the human family. Let us, then, strive after personal goodness for ourselves—inculcate, as far as possible, on the multitudes, the maxims of justice and truth, and fight to the death against ecclesiasticism and tyranny in any form, since they are the representatives of falsehood and evil; but let us be indulgent towards our yet uncivilized species, which, among other titles of merit, has that of always producing one-half of itself, in the shape of emperors, kings, police-agents of every description, and priests—who seem cut out on purpose, with all the choicest attributes of executioners—to promote the glory and well-being of the others.

At Tangier, with my generous host Carpeneto, I lived a quiet and happy life, as far as the life of an Italian exile, far from his country and his dear ones, can be so. At least twice in the week we used to go shooting, game being abundant. Besides this, a friend placed a small boat at my disposal, and we made pleasant and successful fishing-expeditions. The kind hospitality offered me in the house of Mr. Murray, the English vice-consul, withdrew me sometimes from my solitary and savage habits. In this way six months passed by pleasantly enough; all the more so by contrast with the terrible time that had gone before.

At the same time, I was not forgotten in my banishment by all my Italian friends. Francesco Carpanetto, to whom I owed, ever since my arrival in Italy in 1848, an infinity of favours and kindnesses, had hit upon the idea of collecting, among my acquaintances and his own, a sum sufficient for the purchase of a ship, which I was to command. This project quite met my views; for, unable as I was to do anything towards the accomplishment of my political task, I could at least, by engaging in mercantile pursuits, gain an independent livelihood, and no longer be a burden to the generous man who had received me as his guest. I immediately fell in with my friend Francesco's plan, and prepared to set out for the United States, where the purchase of the vessel was to be effected.

About June, 1850, I embarked for Gibraltar, proceeding thence to Liverpool, and from Liverpool to New York. During the crossing I was assailed by rheumatic pains, which lasted through a great part of the voyage, and was at last carried ashore like a bale of goods at Staten Island, New York.

These pains continued for a couple of months, which I passed partly in Staten Island and partly in New York City, at the house of my dear and valued friend, Michele Pastacaldi, where I enjoyed the charming society of the illustrious Foresti, one of the martyrs of the Spielberg.

Carpanetto's plan could not, however, be carried into effect for want of contributors. He had got three shares, of 10,000 francs each, taken up by Piazzoni and the brothers Camozzi of Bergamo; but what ship could be bought in America for 30,000 francs? Nothing larger than a small coasting-vessel; and, not being an American citizen, I should have been obliged to engage a captain of that nation, which did not suit me.

At last it became necessary to do something. An honest man of my acquaintance, Antonio Meucci of Florence, who had determined to establish a candle-factory, offered me a place as his assistant. No sooner

said than done. I could not take a share in the
business for want of funds, as the 30,000 francs above
mentioned, being insufficient for the purchase of a ship,
had remained in Italy; but joined on condition of
giving my services as far as I could.

I worked for some months under Meucci, who treated
me, not as one of his factory hands, but as a member
of the family, and with great kindness.

One day, however, tired of making candles, and
perhaps driven by natural and habitual restlessness, I
left the house with the intention of changing my trade.
I remembered that I had been a sailor. I knew some
words of English, and made my way to the shore of
the island, where I perceived a number of coasting
craft, busy loading and unloading goods. Reaching the
first, I expressed my wish to come on board as a sailor.
The men I saw on deck scarcely took any notice of me,
and went on with their work. Approaching a second
vessel, I made another trial, with the same result. At
last I passed on to a third, which was just being
unloaded, and, asking whether I might be allowed to
help in the work, was told that no more hands were
required. "But I do not ask for wages," I insisted.
No reply. "I want to work to warm myself." In
fact, there was snow on the ground. No one paid any
heed to me, and I was overwhelmed with mortification.

My thoughts went back to the times when I had the
honour of commanding the Montevidean fleet—not to
speak of the gallant and immortal army of that Republic.
What was the use of all that ? No one wanted me.

At last I swallowed my vexation, and returned to work at the tallow. It was fortunate that I had not told the excellent Meucci of my resolution, and therefore my chagrin, being concentrated in myself, was easier to bear. I must confess, besides, that my good employer's behaviour to me had not been the cause of my unseasonable resolve; he was always kindness itself, and so was Signora Ester, his wife. My position in his house, then, was in nowise deserving of pity, and it was only an attack of melancholy that had driven me to leave it. I was perfectly at liberty there; could work if I wished (and naturally I preferred useful work to any other occupation), or go shooting whenever I felt inclined; and often accompanied Meucci himself and various other friends from Staten Island and New York, who frequently favoured us with their visits, on fishing-expeditions. Though there was no luxury in his house, there was no want of comfort as regards either food or lodging.

I must now mention Major Bovi, the same who lost his arm at the defence of Rome, my comrade in several campaigns. He had joined me at Tangier, at Signor Carpeneto's house, towards the close of my stay in that place of refuge; and when I decided on crossing to America, my means not allowing me to take all my friends with me, I left Leggiero and Coccelli behind, with good recommendations, and chose Bovi to accompany me, as, wanting his right hand, he was unable to work.

Coccelli! Why should I not record a brief recollection

of this comrade of mine, so young, brave, and handsome? Coccelli entered the Montevideo legion as a mere boy, and, having great musical gifts, played the key-bugle in the fine band belonging to the legion, and was our trumpeter in the famous charges by which that gallant corps made the name of Italian respected in America. Coccelli followed the legion through all its campaigns, and took part in our Italian expedition of 1848. As an officer he bore an honoured part in the Lombard and Roman campaigns, and accompanied me when, proscribed by the Sardinian Government of 1849, I repaired to Tangier. When I quitted Tangier for America, I left my gun and other hunting appliances with Coccelli. He died very young, of a sunstroke.

My hound Castore also had to be left at Tangier with my friend Mr. Murray, and this faithful companion died of grief at our separation.

At last Franceso Carpanetto came to New York himself, having initiated at Genoa a commercial undertaking on a large scale, to be carried out in Central America. The *San Giorgio*, a vessel belonging to him, had left Genoa with part of the cargo, while he himself went to England to prepare the remainder and send it to Gibraltar, where the vessel was to pick it up. It being decided that I should accompany him to Central America, we at once made preparations for starting, and in 1851, I set out for Chagres with Carpanetto, on board an American steamer commanded by Captain Johnson.

From Chagres we proceeded in a yacht of the same nationality to San Juan del Norte, where we took a canoe and ascended the San Juan River as far as Lake Nicaragua. Crossing the lake, we reached Granada, its port and greatest commercial centre, where we remained a few days, being kindly received by some Italians resident there. Here began my friend's commercial operations, in pursuance of which we visited many parts of Central America, and crossed the Isthmus of Panama several times.

I accompanied my friend in these excursions rather as a travelling companion than a partner in business; in which, I confess, I was a novice. Carpanetto, however, was far from being such; and I admired the activity and intelligence with which he managed every affair which promised to turn out to advantage. I travelled at that time under the name of Giuseppe Pane, already assumed in 1834, to escape from curiosity and the molestations of the police. The basis of Carpanetto's commercial projects was the *San Giorgio's* arrival at Lima, and his intention was to proceed to that city in order to await her. We therefore returned to San Juan del Norte, and thence to Chagres, whence we ascended the river Gruz, in order to reach Panama.

On this last journey, I was attacked by the terrible fever endemic in that marshy region, with its tropical climate. Struck down as if by a thunderbolt, I was never so prostrated by any illness before or since. Had it not been for the kindness of some worthy Italians and Americans whom I met with at Panama—the brothers Monti being among the former—I should probably have succumbed. My good friend Carpanetto watched over and cared for me at that critical time as if he had been my brother.

Once embarked at Panama on board the English steamer which was to take me to Lima, I found a balm in the sea-air, which restored my strength more effectually than any medicine. We passed Guayaquil, where I tried in vain to discover the peak of Chimborazo, which is almost always hidden by the clouds. At Payta we landed, and spent the day. I was hospitably received in the house of a benevolent lady, who had been confined to her bed for several years in consequence of a paralytic stroke, which deprived her of the use of her limbs. I passed part of the day on a sofa beside this lady's couch, as, though my health had somewhat improved, I was still obliged to lie stretched out without moving.

Donna Manuelita de Saenz was the most graceful and courteous matron I ever saw. Having enjoyed the friendship of Bolivar, she was acquainted with the minutest details of the life of the great liberator of Central America, whose entire devotion to the work of his country's deliverance, and the lofty virtues which adorned him, were not sufficient to shield him from the poison of envy and Jesuitry which embittered his later days. It is the old story—the story of all the great men of this world, still a prey to the miserable nonentities who know how to cheat it.

After that day, which, by contrast with so many passed in pain and weakness, I may well call delicious, because spent in the interesting society of this invalid lady, I parted from her deeply touched. Both of us had tears in our eyes, knowing, no doubt, that it was our last farewell on earth.

Having once more embarked, I reached Lima, after steaming along the beautiful Pacific coast. I have used the word "beautiful" in speaking of the western coast of South America between Panama and Lima; but I should have said picturesque, since this coast, with the exception of Panama, Guayaquil, Payta, and Lima, shows along the greater portion of its length scenes which recall the desert shores of Africa. Yet here and there are spots, like the green oases of the Sahara, of astonishing fertility. In that country, where the rains are rare and scanty, springs of fresh water gush out quite close to the sea, and one need only dig two or three feet deep, to find it in abundance. The Andes, those giants of the earth, which are not far from the coast, are the storehouses of this pure water—a greater treasure to the country, perhaps, than the precious metals so well known to abound there.

I had expected to find, on that slope of the great American chain, more living vegetation, and less desolate sandy desert; in short, I had looked for much more beautiful scenery at the foot of the lofty Cordilleras. Born on the slopes of the Alps, I sought in vain, gazing landward, for a lovely valley to be compared to that of my own beautiful Nice.

Nevertheless, that interesting coast is very picturesque, and, if not beautiful as a whole, has beautiful parts, such as Lima, and the valley of Paradise—Valparaiso.

At Lima, where we found the *San Giorgio*, I had a most cordial welcome from the rich and generous Italian colony—especially from the Sciutto, Denegri, and Malagrida families. Signor Pietro Denegri gave me the command of the *Carmen*, a barque of four hundred tons, and I prepared for a voyage to China.

My friend Carpanetto left Lima in the *San Giorgio*, in order to return to Central America and fetch the cargo he had prepared there. I was never again to see this devoted friend, to whom I owed so much kindness and perhaps my life. He died of cholera, a few years later, without being able to complete the undertakings begun so hopefully and with so much sagacity, which ended in nothing but bitter disappointment and death in a strange land, so far from the Italy he loved.

At Lima, before entering on the voyage, I met with an adventure much to be regretted. I stayed, for some time after my arrival in that city, in Malagrida's house, where, not yet recovered from the fever, I received the kindest care and nursing from himself and his amiable lady. At this house, a Frenchman—a thorough-going *chauvin*—was a frequent visitor. Being naturally somewhat unsociable, and perceiving that he was an exceedingly talkative individual, I avoided, as far as possible, entering into conversation with him. One day, however, he fairly cornered me, and, in spite of myself, drew me into conversation on the Roman expedition carried out by Bonaparte's army. The subject was naturally distasteful, and I tried to change it, but in vain; for not only did he persist in continuing it, but expressed himself in abusive terms about the Italians. I replied somewhat severely, though keeping within the limits of decorum, out of consideration for the house I was in, and there the matter dropped. A few days later, being at Callao (the port of Lima), on board the *Carmen*, busy with preparations for my voyage, I received a Lima paper, in which that *chauvin* insulted me. I said not a word, but on Saturday evening, when my work was finished, I went to Lima, found out his house, which was a large place of business, entered, asked him if he knew me, and, on his replying in the affirmative, gave him a thrashing with a light cane I usually carried. As, in the excitement of the affair, I had not taken the trouble to see whether he was alone or not, I found that I had to deal with two antagonists, both stronger than myself. The new arrival, seeing me engaged with his companion, gave me a blow with a stick on the head from behind, which covered my face with blood, while at the same time he tried to stab me in the back with a sword-stick. I staggered for a minute, half-stunned, and was on the point of falling. Had I done so I should have been a dead man, and my adversaries would have had the law on their side, as I had assaulted them in their own house. But, by good fortune, I did not fall. Inflamed by the feeling of the blood running down my face, I became furious, and disarmed the stronger of the two, while the other retreated into the inner room, more scared, surely, by my state of excitement than by my strength, and soon followed by his friend. I remained master of the situation, in a spacious warehouse which did not belong to me ; and left it to seek shelter elsewhere.

The friendship of my fellow-citizens, shown towards me on this occasion, is worth recording. The police at Lima, excited by a furious French consul, were desirous of arresting me by force, but the attitude assumed by the Italians cooled their ardour. They took no undignified action, but all of them—and there were thousands at Lima—were strong and active men. They came in a body to the rescue, and respectfully intimated to the police commissioner that he was not to arrest me. The commissioner made a great ado, but did not carry out the arrest, surrounded as I was by a crowd of quiet but resolute men.

The French consul from the beginning demanded satisfaction from the Peruvian Government, which was explained to consist of nothing less than a fine and an apology on my part. The Sardinian consul, Canevarro, was the intermediary in this negotiation, and did not fail to interest himself in my behalf. The matter was at last concluded, without fine, and without apology.

When I think of our Italian colonies in South America, I feel we have really something to be proud of. These countrymen of ours, on the free soil of those republics, seem to me to be worth twice as much as their brethren at home. The priest, in this favoured clime, crawls about indeed, reptile-fashion, as he does everywhere else—but has no dominion over our kinsfolk, and very little over the sons of that happy nation. The governments are not always good, but, as it is their interest to encourage foreign immigration, they protect the immigrants, especially those of Italian nationality, who have so much affinity with the Iberian race.

In South America the Italian is generally laborious and honest; when some black sheep turns up, the rest keep an eye on him, and, if he commits any crime, they never rest till he is expelled from their community. The seafaring portion of these emigrants of ours are little known—least of all to the Italian Government; but certainly they compose the most energetic section of our immense national marine, in which the Ligurians predominate, and which (though this same Government of ours has not hitherto employed it to the best advantage) ought not at any time to be inferior either to the naval or merchant service of our neighbours.

Not long after this, I set sail with the *Carmen* for the Chincha Islands, south of Lima, where we took on board a cargo of guano for China, returning to Callao to make the last preparations for the long voyage.

On January 10, 1852, I weighed anchor at Callao, bound for Canton. We made the trip in about ninety-three days, always with a favourable wind. Passing in sight of the Sandwich Islands, we entered the China Sea between Luzon (in the Philippine Islands) and Formosa.

Arrived at Canton, as there was no sale for our cargo there, my consignee sent me on to Amoy. When I returned to Canton, finding that the return cargo was not ready, I loaded up with a general cargo for Manilla. From Manilla we sailed back to Canton, where the *Carmen*—which had suffered some damage during the long voyage—was re-coppered, and fitted with new masts ; and, when the cargo was ready, got under way for Lima.

I had made a careful study of the prevailing winds on the two routes by which it was possible to return to Lima. One of these is that to north, the other a southerly one, passing to the westward of Australia ; and, after consideration, I chose the second. Any one who should attempt to cross direct from Canton to Lima, within the torrid zone (which extends for a distance of 23° 28' on either side of the equator, and may, roughly speaking, be calculated at 60°, as the breezes, for the most part, prevail up to Lat. 30° N. and S., and blow from east to west with unfailing regularity), would never perform the voyage, though fully provisioned, as he would always have both wind and tide against him. On the other hand, directing your course away from this zone, towards the poles, you are almost certain of finding variable winds, generally blowing eastward, especially beyond Lat. 50° N. and S. We sailed towards the Indian Ocean, quitting the Eastern Archipelago by the Straits of Lombok, after some difficulty in beating up the strait, on account of the south-west monsoon, which was still blowing hard.

In the Indian Ocean, outside the Straits of Lombok, we found the breezes constant from the east, at a few degrees' distance. Keeping the ship's head to the wind, we continued as far as about 40° S., when, finding the wind westerly, we passed through Bass's Strait, between

Australia and Van Diemen's Land. Touching at one of the Hunter Islands, to take in water, we found a small farm, lately deserted by an Englishman and his wife, on the death of his partner. This information we obtained from a board erected on the settler's grave, which set forth in brief the history of the little colony. " The husband and wife," said the inscription, " unable to bear the loneliness of the desert island, left it, and returned to Van Diemen."

The most important part of the settlement was a little one-storied dwelling-house, rough, but comfortable, carefully built, and furnished with tables, beds, and chairs—not luxurious, indeed, but all bearing the impress of that comfort which seems so natural to the English. We also found a garden—a most useful discovery, as it enabled us to take on board an abundant supply of fresh potatoes and other vegetables.

How often has that lonely island in Bass's Strait deliciously excited my imagination, when, sick of this civilized society so well supplied with priests and police-agents, I returned in thought to that pleasant bay, where my first landing startled a fine covey of partridges, and where, amid lofty trees of a century's growth, murmured the clearest, the most poetical of brooks, where we quenched our thirst with delight, and found an abundant supply of water for the voyage.

From Bass's Strait we sailed between New Zealand and the Auckland Islands, and then, getting in 52° S. latitude, were driven along by strong westerly gales, and made for the west coast of America. Approaching this coast, after many days of successful navigation, we altered the course to port, with a view to getting the south-east trades, which carried us into Lima, after a passage of about one hundred days. Towards the end of the voyage provisions began to run short, and as a precaution the men were put on rations. Having discharged at Lima, we sailed with ballast for Valparaiso, where, on our arrival, the *Carmen* was chartered for a voyage to Boston with a cargo of copper. Having touched at various ports on the Chili coast—Coquimbo, Guasco, Herradura—we completed our cargo with wool, which was stowed on top of the copper, at Islay, in Peru.

Leaving Islay, we sailed southward, rounded the Horn, and, after a very stormy passage in the high latitudes, reached Boston in safety. I had orders to go on from Boston to New York, and, on my arrival at the latter place, received a letter from the *Carmen's* owner, containing a reprimand, which—as it seemed to me undeserved—led me to resign command of the vessel. In justice to Don Pedro Denegri, I ought to add that he treated me with the greatest kindness during the whole time I was so fortunate as to be in his service. But a parasitical Thersites, who had contrived to introduce himself into the house, had succeeded, by unremitting efforts, in blackening my character in the eyes of the principal.

I remained a few days longer at New York, enjoying the society of my dear and valued friends, Foresti Avezzana, and Pastacaldi. During this interval, Captain

Figari arrived at that port, intending to purchase a vessel, of which he asked me to take command on the voyage to Europe. I accepted, and accompanied him to Baltimore, where he bought the *Commonwealth*, and loaded her with flour and grain. I set sail in her, and reached London in February, 1854. Thence I went on to Newcastle, where we took in coal for Genoa; and reached the latter port on May 10 of the same year.

At Genoa, being laid up with rheumatism, I was carried to the house of my friend G. Paolo Augier, where I enjoyed a fortnight's kind hospitality. I then proceeded to Nice, and at last had the happiness of embracing my children after five years' exile.

The interval between my arrival at Genoa in May, 1854, and my departure from Caprera in February, 1859, presents no points of interest. It was spent partly at sea, partly in cultivating a small property I had purchased in the island of Caprera.

CHAPTER XI.

RETURN TO POLITICAL LIFE.

IN February, 1859, through the intervention of La Farina, I was summoned to Turin by Count Cavour. I entered into the policy of the Sardinian cabinet,—then in treaty with France, and disposed to make war on Austria, and flatter the Italian people. Manin, Pallavicino, and other distinguished Italians, sought to bring about an understanding between the Italian democracy and the dynasty of Savoy, so as to attain, through the concurrence of the greater part of our national forces, the fulfilment of the dream of Italian unity which through so many centuries had occupied the elect souls of the Peninsula.

Believing that I still possessed some measure of popularity, Count Cavour, then omnipotent, summoned me to the capital, and certainly found me very ready to fall in with his idea of making war on the inveterate enemy of Italy. It is true that his ally inspired me with no confidence; but what was I to do? There was no help for it.

There weighs on Italy, like an incubus, a terrible consciousness of weakness—assuredly the result of internal discord and priestly influence,—which even now (in the last days of 1859) tells on the effeminate sons of Ausonia, especially the classes accustomed to a life of ease and leisure.

I blush to write it, but it must be confessed—with France for an ally, we went to war with a light heart; without her, we should not have dreamed of such a thing. Such was the opinion of the majority of these degenerate sons of the great nation. And all this through ignorance and unwillingness to make use of the national elements at our disposal, and because our unhappy country's cause is always in the hands of either scoundrels or doctrinaires, accustomed to long palavers and arguments, but not to bold and resolute action.

A people determined not to bow the knee to an invader is invincible; and we have no need to go far afield to seek for proofs. Rome, after the loss of three great battles, with her terrible conqueror at the gates, made her legions march out in sight of Hannibal, and sent them into Spain. Let any one find a similar example in the history of any country in the world! And when the land of our birth can boast such precedents, we may hold up our heads and treat the insolence of foreigners with the contempt it deserves.

At Turin I saw none of the Government except Cavour. The idea of making war on Austria by means of Piedmont was not new to me; nor was that of subordinating every political conviction to the one great aim of making, by whatever means, an Italian nation.

This programme was the same as that adopted on our departure from Montevideo, and when Manin's and Pallavicini's noble resolution of uniting our country into one Italy under Victor Emmanuel was communicated to me at Caprera, it found me still with the same political creed. Was not such the conception of Dante, Machiavelli, Petrarca, and so many more of our great ones? I may say with pride, I have been and am a republican; but, at the same time, I have never thought the popular system so exclusively good that it ought to be forcibly imposed on the majority of a nation. In a free country, where the virtuous majority of the people under no pressure, wish for a republic, the republican system is certainly the best. A republic being impossible for us—at least just now (1859)—whether through the corruption which at present rules society, or the solidarity which prevails among modern monarchies,—and the opportunity presenting itself of uniting the Peninsula by means of the combination of dynastic and national forces, I gave in my absolute adhesion to the project.

After a few days' stay at Turin, where I was to perform the service of enlisting Italian volunteers, I soon perceived with whom I had to deal and what was wanted of me. I chafed at it, but what was to be done? Nothing but accept the lesser evil, and, while unable to do all the good I wished, to obtain what little could be obtained for our unhappy country.

Garibaldi was to keep out of sight; to appear and disappear when wanted. The volunteers ought to know that he was at Turin, so that they might be attracted to the standards; but at the same time Garibaldi was to be requested to hide himself, to give no umbrage to diplomacy. What a condition! To summon the volunteers in large numbers, but to command only a small proportion of them, and those the least fit to carry arms! The volunteers assembled, but were not allowed to see me. Depôts were formed at Cuneo and Savigliano, while I was banished to Rivoli, near Susa.

The management and organization of the corps was confided to General Cialdini. Cosenz was in command at Cuneo, Medici at Savigliano—both excellent officers, who raised the first and second regiments, the nucleus and the pride of the Alpine *cacciatori.* A third regiment, also formed at Savigliano, under Arduino, was composed of the same elements, but failed to make as good a figure as the others, for want of a better leader.

A commission of enlistment established at Turin selected the most athletic and well-grown young men, between the ages of eighteen and twenty-six, for the line regiments, while they left those who were too young, too old, or otherwise inefficient, for the volunteer corps.

With regard to the officers, the authorities were more compliant, and had the good sense to accept nearly all those proposed by me. These had not all been trained in military academies, but nearly every one fulfilled my hopes by showing himself worthy of the sacred cause he was fighting for.

Carrano, Corte, Cenni, and others, formed my staff.

As I have said, General Cialdini was entirely responsible for the work of organization.

Various projects were sketched out by the Government in those early times. The first was that I should carry on operations on the confines of the duchies, which would have produced immense results; but this plan was soon changed—no doubt for fear of letting me get in contact with people who might swell the numbers of the volunteer corps to an excessive degree; so that it was thought better to place me at the extreme left wing of the army. For my part, too, I was glad to see once more the Lombard country and its fine population, so cruelly ground down by foreign tyranny.

I was at first promised the custom-house guards. I cannot think that it occurred to them to give me the guards from the convict prisons! I was also promised some battalions of Bersaglieri; but all this would have made my forces too numerous, and I never had either the one or the other. On the contrary, when the volunteers began to come in in great numbers, his Excellency of the War Office was called upon—for fear I should have too many—to form the corps of *cacciatori* of the Apennines, who were to have joined us, and whom I never even saw till the end of the war.

General La Marmora, the minister of war, who had always been averse to the enrolment of the volunteers, refused to recognize the rank of my officers, so that, in order to give some nominal legality to these rejected ones, recourse was had to the subterfuge of issuing commissions signed by the minister of the interior, and not by his excellency of war. Yet we submitted to it all in silence—we were fighting for Italy, against the oppressors of our brothers.

The current of political events was hastening on, and Austrian insolence showed that the longed-for conflict was not far off. This somewhat expedited the arming of the volunteer corps, whose organization was being actively pushed forward by General Cialdini.

We were by no means ready when the Austrian invasion of Piedmontese territory took place, yet, ready or not, we were eager to march. Cialdini's division was to defend the line of the Dora Baltea; and our destination was Brusasco, on his extreme right, we being intended to protect the high-road from Brusasco (on the right bank of the Po) to Turin.

The minister had sent some guns to the old castle of Varrene,—it was said, to command the road from Vercelli to Turin; and I received orders to defend this position, which would have fettered my movements in case of the enemy's advance. Yet, in any case, we were engaged in the liberation of our Italy—the fulfilment of a lifelong dream! We were as impatient for the hour of battle, my young comrades and I, as the bridegroom is for that which is to unite him to the object of his idolatry. Free from the reproach of every base ambition, we pressed forward, welcoming hardships, dangers, injustice—even the insults and injuries, treacherously inflicted by partisan hostility or jealousy, which sowed our path with thorns, and even attempted to do away with our uniform and extinguish the glorious name acquired on a hundred battle-fields. Yes, we were resolved to tolerate even outrages, provided only that we were suffered to fight the enemies of our idol.

We passed some days at Brusasco, Brozolo, and Pontestura. These first marches began to get the soldiers into training, and we took advantage of the halts in the different villages, to drill them, and accustom them to the various services of outpost and patrol duty.

General Cialdini having been called to the defence of Casale, we had directions to place ourselves under his orders. In making a reconnaissance from this town, we had our first sight of the Austrians.

In a feint made by the enemy on the outer works of the place, the second regiment, under Medici, gave proof of the capabilities of the Alpine *cacciatori*, gallantly charging the Austrians, and driving them before them. Captain De Cristoforis, and Sergeant Guerzoni—who afterwards passed as sub-lieutenant—distinguished themselves on this occasion.

On the day of this attack, a short time before it took place, I had been summoned by the King to his head- quarters at San Salvatore. He received me kindly, giving me instructions, with full discretionary powers, to cover the capital, in case there should be any prob- ability of an unforeseen attack on the part of the enemy, and to proceed, as soon as the danger should have passed away, to harass the extreme right of the Austrian army.

I therefore returned as far as Chivasso in the direction of Turin, where I found orders to place myself and my brigade at the disposal of General Sonnaz. I had an opportunity of admiring the bravery and coolness of that gallant old general, on the occasion of a reconnaissance which was pushed forward into the neighbourhood of Vercelli. The enemy was in the habit of marching out of this town in force, and making raids, plundering all the surrounding country, and spreading terror among its population.

Among other written orders I had received from the King, was one to gather round me all the volunteers remaining in the various depôts, and the regiment of *cacciatori* of the Apennines, composed of young men who had come from the different Italian provinces to serve under me. I wrote to Cavour about the despatch of the Apennine *cacciatori*, but, under one pretext or another—in spite of the order above mentioned—he never would send them; so that I felt convinced there was an unwillingness to increase the number of my soldiers. It was the old grievance, begun at Milan in 1848 by Sobrero; continued at Rome by Campello, who decreed that the corps commanded by me was never to exceed the number of 500; and completed by Cavour, who limited me to 3000.

The three regiments were composed of six battalions, with 600 men in each, forming a total of 3600; but the formation of the depôts, and the fact that my raw levies were unused to marching, reduced their numbers to 3000 before we had crossed the Ticino.

The King, who was certainly better than the men who surrounded him in 1859, sent a second order to march towards Lago Maggiore, and operate on the Austrian right. This was perhaps displeasing to the court cabal; not so to me, who thenceforward found myself free to act—a position to me worth millions. I therefore took leave of my brave old general—to whom, short as our acquaintance had been, I was already united by true affection—and marched to Chivasso, and thence to Biella. The brilliant and sympathetic reception given to my men by the people of Biella was a good omen. We remained a day or two in that friendly city, and then marched on to Gattinara.

The enemy, posted at Novara, having heard that I was marching in that direction, sent about twenty soldiers to cut off the ferry over the Sesia; but an outpost of ours, stationed at that point, prevented this movement.

Here it may not be beside the point to mention an incident very discreditable to us Italians, which should never have been allowed by the people to occur. It is true that the system of terror adopted by the Austrians in Italy had completely cowed the population; while for Cavour's plan of disarming the national guards on the frontiers, no words of condemnation are strong enough. If, therefore, there were manifestations of weakness on the part of our peasants, or of insolence on that of the tyrants from beyond the Alps—who have so long believed themselves absolute masters of our affairs, our property, and our persons—this was only what might have been expected. Preceded by the terror which they knew how to strike into the inhabitants, these lords of Italy extorted from the latter all that they wanted; as the following incident, humiliating to us as it is, sufficiently proves, being all the more surprising that it took place among the brave sub-Alpine population, rich in noble military traditions, and long possessing a brilliant army.

The same detachment of Austrian soldiers that had been sent to cut off the ferry, being unsuccessful in this, returned to Novara, whence they had started; and, so as not to have made their journey altogether in vain, requisitioned a large quantity of provisions, and carts for transport, after which they set out on the carts, completely intoxicated, for their quarters, traversing a space of about fifteen miles of hostile country—where the houses are numerous and close together, and the inhabitants strong and active as in the most favoured regions of the world—without a single Italian being seized with a desire to throw a stone at the drunken band. This ought not to have happened in our country —it is too degrading; and yet it does happen, because the priest has taught the peasants that it is not the Austrians who are the enemies of Italy, but we excommunicated Liberals. And the Government, "by the grace of God," protects the priests! Ten young fellows of that neighbourhood, if they had resolved to attack that triumphal procession with cudgels, might have disarmed or killed them. Such is the power of discouragement and deception, when scattered among a people which, however strong and warlike it may be by nature, is always unnerved by their agency. This does not prevent the same people from furnishing, in time of need, soldiers, who, well officered, are equal to the best in the world.

Having passed the Sesia, we marched on to Borgomanero, where I made my arrangements for crossing the Ticino. At Biella I had already consulted with the gallant Captain Francesco Simonetta as to the passage of that river, and had sent him forward, with some of his horsemen, to make the necessary preparations.* This brave and intelligent officer had some property at Varallo Pombia, and was therefore thoroughly familiar with all places near the banks of the Ticino, as well as greatly loved of the people, so that he was able to take all the necessary measures with a sagacity which was truly admirable.

I informed a few of my principal officers as to my determination, in such terms as to let it be clearly understood that I was resolved on attempting to cross without hesitation. To speak frankly, I was afraid of being recalled, or receiving some counter-order.

From Borgomanero I sent forward to order provisions and quarters at Arona, convinced that in the latter village there would be no want of Austrian spies to inform the enemy of my movements. I reached Arona with my brigade at nightfall, and entered the village with some horsemen, as though we were going to take

* Captain Francesco Simonetta was in command of the few mounted guides we had been able to get together. Like every one else belonging to us, they were in want of everything, and dressed as civilians. It is only due to my own negligence that Simonetta did not die a general.

up our position there, the commissariat officers and foragers having assisted in the deception.

At the same time I sent secret orders along all the different roads leading to the village to prevent our troops from entering it, directing them to march instead towards Castelletto. Having reached Castelletto, and found the boats ready below the village, I sent the second regiment across under Colonel Medici, all the rest remaining on the right bank. The passage was effected in good order—only, as the boats were rather heavy, and very closely packed, they were not easy to handle, and could not land at the same spot, some of them being carried down the river by the current, which caused a little delay in the assembling of the regiment on the Lombard bank. Finally, the rest of us marched on Sesto Calende, made prisoners of a few officers and gendarmes, and at once got the ferry into working order, so that the rest of the brigade could cross. I think this was on May 17, 1859.

We were now on Lombard soil, about to face that dominant Power which for the last ten years had been preparing her victorious army (which she now thought invincible) to complete the work begun at Novara ; perhaps, too, pleasantly dreaming of the whole Peninsula being seized by her eagle's claws.

We were three thousand, very little encumbered, the men's baggage having been left behind at Biella. The carts had orders to remain in Piedmont, except a few intended for the ammunition ; and some mules for this service, and for the ambulance, had been provided by the excellent and indefatigable surgeon-in-chief, Bertani.

From Sesto Calende, I marched with the brigade to Varese. During the night, Bixio with his battalion marched along the shore of the Lago Maggiore to Laveno, with orders to halt on the high-road from that point to Varese.

De Cristoforis remained at Sesto with his company, to keep communications open with Piedmont. This brave officer was—as he had been at Casale—the first to engage the enemy. The Austrians, knowing that we were at Sesto Calende, sent a strong reconnaissance thither, and found only De Cristoforis's company on the spot. That gallant fellow did not count the enemy, but resolutely gave battle, and, after an honourable engagement, fell back on Bixio's division. This had been agreed upon beforehand, as I was convinced that the important post of Sesto Calende could not be held with so small a force. The Austrians, however, with characteristic prudence, did not themselves attempt to maintain it, but retired on Milan.

Meanwhile there was a growing enthusiasm among the Lombard population. A definite and decisive insurrection was not to be expected from these good people. There had been much disillusionment and much suffering; the most spirited of the young men were, for the most part—if they were not forced recruits in the Austrian army—in our own, in exile, or with me. Nevertheless, I was quite satisfied with the welcome they gave us, their eagerness in providing for our wants, and in giving us notice of the enemy's movements and furnishing us with guides where necessary; and especially with the care lavished on our wounded by the kindly Lombard women. The way we were received at Varese on the night following that of our crossing, is a thing very difficult to describe. It was raining heavily, yet I am sure that not a single citizen, man, woman, or child, was missing when we entered. It was a touching sight to behold people and soldiers mingled together in wild embraces. Matrons and maidens, throwing aside their natural reserve, flung themselves on the necks of our rough soldiers in feverish excitement. Not that all my comrades were rough; some of them, indeed, belonged to the first families of Lombardy and other provinces. But all were Italians— vowed, as at Pontida, to the sacred covenant of their country's deliverance.

This manifestation of enthusiasm on the part of the people of Varese—the first of the kind we met with in this period—was all the more satisfactory to us, as we knew for certain that it was entirely spontaneous, and unmixed with hired applause—with voices of spies or police officials.

What, after all, are hardships, privations, and dangers, when thus compensated by the affectionate gratitude of a nation in process of deliverance? Let cold egotists, insatiable traffickers in nations, contemplate this sight, and if they are not touched, let them renounce their claim to be reckoned among the human family, of which they are unworthy to form part.

Varese had pulled down the imperial colours before our arrival, and substituted the national flag, disarming a few gendarmes and imperial officers. We were in a friendly and enthusiastic town, which, compromised as it was, we were under the obligation of defending; though no great defence was possible, with 3000 men opposed to the immense Austrian army. Besides, being obliged to stand on the defensive in a town, we lost that facility of rapid movement—unforeseen, secret, and not to be calculated on—in which lay our real importance on the enemy's flank.

Varese has some strong positions (Biumo, for example), and might have been defended by a superior force, had it—as it did not—possessed some fortifications. Barricades were erected at the principal entrances, and we began to arm some of the citizens with weapons taken by themselves from the enemy.

Urban was the Austrian general destined for our extermination. The first news I had of this ferocious enemy, coming from the direction of Brescia, was that he commanded 40,000 men. There were Austrians at Laveno, and another corps advancing from Milan—one might have been excused for shuddering at the situation.

The obligation we were under to defend Varese, and save it from the vengeance of Urban, who was said to be inexorable, caused me some apprehension. Had I been free to move in any direction outside the town, I should have had little fear of the enemy's numbers; but there was nothing very reassuring in being forced to await them at a fixed point in an unfortified town without a single gun, which could therefore make little or no preparation for serious resistance.

However, there was no help for it; for many reasons Varese could not be abandoned, and we had to decide on awaiting the enemy there at any cost. Once we had decided, every feeling of fear vanished.

Colonel Medici, with the second regiment, occupied the open space where the Como road ended—that is to say, our left; Colonel Arduino, the centre, with the third; and Colonel Cosenz, with the first, was on our right—that is, on the high-road from Milan. I was on the heights of Upper Biumo, with the reserves.

It was known that Urban had arrived at Como, and that other movements of troops, doubtless designed to co-operate with him, were taking place from Milan.

Medici, who to irreproachable courage unites a high degree of military sagacity, had covered his wing with all the works that could be erected in so short a space of time; and it was well he did so, that point being the objective upon which Urban directed the full weight of his attack.

On the morning of May 25, when it was scarcely light, the enemy's column was discovered, advancing on Varese by the Como road. Captain Nicolò Suzini, who had been sent with his company to form an ambuscade about a mile from the city, in a large building overlooking the road, was the first to receive them, which he did with great courage, but, after doing a little shooting at short range, retired to a position on our right.

After overcoming this first obstacle, Urban formed

his attacking column along the road, and, sending forward some lines of sharpshooters, dashed it against our left wing.

But our men were in a position prepared beforehand in cool blood by experienced officers; they were supported by two companies of the first regiment from Marrocchetti's battalion, and the conflict lasted but a short time.

After having let them come close up, our gallant *cacciatori* of the second regiment, cheered on by the brave Medici and Sacchi, sprang out from their shelter, and charged the Austrian soldiers with the bayonet, making them go down the road much faster than they had come up it.

I had imagined that the attack would not be limited to our left front alone, and that, according to all the rules for attacking a position like that of Varese, they ought to have moved their main forces backwards, or to the high ground north of Biumo, though they might, if they wished, have made feints on the high-road on our left. Urban, instead of this, seized the bull by the horns—which was all the better for us, since, few as we were, we could not afford to be distracted by a combined attack on various points at once, especially on the side nearest Milan, where the enemy's forces were considerable.

From the heights of Biumo, where I had placed my head-quarters (the position being a commanding one, and of great value for overlooking a battle-field), I was perfectly aware of every movement on our own part, and on that of the enemy ; the rear—that is, the northern portion of the ground, which I could not see—I caused to be reconnoitred by Captain Simonetta, who I was perfectly sure would perform the duty well.

Having assured myself that nothing was being attempted except the front attack on our left, I descended from Biumo, and gave orders for a part of the brigade to pursue the enemy, while the rest was to continue the movement in good order.

The enemy, with two guns which they had used at the attack of Varese, and a detachment of guides escorting the same, halted at every convenient spot, but continued their retreat on the first appearance of our force, though it is difficult to pursue, without ordnance or cavalry, an enemy whose force is composed of all three branches of the service.

It was not till they reached the position of San Salvatore, beyond Malnate, that the Austrians began to make head against us. At this point an obstinate combat took place, in which many shots were exchanged, and the gallant Genoese carbineers specially distinguished themselves ; the enemy being on one side of a deep ditch at right angles to the road, and we on the other. We had more men wounded in this last than in the first fight, the enemy's position being higher than ours, and thickly wooded.

The enemy, elated with this advantage, procured by the superiority of their cannon and small arms, advanced an infantry corps, which charged our left energetically, and made it fall back some distance. But our side, having occupied farm-buildings overlooking that part of the battle-field, and seeing themselves supported by the reserves marching up to their assistance, charged the enemy with a vigour which drove them into the ditch, whence they did not reappear.

The position occupied by the Austrians on the other side of this ditch was a formidable one, overlooking the road. It was rash to attack it in front, and I tried to think of a way to turn it. This was not impossible, as we had remained in quiet possession of the cowhouse which, overlooking our left, and affording us almost a complete cover, would allow us to cross the upper part of the ditch, and turn the enemy's right flank unhindered.

I had decided on adopting this last expedient, when I was thunderstruck by the news that a strong column of the enemy was marching towards Varese, on our left. I was most deeply mortified, and kept saying to myself, "Can it be possible that Urban's flight was nothing but a stratagem?" I was extremely annoyed, and lost no time in sending orders to Colonel Cosenz, who commanded the reserve, to march at once on Varese, occupy it, and defend it to the very utmost. I made a flank march with my brigade, on the heights to the left, to deceive the enemy, who would be unable to tell whether or not such a march was undertaken to turn their flank; and when I had got out of sight behind the mountain, turned off to the left by a path which leads to Malnate, where the men were assembled in order to march on Varese without loss of time. The news that the enemy's column was marching on Varese being confirmed, I was somewhat surprised, for this column had not only been seen by peasants and common soldiers, but by superior officers. At last we reached Varese, and no more was said about it; the idea vanished amid the acclamations of the kindly people, and was, like a black cloud, driven away by the enthusiasm of the citizens.

I imagine that the column really existed after all, and think that the matter must have taken place in this way: Urban, attacking our left at Varese with his main body, must have sent the force which had been seen, and of which we had heard at San Salvatore, to turn our flank and act conjointly with him. This stratagem had the same result as many by night, and some by day, in places where the ground, as in the present case, is not well known. A combined night-attack of several columns needs, in order to be successful, many favourable circumstances, and a thorough knowledge of the country, with good guides, unimpeachable skill on the part of the leaders of the columns, experienced soldiers, and, finally, a piece of ground with fewer obstacles than that which extends from Varese to Como and, beyond, to the Alps; as, if one leaves the road in this part of the country, either to right or left, the by-paths to be found are extremely intricate. Such, I think, was the reason for the appearance of the strange column, which was nothing else but a force that had lost its way. Destined to turn our left flank, and finding itself entangled among unknown

ditches, it had attempted to get out of them by moving,
now in one direction, now in another, till at last the
men, utterly tired out, had thrown themselves down in
some hidden valley to rest. This was the conclusion I
arrived at from the various reports I heard as to the
enemy's force; and, if our own people had not been
tired out, I would certainly have pursued that stray
column, with a strong probability of overtaking and
capturing it.

Such things happen in our land, where the priests
tell the peasants that heaven is their country, not the
Italy they teach them to hate; while they teach them
to curse the Liberals as heretics, and to bless their
chauvin or Austrian deliverers! Even to-day, unfortunately—I say it with deep bitterness of soul—the
same thing would happen, because the priest is not
kept in his place; to-day, as much as ever, he teaches
love for the foreigner, and hatred of Italy! If that
robber-band of Austrians had found themselves, instead,
in a place where the peasant is taught to love a country
which makes him prosperous, they would certainly
have been dispersed and forced to lay down their arms.

All our own and the Austrian wounded were collected
and sent to Varese. The prisoners, who might in
justice have been forced to expiate with their blood
the murder of our beloved comrades, Ciceruacchio
and Ugo Bassi, and so many others, were, on the
contrary, treated with perhaps even greater care and
kindness than our own men. Not that this is any
credit to us; it is Italy's duty to show humanity

towards her executioners. Forgiveness is the privilege of great souls; and our beautiful country will be truly great when once cured of the cruel plague of Jesuitry.

We marched, then, with the whole brigade, on Varese, to allow the men to get the rest of which they stood so greatly in need.

This was the first fight in which our Alpine *cacciatori* took part, and in it they displayed a valour surpassing all previously formed expectations. Soldiers, for the most part young and unaccustomed to fighting, had faced regular troops trained to despise the Italians, and had put them to flight in each encounter. I augured well for the future from this first victory.

Our losses had been comparatively insignificant as regards numbers, but important and painfully felt, considering the quality of the individuals lost. The greater number of those who followed me were not only well-educated young men of good family—that was comparatively a trifle, for the well-born and well-educated ought to do their duty by their country as well as the proletariat—but there were men of great artistic distinction serving in the ranks as private soldiers.

Dear and noble youth, the hope of Italy, who, in the epic of her resurrection, as yet in the future, was to supply the men who fought at Calatafimi, Monterotondo, and Dijon!

Not a single complaint was heard among the wounded; and if ever a cry found utterance while surgical operations were going on, it was that of " *Viva l'Italia!* " When a people's feelings reach this pitch,

all the papal, foreign, and domestic tyrants may pack
up bag and baggage.

Among the dead was also a son—the first she was
to lose—of that woman for whose sake posterity will
forget the difference between this pitiful age and the
glorious days of Greece and Rome; I allude to the
noble-hearted matron of Pavia, the mother of the
Cairoli. Ernesto, the youngest of the three whom she
had sent to the war, fell fighting, shot through the
chest, on the corpse of an Austrian drummer, killed by
his bayonet. I thought of the heavy sorrow of that
mother, so devoted to her sons, so kind to all who
were happy enough to approach her. On the same day
my eyes met those of the elder brother, Benedetto, a
gallant and modest officer, dear to me as the rest of the
family; his eyes met mine, but not a word was spoken
by either of us. Only I read in that sad look the words,
"My mother!" and thought of all the grief preparing
for that noble heart. And how many others, whose
mothers I did not know, lay mutilated or dying on
that field of slaughter, only longing to see their heart-
broken mothers' faces once more! Poor young fellows!
or rather happy ones, whose blood was redeeming
Italy from her long slavery, and for ever!

The noble-hearted women of Varese made up for
the absence of parents, as far as our wounded were
concerned.

Women of Italy!—I write it with deep emotion; would
you believe it?—I could not tell you about Signora
Cairoli without tears. It is weakness, take it as you

will ; yet I have seen a good deal in my time, of battle-fields, wounded and dying men, corpses, and now—forgive me the presumption of saying so—I no longer feel as strong as I was at twenty, though still as fiery of soul as then, whenever I get a chance of raging for this sacred land of ours. God grant I may close my life repeating as my last words, " *All* Italy is free ! "

Yes, the women of Varese supplied a mother's place to our wounded ; and, it must be confessed, even our enemies shared their pious care. I am not sure whether the fight at Varese took place on the 25th or the 26th of May, though I feel certain that it was on the 27th we marched to Como.

I knew the advantage to be gained by attacking an enemy thrown into confusion by a first defeat, however strong he may be, and did not wish to lose the opportunity of so doing. We left Varese, therefore, for Como, on the morning of May 27, by the Cavallasca road, reaching the latter village after midday. The men had done a great deal of marching, and were tired ; but the hour was propitious. At nightfall one can attack even a superior force with comparatively little danger, especially in a mountainous position like that which was to be the scene of our enterprise, where the enemy's cavalry and artillery could be of little use.

I therefore let the men rest, and began to make all possible inquiries about the enemy's numbers, and the positions occupied by them ; and, receiving intelligence that they were in force in the strong position of San Fermo (which I at once concluded to be the key to all the rest), I directed several companies, under the orders of the brave Captain Cenni, to turn this position on the right. Our second regiment was to attack in front, as soon as the flanking companies should have had time to reach the enemy's flank. The appointed time being over, Colonel Medici, with his usual gallantry, attacked the position in front, while Cenni, with the companies above mentioned, did so in flank.

The enemy bore up bravely against our attack, and fought with obstinate valour. The position was strong, commanding, and well fortified, so that the fight went on with the greatest fierceness for about an hour. At last, surrounded on all sides, the Austrians began to break and fly, and some of them surrendered.

This first longed-for success made us masters of all the dominant positions, which was well; for the Austrians were advancing in force from Camerlata and Como, to the assistance of their detachments on the higher ground.

Medici on the right, and Cosenz on the left, supported by a few companies of the third regiment under the gallant Majors Bixio and Quintini, repulsed the enemy at all points.

The fire of the brave Genoese carbineers, with their improved weapons, contributed greatly to the successful issue of the day. The enemy were numerous, and our brave *cacciatori* had nothing in their favour but the superiority of the ground gained in their first rush. The Austrians were indeed repulsed; but, in a mountainous region like the one where we were fighting, they could always find a position to maintain themselves in, and sometimes one enabling them to beat back our soldiers when they pressed them too closely.

The same configuration of the ground prevented us from overlooking the whole of the battle-field at once, and often we only had intelligence of a partial engagement through the firing heard.

From the heights, the enemy's strong reserve could be seen drawn up in good order in the underlying plain, and also their artillery—twelve guns—which was of no use to them. After the fighting just described, as night was coming on, I attempted to assemble our scattered forces, separated from each other by the inequalities of the ground and the complex nature of the fighting.

The brigade being all collected, we immediately marched along the road which runs in a zigzag course down to Como, the enemy retreating as we advanced. At Borgo San Vito we halted to make inquiries, but it was difficult to find any inhabitants, as they had all disappeared, in fear of ill-usage. At last we resolved to enter the town.

The people, terrified from the first, and not knowing to which army the invaders belonged, as the night was very dark, kept their doors and windows closed, and not a soul was to be seen. But when they discovered by our accent that we were Italians, their brothers, there took place a scene which beggars description, and ought to have had the sun shining on it. It was like the explosion of a mine; in a flash the town was lit up, the windows crowded with people, and the streets almost blocked. All the bells sounded the tocsin at once, and contributed not a little, I think, to the consternation of the flying enemy.

Who can describe the touching scene witnessed at Como that night, and who can remember it without emotion? The people were frantic. Men, women, children, had seized upon my soldiers—embraces, tears, shrieks, delirium, were the order of the night. The few horsemen, marching with me at the head of the column had to make serious efforts not to be overthrown and pulled out of their saddles, especially by the girls, whose beauty seemed to authorize them to assume the mastery over their deliverers.

There was no certain intelligence of the enemy. Some said they were quartered in such or such a place; others, that they were on the march towards Camerlata. The fact is, that while we were entering on one side they were leaving by the other, and not finding themselves secure at Camerlata, they proceeded in confusion towards Milan, leaving behind them, in the depôts at Camerlata, a great quantity of victuals and arms.

The poor gallant Alpine *cacciatori* bivouacked about the streets and squares of Como, and had good reason to be tired; for, leaving Varese in the morning, they had marched all day, and afterwards fought and marched half the night. This was a wonderful feat for young fellows quite unused to the fatigues of campaigning. Only patriotic enthusiasm could have kept them on their feet. I, who was a tough old veteran, after having arranged the formation of some barricades at the end of the street nearest Camerlata, and having looked with affectionate emotion at my weary comrades stretched out in the streets and squares, accepted for a moment the shelter offered me in, I think, the Rovelli house.

The enemy had received a heavy blow. From the nature of the ground, from the various fights that had taken place, and from the fact of night having overtaken us, it was to be supposed—which was, in fact, the case—that they were much scattered, and therefore demoralized. However, convinced that they had about 9000 men, twelve guns, and a respectable cavalry force, while we had less than 3000 men, with a few mounted guides, and not a single cannon; and considering the position of Como, in a depression surrounded on all sides by formidable heights;—I was quite right to occupy my mind with what might happen on the following day, if we had to deal with an enterprising enemy. All these thoughts disturbed my short interval of repose, and the dawn found me riding towards Camerlata, to get intelligence of the enemy. They had evacuated that important point—such was the sum of the information I received; and it was very welcome, my brave fellows being so worn out that it was not desirable they should have to fight that day. We occupied and garrisoned Camerlata and the *cacciatori* rested all day, to their great satisfaction.

The victory had been dearly purchased. Our dead and wounded were not many, but such as we could ill spare. The gallant De Cristoforis had paid with his life for the impetuous daring with which he led his company to the front attack on the position of San Fermo, and his loss was one which we felt cruelly. Young, handsome, modest as a girl, he had all the gifts which go to make heroes and great captains. De Cristoforis was from the same district as Anzani, Daverio, and Manara; born, like them, in an enslaved country, he had, like them, proved that a people which produces men of that stamp must be the slave of none. As was the case with these others, his personal courage was a slight thing compared with the choice qualities of soul which adorned him. The country of the Scipios and the Gracchi, the nation which records in its annals the Vespers and Legnano, may be turned from the right way, crushed down for a moment—for a moment trodden underfoot by foreign arrogance, or prostrated by the contagious corruption of impostors—but it will never want sons to astonish the world.

And Pedotti! He had not the presence of De Cristoforis, being of insignificant stature, but was of like valour; and he too had paid his tribute to his country, when he lay dead among the brave men who led the front attack. Pedotti, too, formed part of that chosen band of young Lombards belonging to the first families, who had come to swell the ranks of the volunteers at the very beginning of the enlistment. He first spent his money lavishly in the purchase of arms, and afterwards gave his life for his country. Cartellieri too, second to none of the band in gallantry, had from 1848 onward been found wherever there was fighting going on for Italy.   Brave young hearts ! the lives you gave so freely form the eternal foundation on which will be built up the country you loved so well ; and the women of coming generations will tell their children of your glorious deeds, and teach them to bless your sacred names.

I have forgotten the names of many of my comrades who fell in that truly glorious action, in which a few raw and inexperienced lads scattered, with their impetuous onset, the far more numerous ranks of the ferocious Urban, who fled as far as Monza without turning back to see who had defeated him.

The possession of Como improved our situation by the acquisition of means of every kind—of credit, and of reinforcements in men and arms. The steamers, thanks to the good-will of the company and of their commanders, were ours, so that we were masters of the lake.   All the villages of the lake, and the districts of Lecco and the Valtellina, had pronounced in our favour ; everywhere men were asking for weapons to join in the patriotic enterprise. We were, however, still in want of arms, and yet more of ammunition, a great deal having been consumed in the preceding fights ; and not only were we at a distance from Piedmont, our base of operations, but communication with it might be said to be almost entirely cut off. The patriotism of some of the citizens made up for the want of communication with Piedmont as regards news ; but as to arms and ammunition, it was difficult, if not impossible, to get them.   This put it into my head to approach the Lago Maggiore once more, and at the same time attempt a *coup de main* on Laveno. The Alpine *cacciatori* were therefore soon on the road again from Como to Varese. Major Bixio, a distinguished and resolute officer—one of those, like Cosenz and Medici, to whom the arrangement of any enterprise may be entrusted, in the certainty that they will do their duty—was instructed to advance and reconnoitre Laveno; but the intended attack did not fall to his share, as, when I approached that point, it was suggested to me that the operation might be supported from the lake, and Bixio was the best man to be placed in charge of any manœuvre to be executed on the water, as, in addition to his gallantry as a soldier, he was an experienced captain.

Remaining but a short time at Varese, we marched to Gavirate; and afterwards écheloned the brigade from Gavirate to Laveno. I might have attempted a serious night-attack on Laveno with the whole of my troops; but I knew, from intelligence I had received, that Urban was on our track with greatly increased forces, and was therefore firmly resolved not to engage with my whole strength, having a formidable enemy at a short distance in the rear. I therefore confined myself to a partial surprise, and entrusted it to two companies of the first regiment, under the orders of Captains Bronzetti and Landi. Major Marrocchetti was to support them with the rest of the battalion, and Colonel Cosenz with the rest of the regiment. In the mean time, I had received two small mountain howitzers and two light cannon, with some ammunition, under the charge of the gallant Captain Griziotti

The operation on Laveno did not succeed. Captain Landi, who was the first to attack, entered the fort about one in the morning, with a score or so of men; but, not being followed by the rest of the company, was obliged to evacuate it—the rather as he himself was severely wounded. Captain Bronzetti, being led astray by his guides, did not arrive in time to take part in the attack; so that our men were driven back, and obliged to take position again in the open, where it was easy for the enemy to wound some of them by shots from behind the parapets. If the rest of the company had entered with Captain Landi, and been immediately followed by the other company under Bronzetti, the fort, with about eighty Austrians, would certainly have remained in our hands. Having taken this fort, which commanded all the other positions, and the steamers, I could easily have occupied Laveno, and thus kept open the communication with Piedmont.

Not only was the assault on the fort a failure, but also that from the lake with the steamers, Major Bixio having been unable to induce the revenue boats on the Piedmontese side to accompany him. We therefore had to think of retreat as soon as the enemy, perceiving, at dawn, that our attack was unsuccessful, opened a tremendous fire on the retreating companies and the reserves. The forts and the steamers kept up a desperate cannonading, as if in revenge for the fright they had had during the night. They fired off rockets —the favourite plaything of the Austrians—in enormous quantities. A plaything indeed, for never in my life have I seen man or animal wounded by one of these bugbears. The wish of the Austrians being to rule Italy through fear, their favourite weapons have been these rockets, which frighten without doing any injury, and fire, which both frightens and injures. Let our countrymen bear this in mind! I hope that those populations who, to their sorrow, are still saddled with these tyrants, will get rid of them as quickly as possible; and then we shall see no more of the rockets or conflagrations. But if, perchance, matters should take a different turn, let us remember the rockets, the burning towns, and the murders they have committed.

South of Laveno there is a wooded height, which overlooks all the positions of that town, as well as its harbour on the lake. I had sent the little artillery we had to this spot, where it served to keep the steamers at a distance. So that our retreat was made in pretty good order.

Captain Landi behaved with his usual gallantry. Having led the van of his company right into the fortress—the darkness of the night, perhaps, being the reason why the rest lost their way—he remained there, severely wounded. If Bronzetti, likewise a man of perfect courage, had been as fortunate, the success of the enterprise would have been assured. Lieutenant Spegazzini and Sparvieri were also wounded while fighting bravely.

On the evening of the same day, I was informed that Urban had entered Varese. This was somewhat of a check to my plans. I was cut off from Como, and there was no time to be lost. I threw myself into Val Curia with my brigade, and, crossing Val Gana, descended in sight of Varese, and reached the foot of Biumo Superiore with the vanguard.

Night was coming on, so that we could attack the enemy without much risk, and with a secure retreat into the strong positions of Val Gana in case of failure.

From the heights overlooking Varese on the north, I had made accurate observations of all the positions occupied by the enemy; and from what I could see, the latter seemed to me to be very numerous, though fewer than represented by the inhabitants—not less than twelve or fifteen thousand. I could see their artillery, and could also see that—as was natural—they had occupied all the dominant positions.

My wish to attack Urban and liberate Varese was very great; but I knew that the Austrian general would be willing to avenge on the poor inhabitants any defeat he might sustain, and also that it was quite in his power to do so. All things considered, I did not attack, but resolved to lead the brigade back to Como.

At Malnate there was also an Austrian corps, so that we could not follow the main road from Varese to Como, and I was obliged to proceed by a more mountainous path, which, thanks to the excellent guides I obtained from the *podestà* of Arcisate, we were able to traverse, in spite of a deluge of rain, which continued without a single minute's intermission through our whole march. This was a new proof of the courage and endurance of my young comrades.

We passed within a short distance of Malnate, but in such a storm, that we were in no danger of coming upon Austrian scouts. The column had been stretched out to its greatest length, and once I attempted to check the leading ranks, but found it impossible; it was only by continuing our march that we could at all bear up against the storm and the cold, which were very trying to my poor fellows. It was a long and toilsome march; several streams and torrents, swollen by the rain, were difficult to cross, especially for the rear of the column, and the waggons.

At last we reached Como, where, as the good inhabitants welcomed our *cacciatori* with their usual kindness, past dangers and fatigues were soon forgotten. Our return to Como, however, did not take place a day too soon, as the people of the district were becoming disheartened through our absence. All kinds of falsehoods had been put in circulation by the Austrians and their masters in this craft, the priests, who showed an especial talent in making masses of hostile troops appear and disappear at every point of the horizon.

The municipal authorities of the town had retreated to the lake, as well as several companies whom I had left behind when starting for Laveno. The wounded also had been transferred to Menaggio, which was most unseemly.

All this had frightened the inhabitants. If any hostile force, however small, had appeared at Como during our absence, the place would have returned to its Austrian subjection. This news was brought me by a beautiful and high-spirited young girl, who drove out from Como to tell me of the deplorable state of the town, and entreat my speedy return, and appeared to me, in her carriage, like a lovely vision, on the road between Rubarolo and Varese, while I was marching on the latter town to attack Urban.

At Como, works of defence were planned on all important and commanding points in the environs, and the population lent themselves with alacrity to the work; but the battle of Magenta, which took place about this time, completely altered the aspect of affairs. That battle, as was natural, electrified the public mind, and made our position easier, while that of Urban, at Varese, had become very critical; indeed, with a few more thousands, we should have had no difficulty in making him lay down his arms. However, considering that my brigade at that time consisted of about 2000 men capable of fighting, I certainly could not run the risk of being crushed by throwing myself in the way of an enemy who so far outnumbered us. In spite of these considerations, I had, it is true, one morning resolved to throw my corps across the roads which Urban had to follow in order to fall back on Monza; but I abandoned the plan for various reasons, chiefly because Urban, knowing that we were on the Monza road, would have taken that to Como, the most important, and the safest for us, from every point of view.

As the steamers had made us masters of the Lake of Como, there was no longer a single point on the lake where the abhorred Austrian colours had not been hauled down, and the tricolour hoisted in their stead. The important town of Lecco opened up to us the great road of the Valtellina, and also that to the east, leading to Bergamo and Brescia, with which towns our gallant Gabriele Camozzi was already in close communication.

Gabriele Camozzi is one of those fine characters in whom Italy was rich at the time of her revolutionary struggle—characters which one is always fortunate in finding, and which, just at critical moments, are sure to make their appearance in some striking manner. I had seen him for the first time at Bergamo, and had been strongly attracted by that winning, modest, and resolute countenance. The attraction proved mutual, for, in the hour of need, I found Camozzi ready with 10,000 francs, to help me in my straitened circumstances.

About the time of the battle of Novara, we find Camozzi in the neighbourhood of Bergamo, collecting three or four hundred men, many of them his own tenants, to march to the assistance of Brescia—the heroic city whose people were fighting to the knife against the numerous and well-trained soldiers of Austria, keeping up the conflict for several days. A sublime example which, had it been followed by all Italian cities, would ere this have taught our insolent neighbours that this land is no longer their country residence, and that there is no power on earth capable of subduing a nation which possesses such sons.

Yes, Camozzi and his comrades' marched alone to succour the valiant people of heroic Brescia. It was a noble act of impetuous courage, this attempt to help and cheer their brethren in danger and conflict, or at least to share their unhappy fate. I was at a distance when I heard this about Camozzi, and was deeply touched with admiration and respect (1849).

To-day (1872) Italy ought no longer to fear foreign invasion. Who on earth can conquer a nation able to arm over two million citizens? But none the less is it a good thing to recall the example of the gallant Bergamaschi.

Gabriele Camozzi, as already mentioned, was in correspondence with Bergamo and the surrounding villages. It is therefore superfluous to say how valuable his coöperation was to me.

I have already indicated above the reasons which prevented my throwing myself on Urban's line of retreat. Not having embraced that resolution, yet unwilling to remain idle, I contemplated operations on the line of Lecco, Bergamo, and Brescia, as being better suited to our usual mode of action, and the slender force to which the brigade was reduced.

We continued to encourage insurrections in such important places as these, while always keeping our own liberty of action. Having, therefore, decided on this last plan, I began to embark part of the brigade on board the steamers from Lecco. At that moment I received a communication from General Fanti, asking me whether I thought it possible to operate against Urban conjointly with the forces commanded by him. I do not know who brought this communication, but as

I did not see the messenger, and was not asked to send an answer, I continued my march towards Bergamo, leaving to the allies the task of pursuing Urban, then in retreat for Monza and the Adda.

From Lecco we continued our march for Bergamo, where the Austrians were. On the way we took prisoner an Austrian officer, who was making a circuit of the neighbourhood to exact a contribution of 12,000 zwanzigers, threatening, in case of refusal, the destruction of the villages—a frequent compliment on the part of these gentle masters, accustomed to put their threats into immediate execution. This time they were paid in the iron coin with which Camillus paid the Gauls in Rome.

On approaching Bergamo, at an early hour in the morning, we heard from the inhabitants that the enemy were just evacuating the city, and that, however quickly we might march, we could not come up with them.

We occupied Bergamo, where we found some guns and a great quantity of ammunition, though the enemy had attempted to destroy everything.

A curious incident occurred at Bergamo. At the beginning of our occupation, we received notice from the railway station that a corps of 1000 men was leaving Milan to reinforce the garrison of Bergamo. I assembled the brigade in the station, hiding the men in the cuttings and the various buildings, as well as at all points in the neighbourhood that could be occupied with advantage. It was indeed quite true that a train full of Austrian troops was approaching, but a *cantonnier* of Austrian nationality, who happened to be at Seriate, about two miles away, warned the enemy of our presence in Bergamo; so that they did not pursue their way, but stopped at Seriate, probably undecided what to do.

Captain Bronzetti, sent with his company to reconnoitre in that direction, resolutely charged and routed the Austrian force, though ten times as numerous as his own. When I arrived, with some troops to support Bronzetti, the Austrians had disappeared. Let this prove to our countrymen that such masters as these certainly did not deserve to have us as slaves; and also serve as a specimen of the demoralized state of the murderers of Ugo Bassi and Ciceruacchio.

We had a few men wounded in this truly extraordinary encounter, among them the brave Lieutenant Gualdo, who was obliged to have his leg amputated.

We did not remain long at Bergamo, but, hearing that the enemy were levying contributions on the village of Bassa, marched down with the brigade, and succeeded in saving the poor peasants from depredation. After this we went on towards Palazzolo, whither I had sent on Cosenz with his regiment. Having reached Palazzolo, and hearing that the enemy was on the Brescia road, I determined to hasten our march to that city, which, as I learnt from some messengers who came to bring me the news, and ask for help in the name of the Brescians, had already been evacuated, but feared a return of the enemy, who were still in the neighbourhood.

My poor *cacciatori* had reached Palazzolo tired out by forced marches, but I counted on their gallant spirit, and not in vain. I had inquiries made by the commanding officer of each corps, in order to find out whether the men felt able to go on as far as Brescia the same night, and with one voice the cry was raised by these brave champions of Italy, "To Brescia! to Brescia!" So that about 9 p.m. they were again on the march, with the same readiness and cheerfulness as ever, forgetful of hardships and weariness. My brave young comrades! At this very moment while I write of you, thus giving you the only proof of affection in my power just now, you are exposed to the abuse and misrepresentation of pedantry and envy,—of the men who did little or nothing for Italy, while you were doing all that patriots could. At this moment the place of your gallant officers is taken by the Thersites of the Italian Iliad, who revel gorgeously, while the greater number, and the best, of our friends, rejected as if they had been enemies, are wandering and begging their bread through those same districts where, by your side, they fought the plunderer of our land. Well, my poor, noble brothers-in-arms, our country cannot refuse you her applause for the many glorious labours undergone; and she hopes that, in the hour of danger, though rejected and hardly treated by scoundrels, you will yet return, with the same dash and the same alacrity, to fight against her enemies. Those who show so much interest in depreciating you, and putting out of sight the glorious uniform which dazzles them, and which so poorly adorned you at Varese, at Como, and at Seriate, cannot refuse to feel a certain admiration for your deeds, and above all for your endurance in bearing the hardships and fatigues of the forced marches from Varese to Como, and from Palazzolo to Brescia.

Half-way from Palazzolo to Brescia, at a place whose name I do not remember, we found the enemy. We were not to attack, but to avoid them, as, with the small probability of success which their superior numbers afforded us, our enterprise would have been retarded by so doing. We therefore took a road to the left, which was very good, and not much longer. The Brescians, informed of our approach, sent out a quantity of carriages to meet us and convey those too tired to walk; and on the following morning we reached the city, where we found, as at Bergamo, the whole population assembled to welcome us, with even more enthusiasm—with an enthusiasm, indeed, which might be called Brescian; that is to say, unique.

Palermo, Genoa, Milan, Brescia, Messina, Bologna, Casale! when all Italian cities are resolved to treat the enemies of your country as you have done, this our country will no longer be a land of masters and slaves, but of free men respected by all.

In the citadel of Brescia, as in that of Bergamo, we found many guns and a great quantity of ammunition. We spent some days in this city, so as to let the men rest, and then marched on towards Rezzate and the Chiese. It was thought that the enemy were retreating by way of these places; but the numerous patrols which approached the high-road from Brescia to Ponte San Marco, along which we were passing, indicated that they were still in force at Castenedolo.

At Rezzate, I received from the King's head-quarters the order to occupy Lonato, with the notice that two cavalry regiments and a battery of artillery, under the orders of General Sambuy, would be sent to assist me in this operation.

With the enemy in force at Castenedolo, I certainly could not pass the Chiese at Ponte San Marco, and made inquiries as to a passage higher up. In consequence of the information received, I determined on repairing the bridge of Bettoletto, destroyed by the Austrians a few days before.

The King's orders, though at first received with joy, placed me in some degree of embarrassment with regard to the regiments of cavalry and artillery which were to join and act in conjunction with us. By marching with the whole brigade to the Chiese, I should leave the high-road open ; and the artillery and cavalry, without our support, would then certainly be exposed to great danger. I therefore resolved to leave the first and second regiments écheloned on the high-road, fronting the enemy at Castenedolo, and keeping an eye on them, while I posted myself with part of the third, the company of Genoese Bersaglieri, the four guns, and the Guides, on the Chiese, in order to construct the bridge at Bettoletto. The bridge was nearly finished, when I received information that the enemy had attacked our two regiments left on the high-road. I left the works at the bridge, and betook myself at a gallop to the scene of action.

The first regiment which had been attacked had, under the brave Colonels Cosenz and Türr, repulsed the enemy with much gallantry, driving them back on their main body at Castenedolo; but, overcome by numbers, had been obliged to beat a retreat, and it was in this state, and somewhat disordered, that I found it on reaching the battle-field.

Colonel Türr, who was on the left—the point I reached—had been wounded and carried away from the field. With my brave staff-officers, Cenni, Trecchi, Merryweather, I restored some order among our gallant *cacciatori*, who once more made head against the enemy, but were again obliged to fall back before the superior weight of the Austrian force, which not only pressed them hard in front, but tried to turn their flank and surround them. The retreat, however, took place in good order, under cover of the second regiment, which had been summoned by Major Carrano, my chief of staff.

Among the gallant officers who fell in this affair we had to deplore the loss of Major Bronzetti, who had earned, in all our encounters, the title of " Bravest of the Brave." He was carried off the field with three bullet-wounds, and died a few days later.

Gradenigo, a descendant of the famous Venetian patricians, an officer of admirable bravery and coolness, had been killed at the head of his men, while charging the enemy. Aporti, my former comrade at Rome and in Lombardy, as valiant in fight as he was gentle and lovable in the ordinary intercourse of life, had fallen among the enemy, and was left behind in the retreat; being unable to move, on account of a broken thigh, which was amputated shortly afterwards.

I do not know whether time will enable me to recall the names, for the present vanished from my memory, of so many of my brothers-in-arms, martyrs for Italy, who fought so gloriously, and fell on the battle-field that day—a memorable one for the Alpine *cacciatori*.

The engagement of this day, known as the fight of Treponti, was the most hardly contested and the most murderous in which our first regiment—to whom the main honour of the day is due—took part. The second sustained the glory acquired in previous encounters; and the companies of the third, under the brave Major Croce, showed themselves worthy to fight beside their gallant comrades.

Lieutenant Specchi was wounded in one arm while covering the retreat with his usual bravery. A detach-ment of the Genoese company, which I had led from the Chiese, arrived in time to support our men and signalize the courage of that chosen band. Stallo, Burlando, Canzio, Mosto, Rosaguti, Lipari, distinguished themselves as usual. The Austrians ceased to advance, and all the Alpine chasseur corps that had taken part in the conflict, tired as they were with the march and the sustained fighting, reconcentrated themselves on the high-road near Treponti, collecting the wounded.

This fight would not have taken place under such unfavourable conditions, had we not had the honour of being under direct orders from head-quarters, which obliged us to divide the brigade, leaving behind two-thirds, for the protection of the advancing cavalry and artillery, which never appeared at all. It was the first time in the campaign that I was in direct communication with the King's head-quarters, and certainly I had no reason to congratulate myself on the result. Did they, or did they not, know that Lonato was the head-quarters of the Emperor of Austria, and the centre of an army of 200,000 men? And, if they knew it, why send me to Lonato with 1800? To admit that the fact was not known, would be to have a very unfavour-able idea of the King of Sardinia's staff, who, whatever might be their other shortcomings, were not negligent in the employment of spies. And why promise to send me two cavalry regiments and a battery, to secure the safety of which, my little brigade ran the risk of utter destruction, while all the time not only was nothing sent, but, from that-day to this, I have never heard another word of that cavalry and artillery? Was it, then, a plot in which they wished to entangle me, to secure the ruin of a handful of brave men who were too much for the nerves of certain great masters of the art of war. I began at last to be convinced that the King's staff had wished to play off a joke upon us, but a somewhat tragic joke; and this showed me that it was an insane idea to want to occupy Lonato, and that I had better attend to our own affairs without awaiting orders from above. I was confirmed in this opinion by the answer I received from General Cialdini when, in the evening, I reported to him the day's events. He said, "You will fare badly, if you trust to such men." It was therefore clear that I could only count on myself and my comrades for any further arrangements to save us from falling into the clutch of the enemy's army, which was still entire and not far off, as subsequent events soon proved. During the action already described, having observed that the enemy were gaining ground on the right, I thought, with some reason, that they were trying to cut out our force on the Chiese. I therefore sent orders to Colonel Arduino to leave the bridge already constructed, and retire to the mountains, which were a short distance from Novolento. The colonel, taking my order too literally, not only retired on Novolento, but, having sent the artillery towards Brescia by way of Gavardo, took the mountain-paths with the infantry, and retreated in the same direction.

Having given Colonels Cosenz and Medici the necessary directions for concentration on certain points, I set off at a gallop to join Arduino, and put him in communication with the other corps, on the slopes of the mountains, which offered positions capable of being maintained against a superior force.

Being just then without a staff, as Cenni's horse had been killed, and the rest whose horses were not tired out had already been sent away elsewhere, I went on alone, making inquiries of all the people I met. Almost all the inhabitants had either fled or hidden themselves, to escape the annoyances and depredations to which they were subjected both by friends and foes. Moreover, what are called glorious battles have, naturally enough, little interest for those not immediately concerned ; and the rustic population has, hitherto at least, always shown itself indifferent to Italian battles, even where we have not found it hostile. All the intelligence I obtained represented the men I was in search of as at a great distance, so that it was only thanks to my excellent mare, which had galloped all day, that I was able to overtake them. Without her I should, to my great mortification, have had to go on seeking that fraction of the brigade in the mountains near Brescia for another whole day, or only come up with them in the city itself.

That evening, the brigade remained écheloned from Rezzate to Nuvolera and Nuvolenta, while the king's army was advancing along the Brescia road. General Cialdini, with whom I was connected by ties of friendship, had done his best, on hearing of our engagement at Treponti, to push on, being, as he was, in the van of the royal army. He told me that he had sent some of his light forces to support us ; but they were worn out with the long march, and only arrived when the battle was over.

We remained for some days écheloned in the above-mentioned positions. Our presence, and the progress of our army, kept the population of Gavardo and Salò well-disposed ; and, moreover, the Gavardo people having restored the bridge over the Chiese, which also had been destroyed by the Austrians, I intended to push on to Salò, passing over this bridge. We therefore assembled all the brigade at Gavardo, passing the Chiese in the night, and directed our march towards Salò. Major Bixio had orders to occupy this town on the Lake of Garda with his battalion during the night; and the brigade remained on the heights overlooking the north road, making its entry into Salò on the morning of the following day.

While arranging the project of marching towards the Lake of Garda, I had at the same time sent for some boats from the lakes of Como and Iseo, which arrived with us at Salò. I had procured these boats under the not unnatural impression that the enemy, when abandoning the western side of the lake, would have withdrawn or destroyed the boats; though we found afterwards that they had done neither the one nor the other.

We occupied Salò for several days, the most important event of our stay there being the destruction of an Austrian steamer. While we were there, this vessel came every day to make observations, and for this purpose always backed into the innermost part of the harbour, keeping her bow towards the entrance, so as to be ready for retreat in case of need. Having seen this manœuvre take place every day, I asked the commander of a strong detachment of the army, which happened to be at Gavardo, for half a field battery, containing, among other pieces, two howitzers. The half-battery having arrived, I placed it on the right-hand side of the entrance to the harbour, in a position that could not have been more suitable, had it been constructed on purpose. The pieces were placed on the lake-shore, and covered with bushes, which completely concealed them from outside, while leaving them free to open fire on the lake in any direction. On the opposite side of the entrance to the harbour, I had sent the Genoese Bersaglieri under Captain Paggi, to hide among the bushes. The steamer entered the harbour, and, backing in the usual way, came within range of the Bersaglieri, who opened fire on it with their improved rifles. As a result of their fire, the steamer withdrew from that side, and approached the masked half-battery on ours. After a few shots from our gunners, fire was seen on board the steamer, which they did not succeed in extinguishing. The vessel attempted to gain the other side of the lake with all speed, but did not succeed, sinking within a short distance. I am sorry not to remember the name of the brave artillery officer who pointed those guns, but glad to record here a word of praise for our Italian artillery, certainly second to none in the world.

General Cialdini, under whose orders I had been placed by the King, directed me to march into the Valtellina with my brigade. I sent forward Colonel Medici in this direction, and he collected all our detachments within reach of that valley, driving the Austrians back on the Stelvio.

I followed with my brigade into the Valtellina, crossing the Lake of Como from Lecco to Colico by steamer. We occupied the valley as far as Bormio, whence Medici, pushing on towards the Stelvio, obliged the enemy to withdraw from Lombard soil.

Our young Alpine *cacciatori*, led by Medici, Bixio,

Sacchi, and others, gave fresh proofs of courage, and endurance in this new kind of warfare, among the gorges and precipices of the Alps, covered with eternal snow, where the enemy, being nearly all Tyrolese, were familiar with the ground and the climate. We were therefore masters of the Valtellina, while General Cialdini, with the fourth division of the army, occupied Val Camonica and Val Trompia, as far as the Lake of Garda, and Colonel Brignone, of the same division, occupied Val Camonica itself.

I do not think it beside the point to say a word here about the fate of that fourth division, beyond doubt one of the best in the Italian army, and commanded by most distinguished officers. Was it detached from our army because the appearance of a strong body of Austrians was feared from that part of the Tyrol? Or was it for the sake of diminishing our army, and causing it to play a less conspicuous part in the decisive battle which must inevitably be fought on the Mincio? Or was it in order to keep a watch over the corps of Alpine chasseurs—growing just then at a portentous rate—and deprive it of that independence which, though seemingly not displeasing to the King, did not please certain exalted personages?

I think the first supposition is not altogether wrong with regard to that fox of a Bonaparte, and that the removal of the division from the army was a mere pretext for depriving the latter of a brave leader and an excellent division. Besides, the Alpine *cacciatori*—who, though reduced, after the affair at Treponti, to 1800

men, had increased as if by magic in little more than
a month to about 12,000, and were adding to their
numbers daily,—did not fail to give umbrage to those
insignificant bigots who maintained that the volunteers
were no use, by having the impudence to become
formidable to them. These men, overloaded as they
are with guilt, are afraid of us, and have plenty of
reason to be so. They call us revolutionaries, and
honour us in so doing; nor will we renounce that
honourable title, so long as there are base wretches
on earth who, in order to revel in luxury themselves,
keep the better part of the nation in slavery and misery.
This sending the fourth division away may have had its
origin in the crooked soul of the third Napoleon, and
been reflected in the mind of the King and his servile
courtiers. The fact is that the battle of San Martino
took place, and the Italian army, composed in all of
five divisions, wanted the fourth, which might have
carried out a brilliant *coup de main* and made the hard
struggle sustained by our side easier. The fear, real or
pretended, of Austrian troops descending from the Tyrol,
was evident to me from the hour of my arrival at Lecco,
where I found a detachment of French sappers and
miners, with a superior officer, occupied in mining the
main road from Lecco into the Valtellina. It is true
that this officer had orders to come to an understanding
with me as to what was to be done; and I, having no
information of any hostile troops advancing in that
direction, begged him to desist from his work of destruction. I believe that General Cialdini had orders—

emanating, no doubt, from the same source—to destroy roads and bridges in the upper valleys; like orders being transmitted to Colonel Brignone, who occupied Val Camonica, and to me in the Valtellina.

The colonel reluctantly had some roads broken up, and I had the points most suitable for demolition, in case of need, studied by engineers; but nothing of the kind was actually carried out, as it seemed to me an act of untimely fear to ruin bridges and roads absolutely necessary to the poor dwellers in the valleys, unless we had intelligence of the enemy's presence in large numbers. Meanwhile the great battles of Solferino and San Martino were taking place; and soon after, the peace of Villafranca, looked on by many as a calamity, and by me as a fortunate event, was concluded.

At the armistice—afterwards the peace of Villafranca —the 1200 Alpine *cacciatori*, in five regiments, occupied the four valleys of Valtellina, Camonica, Sabbia, and Trompia, as far as the Tyrolese frontier. General Cialdini had retired with his division on Brescia. In addition to the five regiments of Alpine *cacciatori*, there had arrived, at last, the regiment of *cacciatori* of the Apennines, which Cavour, in spite of the King's orders—received at the beginning of the campaign— had always, under one pretext and another, refused to send me till the war was over.

With the Apennine *cacciatori* arrived also Colonel Malenchini, the same who, when the Italian youth began to migrate into the ranks of the Piedmontese army, had come from Tuscany with 900 men. Malenchini was a great acquisition to me, both on account of the affection with which his soldiers regarded him, and the truly kind friendship which he entertained towards me. A little later came Montanelli, a man whom I had taken into my affection from the moment I made his acquaintance—at Florence in 1848—and who deserved the respect of every one for his truly heroic self-denial. He was a private soldier in the corps of the Apennine *cacciatori.* Montanelli, Filopanti, and Massimo d'Azeglio are three men who have always inspired me with a real respect for their courage and talent. In them I venerate the ideal of the great citizen. Two of them may, for the moment, have been doctrinaires; but they grudged no personal risk in the hour of danger. At Curtatone, and at Vicenza, those two illustrious political leaders were wounded, fighting as private soldiers among the Italian patriots. I have myself seen Filopanti, the great astronomer, the irreproachable member of the Roman Constituent Assembly, fighting, musket in hand, at the defence of Rome. Italy may well be proud of having produced such men. Montanelli, amid the Tuscan youth at Curtatone, and Massimo in the ranks of the combatants at Vicenza, are figures which loom gigantic; and the honourable scars gained on the battle-field adorn with a halo of eternal glory the authors of " La Costituente Italiana," and " Niccolò de' Lapi."

When Malenchini marched into Piedmont with his Tuscan youth, he quitted the post of minister of war at Florence, which public opinion, then omnipotent, had justly assigned him.   He resigned this position as soon as he heard of the fighting in Lombardy, and hastened to the spot, eager for the chance of striking a blow for his country.   Such self-abnegation is often carried too far by modest and deserving patriots; the superior posts, nobly deserted by them, being usually filled by intriguers only capable of working mischief to the country.

The armistice of Villafranca, which was universally understood to be preliminary to a peace, left the Alpine *cacciatori* in a position unsuited to their character.   Enthusiastic young men, who had given up their professions and the comforts of their life to get the chance of fighting for Italy, were certainly not suited for the quiet life of a garrison, the monotonous routine of quarters, and, above all, the excessive discipline enforced on royal armies in time of peace. It was therefore understood that, from the very beginning of the armistice, the Alpine *cacciatori* would become an exotic plant in the midst of the standing army, subject to the permanent hostility of La Marmora's ministry.   The news from Central Italy, on the other hand, offered some warlike prospects.   It was said that the Duke of Modena was keeping himself in readiness to invade the duchy; and that the Pope's Swiss guards, after the slaughter of Perugia, were eager to throw themselves upon Romagna.

CHAPTER XII.

IN CENTRAL ITALY.

ONE very natural desire was manifested in Central Italy, then in full blast of hostility against its rulers—to secure the services of the Alpine *cacciatori.* This corps fully deserved the esteem of the country; the independent character of its component elements seemed to guarantee, with a fair degree of probability, that it would not be indiscriminately fettered by dynastic interests. There needed no great stimulus to urge it on against priests and petty tyrants.

Montanelli and Malenchini not only spoke to me of this plan, but made a journey into Central Italy, on their return from which they entreated me to betake myself thither, in accordance with the request of the governments of Florence, Modena, and Bologna, who also offered me the command of their troops.

When I told Montanelli that I would demand my discharge, and march without delay, he embraced me with emotion. Malenchini then arrived with a letter from Ricasoli, summoning me into Central Italy to command the whole army *or a part of it.* This expression showed me the existence of some amount of distrust, but, as I have never made any stipulations in serving the cause of peoples—above all that of my own country—I did not say a word. The good Malenchini, however, told me that Farini, with whom I had spoken at Modena, and Pepoli, whom I had seen at Turin, assured him that they would give me the command of all troops stationed there.

I therefore sent in my resignation as a Sardinian general, and set out, by way of Genoa, for Florence. In the capital of Tuscany my misgivings began to be realized; for I perceived that I had to deal with the same class of men with whom I had come in contact on my first arrival in Italy. At Montevideo, I had abandoned the supreme command of an army which had been fighting heroically for six years; yet, on my reaching Italy with my poor but valiant seventy-three, I spent some months in wandering from Nice to Turin, from Turin to Milan, thence to Roverbello, and then back to Turin; and after all this waste of time, succeeded at last, a short time before the capitulation of Milan, in obtaining the command of a few sweepings of the barracks, with the grade of colonel. And this command was only given to me when the war had taken a disastrous turn, and, in fact, just for that very reason. I had come from America to serve my country, were it only as a private soldier; the rest mattered little to me. On the other hand, it mattered a great deal to me that I should see Italy honourably served, and not left a prey to a certain crew of worthless scoundrels. At Rome, a minister, Campello, kept me and my men at a distance from the capital, and his beggarly suspicions would not allow my force to exceed the number of 500. In Piedmont, at the beginning of 1859, I was kept as a flag to attract volunteers; the volunteers flocked to the standard fast enough, but those between the ages of eighteen and twenty-six were destined for the line regiments, Only those who were too young, too old, or in some way deficient, were sent to me, on whom the obligation was laid not to appear in public—to avert a diplomatic scare, so it was said. Once on the field of battle, moreover, when I might have been able to do something, I was refused even those volunteers who had flocked at my call.

At Florence, it was not difficult to understand that I had to deal with the same kind of men. They began to speak of the possibility of General Fanti's accepting the supreme command, which they had been holding out as a bait to me. Poor miserable rascals! Perhaps I ought to have accepted nothing, and returned to private life; but, as I said before, the country was in danger. And what then? Was it my custom to demand anything for myself, when so noble a cause was in question? I accepted the command of the Tuscan division.

When I entered the Palazzo Vecchio, the people received me with acclamations; these, naturally, were not very welcome to the Government, who requested me to calm the people, and start as quickly as I could for Modena, the head-quarters of the division.

At Modena, I saw Farini, who received me well, and placed under my orders the organized forces of Modena and Parma. Farini, a man of superior intelligence and not too scrupulous, was, like all the rulers of Central Italy, much liked in the capacity of dictator of those beautiful provinces; and the idea of having a man beside him whose popularity matched his own, did not please him much. Ricasoli I thought from the beginning more open and less cunning than Farini; but, unhappily, he seemed to feel the same repulsion for me, attributing it to my excessive rashness. Cipriani, the Governor of Bologna, was an out-and-out Napoleonist, and as such could have little in common with me. Between this last and myself, therefore, a frank mutual antipathy had manifested itself ever since my first arrival in Central Italy; and there was no danger of his making arrangements to hand over to me the command of the troops, in that part of Romagna governed by him. The call I received from these gentlemen was therefore instigated by the small measure of popularity I enjoyed, on which they hoped to ride into favour themselves—nothing else, as we shall soon see.

Farini—"just as a joke," as he used to say—had one day, writing to Fanti, offered him the command of the Central Italian troops. Fanti, with that coolness peculiar to him, did not accept definitely, but held out hopes that he would do so, when once his position with regard to the Sardinian Government had been settled. The fact is that my presence in the centre was most welcome, both to the people and the army; and the more evident this feeling was, the more intolerable it became to the Government. The latter, therefore, used all their efforts to hasten the arrival of General Fanti, who, holding, as he did, the position of my military superior, was the only one who could restrain my ardour in a just cause, and quiet the fears of the new rulers, just as jealous of popular favour as the old ones. Although a born revolutionary—since any one who suffers cannot remain either silent or steady (and what man who sees his country enslaved and plundered does not suffer?)—I have, notwithstanding, never refused to subject myself, when necessary, to that needful discipline indispensable to the success of any and every enterprise; and, convinced as I was that Italy ought to march with Victor Emmanuel in order to free herself from the foreign yoke, I thought it my duty to obey his orders at any cost, even to the silencing of my republican conscience. Nay, more; I thought that, quite apart from any consideration of his fitness for the post, Italy ought to confer the dictatorship on him, till such time as her territory should be completely free from the foreigner. Such was my conviction in 1859; it has since been somewhat modified, because the monarchical form of government has many defects, and because we could have done immense things by our unaided efforts; though, as a matter of fact, we have always preferred kneeling at the feet, now of one, now of another, pitifully and disgracefully supplicating for what, after all, is our own. This being premised, a hundred thousand men would have gathered round me in Central Italy during the latter part of 1859; and with their appearance European diplomacy would certainly have taken a favourable turn, or one might even, with only the 30,000 thus assembled in the Duchies and Romagna, have decided the fate of Southern Italy in a fortnight—in short, done what was done by the Thousand a year later.

The Governments would have remained at their posts, and in the mean time administered the affairs of their several provinces, and filled a place secondary, indeed, but glorious in our operations. This was not their own opinion ; and therefore they plotted together to humiliate me, and nullify my action; two of them from base personal considerations, the third, probably, in obedience to the orders of the man whose wish—though in this I may be mistaken—is anything but the unity of Italy (1859).

Meanwhile, I dragged on a deplorable existence for some months, doing little or nothing in a country where so much could and ought to have been done. Organizing troops is the most tedious of occupations for me, who have an innate antipathy to the soldier's trade; who have at times, it is true, because born in an enslaved country, taken it up, but always with reluctance, and with the conviction that it is a crime for men to be forced to butcher one another, in order to come to an understanding.

Being obliged to confine myself to the Tuscan division, I occupied myself in improving its condition. Then Fanti came ; and a great deal of nonsense was current at the time of his arrival ; for instance, Farini assured me that Fanti would assume the ministry of war, and that I should take command of the troops. Valerio arrived, sent by the Piedmontese ministry, and said to me,

" Remember, if you are not satisfied, Fanti does not wish to accept." I replied, " I am not satisfied," and Fanti accepted nevertheless.

In short, the point for these gentlemen was to get rid of my personality, without entirely eliminating my name, which they needed, in order to make themselves attractive in the eyes of the people. They thought they had found a way out of their difficulties by naming me second chief of the troops of the league ; this league consisting of three provinces of the Peninsula, whose powerful Governments, for fear of displeasing certain patrons, did not dare to call themselves Italy !   This is the way in which we build up the constitution of this humble and disgraced country of ours.

Here began the base intrigues intended to disgust me. Fanti refused to accept my gallant officers of the Alpine *cacciatori*, summoned by me with the Governor of Modena's consent, while officers of every other kind were welcomed.   My poor *cacciatori*, who had come in crowds, ever since they had heard of my presence in Central Italy, to increase existing corps and form new ones, were very hardly treated.   Arriving, for instance, from the remotest parts of Lombardy, without shoes, in their linen jackets, quite worn out by the march, they were rejected on account of some slight defect of age, stature, or physical constitution.   No one so much as dreamed of asking them whether they had had anything to eat, or whether they had means to get food and return home.   The governor, Cipriani, acting on an understanding with Fanti, sent me to Rimini, to fit out two merchant vessels for fighting, and had me escorted by a brother of his, who corresponded with him in cipher, without my knowledge. At Rimini, all orders were given to General Mezzacapo, who happened to be my subordinate.

I appreciated all the difficulties of my position, and had, as it were, to swallow poison, in the hope of being of some use to my unhappy country. Fortunately, I was somewhat indemnified for the intrigues of a cowardly crew by the affection of the people and of my soldiers.

At one time I flattered myself that I was able to modify the difficult situation, and even be of some use, by trying to win over Fanti; and used every effort to gain his friendship. But it will soon be seen how mistaken I was, and what base advantage was taken of my good faith.

The Marches and Umbria, too, were impatient of the Papal yoke, and previous to my arrival had concerted a rising with Cipriani. This was the reason for the arming of the two steamers at Rimini, and I had instructions to second a movement in that district.

My presence at Rimini, it is true, excited the enthusiasm of the people; but, frankly speaking, it was wished —especially by Cipriani—to present the appearance of action, and not only do nothing, but fetter, and even undo, the action of others. With me, in the meanwhile, artifice was used. It was suggested, whether by Cipriani or Fanti I do not know, to swear in the volunteers for eighteen months. Now, from the beginning of the events which had brought about the new state of things, the volunteers had joined on the understanding that they were to serve till six months after the conclusion of the war. All these brave young fellows had entered of their own free will, and would not have uttered a word of objection if the duration of the war had forced them to serve for ten years. But they did not like the eighteen months' fixed service, as I knew well, and had represented first to Cipriani, and then to the commander-in-chief. No notice was taken of my remonstrances, and they nearly lost the whole Mezzacapo division by this ill-judged measure. When I was at Bologna, I was summoned by Intendant Mayer of Forlì and Colonel Malenchini, who were seriously alarmed by the number of desertions and requests for leave of absence in the corps stationed on the line of Cattolica. I hastened thither, and succeeded in partly stopping the dissolution of the corps; but while I was employed at this work, Mezzacapo was using his utmost efforts to get the counteracting measure adopted—that is, to have the men sworn in for eighteen months—perhaps by order of Fanti. He did this for the pleasure of thwarting me; perhaps also in the hope of disparaging me in the eyes of those who did not know me. I asked for some delay in administering the oath, but in vain.

Meanwhile, the agitation among the people of Umbria and the Marches still went on. The gallant old brigadier Pichi, a native of Ancona and a veteran of Italian liberty, kept up a constant correspondence with the oppressed populations, while negotiations were opened with the kingdom of Naples and with Sicily..

With less opposition on the part of the Governors and their generals—who, if they had been paid by the enemy to work mischief, could not have done worse— we might have risked everything and proceeded on a triumphal march to the south of Italy, more easily and completely than was done a year later. It is true that I had instructions from General Fanti, expressed pretty nearly in the following terms :—" If you are attacked by the Pontifical troops, you are to repulse them, and invade their territory; or, in case of insurrection in a city like Ancona, to invade in support of the insurrection." The first alternative was impossible, as the Pontificals were certainly not thinking of attacking us. The second had also become very improbable, as our adversaries were on the watch, and had strengthened the garrisons of Ancona, Pesaro, and other towns. Nevertheless, arms were introduced into Ancona and the Marches, and the people's spirits kept up. The young soldiers who formed the vanguard would have greeted an order to march forward with frantic cries of joy: so great was the general eagerness to rush to the liberation of our brothers. But that fatality weighed on our poor country which, under one form or another, has kept her back for so many centuries. At all times she has been tortured by varying forms of internal discord, and to this evil is added, at the present day, that of a flock of doctrinaires, who, having seized the helm of state, and being supported by all whose object is to prevent Italy from becoming great (1859), do their utmost to deaden her generous impulses.

While I was preparing for action, secret orders were sent to my subordinates not to obey me. General Mezzacapo, in particular, had a despatch from Fanti to this effect: "No one is to move without an order. Send this on to General Roselli." Not only had my subordinates, Mezzacapo and Roselli, orders not to obey me, but my very staff was told to go and place itself at the disposal of Colonel Stefanelli, the head of the Tuscan division.

Such was my position at Rimini when General San-front arrived there, sent by the King. He found me thrown into deep perplexity and indignation by the treacherous conduct of my opponents, and if he had not come, I know not what desperate course I might have resolved upon. I accompanied him to Turin, and had a conference with Victor Emmanuel, which resulted in his promising to advise General Fanti to tender his resignation, as suggested by the Governments of Florence and Bologna, and declaring that Cipriani's presence in Romagna had become absolutely injurious; and that I, at the head of the Central Italian forces, should have done the best for the common cause by acting as I thought fit. Yet he did not give his consent to the invasion of the Pontifical territory—the usual reserve, very natural in his position, in presence of a revolutionary—just as, a year later, he successively refused his consent to the Sicilian expedition, the passage of the Strait, and the march on Rome which ended at Aspromonte. I left Turin well content, and assuredly lost no time in getting to Modena, where I found Farini and Fanti, to whom I frankly detailed the result of my mission.

My opponents, however, were not asleep. A telegram from the Minister of War warned Fanti not to accept his dismissal; and in the mean time they were working on Victor Emmanuel, in order, if possible, to change the character of his feelings towards me.

The first measure to be taken in Central Italy was that of removing Cipriani from the government of Bologna. As I gave those gentlemen to understand, he had to be removed, by persuasion or by force. If we were to carry on operations in the Papal State, it would never do to have in our rear a hostile governor, whose efforts were directed to no other end than that of hindering the arming of the nation. The measure which concerned Cipriani was favourably received by all, every one being interested in his removal, especially Farini and Fanti. The latter, when informed by me of the King's resolution, was not the man to resist it; but Napoleon, Cavour, Minghetti, and others, were too much interested in supporting him. Rattazzi, perhaps the only one of these political intriguers who might have supported me, was weak, irresolute, and probably also, to some extent, under Napoleon's influence.

Here, then, was Victor Emmanuel thwarted—unless all his professions were hypocritical—in his good intentions, and forced to yield once more to Cavourian power and insolence, as he had done at the beginning of the war, when he gave orders for my troops to be reinforced with that regiment of Apennine *cacciatori*, which was afterwards sent to me only when the war was over.

Farini, the old fox, was acting with his usual cunning. To Minghetti's question, "Who should succeed Cipriani?" I had replied, "Farini." And, indeed, by this means there were two advantages to be gained. The first was that of uniting Romagna and the duchies of Parma and Modena under a single government; the second, that with Farini, a man of superior intelligence, and, after all, with an Italian heart, one could obtain what could never have been obtained under his predecessor—a chance of pushing on the work of national armament and national unity.

Since my first arrival in Central Italy I had understood Farini, and, though I did not distrust him as an Italian, he inspired me with no great confidence as a personal friend; besides which, I had lately become aware that he was not acting sincerely by me. My last words to Farini, in the palace at Bologna, were these, "You have not been open with me;" and, as his reply showed some degree of annoyance, I added, "Yes, it is you who are chiefly to blame for this stew."

I must confess, however, that Farini did good work during his dictatorship at Modena, and continued to do the same at Bologna. In other parts of Italy, no one has been able to match the energetic measures in the way of arming and organization, which he and Frapolli carried out at Modena.

For all this, however, the dictator was as little straightforward with me as he had been before; and,

while he fully agreed with me as to what ought to be
done at Bologna, he being at the head of the civil
administration, while I directed the military department, I perceived from the expression of his pale face
that he received adverse hints from outside, and was
disposed to act according as the wind might blow
from Piedmont. The wind had ceased to blow in my
favour from Turin. My opponents had gained the
upper hand in the King's mind ; and no doubt he was
also influenced from Paris, where Cipriani's removal
from power at Bologna, and my appearance in command
of the Central Italian troops, were anything but pleasing.
In their place, I should have said, " Garibaldi, retire ! "
but these men were incapable of so much frankness,
and tried instead to get me out of the way, by every
kind of opposition and the most contemptible strata-
gems. My influence on the soldiers and the population
—so, at least, it seems to me—placed me in a position
where I could have acted in spite of my adversaries ;
and certainly I was not afraid to fling myself into the
vortex of revolution, where, indeed, there was every
chance of success.

But that revolution would have had to be initiated
by me. I should have had to loosen every tie of discipline in soldiers and people ; while before and behind
me, at Rome, Piacenza, and elsewhere, was the French
intervention. In short, the thought that I might compromise the sacred cause of my country kept me from
action. I expected something from the King, according
to our agreement ; if he did not authorize our under-

taking, I thought he would tacitly consent to it, leaving me the whole responsibility, and ready to restrain me, should the necessity occur. All this I was willing to submit to, and was quite ready for any event that might take place. But no sign was given. At last I sent Major Corte to Victor Emmanuel, and then I was summoned to Turin. Reaching the capital, I presented myself to the King, and at once became aware of the change that had passed over him since our last conference. He received me with his usual kindness, but gave me to understand, in a few words, that outside requirements obliged him to maintain the *status quo*, and that he thought better to keep me out of sight for some time.

The King wished me to accept a commission in the army. I declined with thanks, but accepted an excellent fowling-piece, of which he insisted on making me a present, and which he sent me by Captain Trecchi, of my own staff, when I was already in the train for Genoa. Arrived at Genoa, I proceeded to Nice, where I spent three days with my children, returning in time to catch the steamer which left Genoa for La Maddalena on November 28, 1859.

I had my luggage on board, and was on the point of starting, when, happening to be in the house of my friend Coltelletti, I was waited on by a distinguished Genoese deputation, headed by the syndic of the city, Signor Moro, who gave me to understand that my departure would, under the circumstances, be ill-advised. I was persuaded to stay, and accepted the hospitality offered by my friend Signor Leonardo Castaldi, in whose villa at Sestri I passed some days. At that time the mobilization of the national guard was all the talk, and Colonel Türr told me that the King wished to see me, in order to make some arrangements on this head.

I reached Turin and saw the King, who was always kind to me. I also saw the minister Rattazzi, who, I can assure the reader, inspired me with little confidence. I entered into an agreement with both of them, that I should be entrusted with the organization of the mobilized National Guard of Lombardy. I was satisfied with this arrangement for two reasons—firstly, I could in this way prepare a strong contingent for the new war into which I felt sure that Italy would be plunged ; and, secondly, I could incorporate with this national guard many of my old comrades, who were now, most of them, wandering from place to place, without means of subsistence.

While awaiting at Turin the nomination which was to put it in my power to begin the work of organizing, I was visited by the excellent patriots Brofferio, Sineo, and Asproni, with some other liberal deputies, who explained to me that they wished to profit by my stay in the capital, to reconcile the different sections into which the advanced party had for some time been split up, and which were waging with each other a war both unseemly and injurious to the Italian cause. A common complaint in our poor country !

At first, feeling that my success in the scheme proposed to me was very doubtful, and rather averse to any association which did not include the whole nation, I refused to enter into it; and it would have been better had I kept to this resolution. But as they persisted in their request, and explained to me that their scheme, if it succeeded, would be a great benefit, I at last accepted, and we decided on the founding of a society with which, under the name of the " Armed Nation," all existing associations should be incorporated.*

So far everything had gone well, and all members of the different societies who presented themselves to me gave in their adhesion to the idea of fusion, and seemed perfectly satisfied.

A meeting of the society *Libera Unione* was to sanction the act of reconciliation; but, so far from this being the case, those same men who, in conversation with me, had shown themselves quite satisfied with the proposed reconciliation, put forward ideas of quite an opposite character, and, under one pretext and another, declared it to be quite impossible. It had been an old idea of mine, and I became more and more convinced of its justice, that nothing but a rope's end will serve to persuade us Italians to pull together. All our labour, therefore, was not only in vain, but worse still. The foreign ambassadors, strong in the weakness of the Government, or, as was said, instigated by Cavour and

* I do not know when will be realized this dream of my life, which, with the elimination of the priests, would make Italy a power of the first rank.

Bonaparte—then omnipotent—asked for explanations; and, in consequence, the ministry, with the exception of Rattazzi, sent in their resignations *en masse.* The pretexts were the " Armed Nation," the mobilization of the national guard, and, if I may take the liberty of saying so, the fact that my unfortunate self was mixed up with these.

The *Nazione Armata* was a thunderbolt for that miserable diplomacy which longs to see Italy weak— a *chauvin*, Bonapartist diplomacy which has for its perpetuator the little monarch of the French Republic.*

* Thiers, Bonaparte, Chauvinism—all names indicating the ridiculous pretensions of clerical France to domineer over Italy, which will, no doubt, be a constant source of ill-feeling between two nations that might, with a little mutual forbearance, live in harmony as friends. I do not wish to end this second period of my recollections without recording two facts which concern myself, and prove the malice of the man of December 2, and his accomplices—not to mention the extent to which he interfered in our affairs. At Gavardo, where I passed the Chiese in order to reach Salò, in the campaign described above, I was waited on by a certain N—— A——, sent from the Emperor's head-quarters, with the following message :—" I am charged to offer you all you need for yourself and your men ; money and articles of every description will be placed at your disposal—only ask. The Emperor knows the many wants of your soldiers, and wishes to remedy them. He cannot bear the idea of the distress in which you are left." I replied that I was in need of nothing. It must be understood that this was an undisguised bargain ; the sale of Nice was being negotiated—nay, the town was already sold—and they wanted one more accomplice to the business—a Nizzard. At fifty-two—save the mark !—and when a man has seen a little of the world, he is not so easily gulled. Yet so great was the corrupting cynicism of Napoleon III., and so many were the cowards who had prostrated themselves before that image of corruption !

The second fact is the following. After the events in Central

Let this show my countrymen that, if we wish to pass for lions, instead of, as hitherto, rabbits—to overawe our insolent neighbours—we want the whole nation armed : that is, two millions of soldiers—and the clergy honestly employed in draining the Pontine Marshes.

The King sent for me, and told me that it was necessary to lay aside all our projects.

Italy already described, I resigned the command of those troops. Whether or not Bonaparte had a hand in all these intrigues, may be seen by the following letter to the Pope :—

Letter from Napoleon III. to the Pope.

" My efforts only succeeded in hindering the spread of the insurrection ; and Garibaldi's resignation has preserved the Marches of Ancona from certain invasion."

P.S.—It is only through forgetfulness that I have not mentioned Colonel Peard, commonly called *Garibaldi's Englishman.*

This gallant Englishman appeared among our volunteers in 1859, armed at all points, provided with a valuable carbine, and exciting universal admiration by his skill as a marksman and his extraordinary coolness in the greatest danger. Modest and unpretending, he would not accept a *soldo* of pay. He was on the spot every time our volunteers entered the field. He distinguished himself greatly in 1859 and '60. The coming of that splendid English contingent, which, though late in arriving, gave excellent proof of its mettle in the last actions on the plains of Capua, was greatly due to his exertions. If Bonaparte and the Sardinian monarchy had not prohibited our march on Rome after the battle of the Volturno, the English contingent, whose numbers increased every day, would have greatly helped us in winning the immortal capital of Italy. Major Dowling, of the artillery, and Captain Forbes, both English, fought gallantly in the ranks of the volunteers. Along with them, I should be glad if I could point out to the gratitude of my country all those brave fellows who gave their lives to serve her. Deflotte, whom we ought to look upon as one of our martyrs, and Bordone, now a general, also deserve our entire gratitude.

THIRD PERIOD.

CHAPTER I.

THE SICILIAN CAMPAIGN, MAY, 1860.

SICILY! a filial and well-merited affection makes me consecrate these first words of a glorious period to thee, the land of marvels and of marvellous men. The mother of Archimedes, thy glorious history bears the impress of two achievements paralleled in that of no other nation on earth, however great—two achievements of valour and genius, the first of which proves that there is no tyranny, however firmly constituted, which may not be overthrown in the dust, crushed into nothingness by the dash, the heroism, of a people like thine, intolerant of outrages. This is the impression left by the sublime, the immortal Vespers. The second belongs to the genius of two boys, who have made it possible to believe in the discoveries of the human mind in the boundless regions of infinity.*

* Two Sicilian boys, not over fourteen years of age, recently succeeded in mentally extracting the algebraic root of the thirty-second power, in the course of a few minutes—a truly stupendous operation.

Once more, Sicily, it was thine to awaken sleepers, to drag them from the lethargy in which the stupefying poison of diplomatists and doctrinaires had sunk them—slumberers who, clad in armour not their own, confided to others the safety of their country, thus keeping her dependent and degraded.

Austria is powerful, her armies are numerous; several formidable neighbours are opposed, on account of petty dynastic aims, to the resurrection of Italy. The Bourbon has a hundred thousand soldiers. Yet what matter? The heart of twenty-five millions throbs and trembles with the love of their country! Sicily, coming forward as champion and representative of these millions, impatient of servitude, has thrown down the gauntlet to tyranny, and defies it everywhere, combating it alike within convent walls and on the peaks of her ever-active volcanoes. But her heroes are few, while the ranks of the tyrant are numerous; and the patriots are scattered, driven from the capital, and forced to take to the mountains. But are not the mountains the refuge, the sanctuary, of the liberty of nations? The Americans, the Swiss, the Greeks, held the mountains when overpowered by the ordered cohorts of their oppressors. " Liberty never escapes those who truly desire to win her." Well has this been proved true by those resolute islanders, who, driven from the cities, kept up the sacred fire in the mountains. Weariness, hardships, sacrifices—what do they matter, when men are fighting for the sacred cause of their country, of humanity?

O noble Thousand! in these days of shame and misery, I love to remember you! Turning to you, the mind feels itself rise above this mephitic atmosphere of robbery and intrigue, relieved to remember that, though the majority of your gallant band have scattered their bones over the battle-fields of liberty, there yet remain enough to represent you, ever ready to prove to your insolent detractors that all are not traitors and cowards—all are not shameless self-seekers, in this land of tyrants and slaves! "Where any of our brothers are fighting for liberty, thither all Italians must hasten!"—such was your motto, and you hastened to the spot without asking whether your foes were few or many, whether the number of true men was sufficient, whether you had the means for the arduous enterprise. You hastened, defying the elements, despising difficulties and dangers and the obstacles thrown in your way by enemies and self-styled friends. In vain did the numerous cruisers of the Bourbon armament surround as with a circle of iron the island about to shake off their yoke; in vain they ploughed the Tyrrhene seas in all directions, to overwhelm you in their abysses—in vain! Sail on, sail on, argonauts of Liberty! There on the utmost verge of the southern horizon shines a star, which will never suffer you to lose your way—which will lead you in safety to the achievement of your quest. The star seen of the mighty singer of Beatrice—seen of the great ones who came after him, in the darkest hour of the tempest— the Star of Italy! Where are the boats which received you at Villa Spinola, and carried you across the Tyrrhene Sea into the small port of Marsala ? Where ? Have they been jealously preserved, marked out for the admiration of foreigners and of posterity, as the symbol of the greatest and most honourable enterprise ever undertaken in Italy? Not at all; they have disappeared. Envy and contemptible littleness of mind on the part of Italy's rulers produced a wish to destroy these witnesses to their shame. Some say they perished in a purposely contrived shipwreck. Others suppose them to be rotting in the recesses of some arsenal, Others, again, assert that they have been sold, like worn-out clothes, to the Jews.

Yet sail on, sail on fearlessly, *Piemonte* and *Lombardo*,[*] noble vessels manned by the noblest of crews ; history will remember your illustrious names in despite of calumny. And when the survivors of the Thousand, the last spared by the scythe of time, sitting by their own fireside, shall tell their grandchildren of the expedition—mythical as it will seem in those days—in which they were found worthy to share, they will recall to the astonished youth the glorious names of the vessels which composed it.

Sail on ! sail on ! Ye bear the Thousand, who in later days will become a million—in the day when the blindfolded masses shall understand that the priest is an impostor, and tyrannies a monster anachronism. How glorious were thy Thousand, O Italy, fighting against the plumed and gilded agents of despotism, and

* The two steamers which carried the Thousand to Marsala.

driving them before them like sheep!—glorious in their motley array, just as they came from their offices and workshops, at the trumpet-call of duty—in the student's coat and hat, or the more modest garb of the mason, the carpenter, or the smith.[*]

I was in Caprera when I received the first news of a movement at Palermo. Sometimes the talk was of an insurrection which was being propagated, sometimes it was said that the first outbreak had been suppressed. Rumours, however, continued to reach us, of a revolution which, whether suppressed or not, had certainly taken place. I had notice of what had occurred from my friends on the continent. I was asked for the arms and the funds of the "<u>Million of rifles</u>"—the name which had been given to a subscription for the purchase of arms.

Rosalino Pilo and Corrao were preparing to start for Sicily. Knowing the character of those in whose hands was the destiny of Northern Italy, I had not yet shaken off the scepticism into which I had been hurried by the events of the last few months of 1859, and advised them not to act unless we received more positive news about the insurrection. Like the middle-aged man I was, I threw cold water on the strong and

---

[*] From my heart I wish I could have added "of the peasant," but I will not distort the truth. This stalwart and laborious class belongs to the priests, who make it their business to keep it in ignorance. I do not know a single instance of one of its members being seen among the volunteers. They serve in the army, but only when forced to do so; and form the most effectual tools of despotism and priestcraft.

ardent resolutions of youthful will. But it was written in the book of destiny that cold water, dogmatism and pedantry should be powerless to obstruct the triumphant march of Italy's fortunes. Though I counselled inaction, action was going on, and the news at last reached us that the Sicilian insurrection was not quelled. I counselled inaction, it is true; but should not the Italian be found wherever the struggle of the national cause against tyranny is going on?

I left Caprera for Genoa, and had some talk on Sicilian affairs with my friends Augier and Coltelletti. Then, at Villa Spinola, in the house of my friend Augusto Vecchi, we began to make arrangements for an expedition.

Bixio was certainly the prime mover in this astonishing enterprise. His courage, activity, and experience of the sea, especially in the neighbourhood of Genoa, his native place, were of enormous value in facilitating our proceedings.

Crispi, La Masa, Orsini, Calvino, Castiglia, the Orlandi, Carini, and others, were the most enthusiastic for the expedition among the Sicilians, and also Stocco and Plutino of Calabria. All were agreed that, whatever happened, if the Sicilians were fighting, we must go, whether there was any probability of success or not.

However, a few discouraging rumours came very near putting an end to the whole thing. A telegram from Malta, sent by a trustworthy friend, announced that all was lost, and that the survivors of the Sicilian revolution had taken refuge in that island.

We were near desisting from the enterprise, though I ought to acknowledge that the faith of the above-mentioned Sicilians never failed, and that they were still determined to try their luck under the guidance of the gallant Bixio, and at least to ascertain, on Sicilian ground, how matters stood.

Meanwhile Cavour's Government was beginning that system of petty intrigue and contemptible opposition, which pursued our expedition to the last. Cavour's followers could not have said, "We do not want an expedition into Sicily;" public opinion would have declared them reprobates, and that fictitious popularity, gained by the wholesale purchase (with the nation's money) of men and newspapers, would probably have been shaken.

I could therefore prepare some help for our friends fighting in Sicily, with little fear of being arrested by these gentlemen, and with the support of the people's generous feelings, deeply stirred as they were by the manly resolution of the brave islanders. Only despair, and the iron resolution of the men of the Vespers, could push forward such an insurrection. La Farina, deputed by Cavour to watch our movements, showed his want of faith in the enterprise, and made use, in order to dissuade me from it, of his knowledge of the Sicilian people, being himself a native of the island. He alleged that the insurgents, having lost Palermo, were hopelessly ruined. However, a Government notice which he himself gave us, helped to strengthen us in our resolve of immediate action. At Milan we had some 15,000 good rifles, in addition to the pecuniary means at our disposal. At the head of the management of the "Million rifles" fund were Besana and Finzi, both trustworthy men. I sent for Besana, who arrived at Genoa with a sum of money, leaving orders for rifles, ammunition, and other necessaries of war, to be sent to us from Milan. At the same time Bixio was in treaty with Fauché, of the Rubattino Steamship Company, for our passage to Sicily. The affair went off all right, and, thanks to the activity of Fauché and Bixio, and the noble impetuosity of the Italian youth, who hastened from all sides to join us, we found ourselves, in a few days, quite ready to take the sea, when an unexpected incident not only retarded our enterprise, but almost rendered it impossible.

The men sent by me to receive the rifles at Milan found at the doors of the depôt the royal carbineers, who intimated to them that they were not to take away a single rifle. This order had been given by Cavour.

This obstacle, though it did not fail to thwart and annoy us, could not make us desist from our project; and, as we could not have our own arms, we attempted to get others elsewhere. We should certainly have procured them in one way or another, when La Farina offered a thousand rifles and eight thousand francs, which I, unwilling to bear malice, accepted.

It was a cunning act of liberality on the part of those highly placed foxes, since in reality we were deprived of the good guns which had remained at Milan, and found ourselves forced to use the very inferior article procured by La Farina.

My comrades of Calatafimi can describe the wretched arms with which they had to meet the good Bourbon carbines in that glorious conflict.   All this delayed our departure, so that we were obliged to send home many volunteers, their numbers becoming too great for an insufficient means of transport, and because we had no wish uselessly to arouse the suspicions of the police— the French and Sardinian not excepted.   The firm determination to do something, and not desert our Sicilian friends, at last overcame every obstacle.   The volunteers who had been destined for the expedition were recalled, and came at once—especially from Lombardy.   The Genoese had remained in readiness all the time.   The arms, ammunition, provisions, and a small quantity of baggage, were embarked on board some little boats. Two steamers, the *Lombardo* and the *Piemonte*, the former commanded by Bixio, and the latter by Castiglia, were fixed on ; and on the night of May 5 we left the harbour of Genoa, in order to take on board the men who were awaiting us, divided between La Foce and Villa Spinola.

We did not fail to meet with some difficulties, inseparable from an enterprise of this kind.

To board the two steamers at anchor in the harbour at Genoa, just under the Darsena, to overpower the crew and force them to assist us, then to get up steam and take the *Lombardo* in tow of the *Piemonte*, and all this by moonlight—these are actions easier to describe than to perform, and needing great coolness, skill, and good fortune to execute them successfully. The two Sicilians, Orlando and Campo, who formed part of the expedition, and were both engineers, were of the greatest use to us on this occasion.

By dawn all were on board. The joy of danger and adventure, and the consciousness of serving their country's sacred cause, were stamped on the countenances of the Thousand. There were a thousand of them, nearly all Alpine *cacciatori*—those same men whom Cavour, a few months ago, had abandoned in the heart of Lombardy during the Austrian war, and to whom he had refused to send the reinforcements ordered by the King. They were those same Alpine *cacciatori* who were received by the ministry at Turin— being, unhappily, compelled to apply to the latter—as if infected with the plague, and as such driven away; the same Thousand who twice presented themselves at Genoa to run a positive risk, and who always will present themselves wherever there is a chance of giving their lives for Italy, asking for no other reward than the approval of their consciences.

They were glorious, my young veterans of Italian liberty; and I, proud of their faith in me, felt capable of attempting anything.

CHAPTER II.

THE FIFTH OF MAY, 1860.

O NIGHT of May 5, illumined by the countless fires with
which the Omnipotent has adorned the infinity of
space!—beautiful, tranquil, solemn, with that solemnity
which thrills noble hearts hastening to the deliverance
of the slave! Such were the Thousand.

Assembled on the eastern shores of Liguria, they
stood about in groups, grave, overawed by the greatness
of their enterprise, but proud of its having fallen to their
lot, though suffering and martyrdom might follow.

Glorious was the night of the great enterprise. Among
those noble ranks its music was felt with that undefined
but sublime harmony with which the elect are blessed
when contemplating the Infinite in boundless space. I
have heard that music on all nights which resemble the
nights of Quarto, of Reggio, of Palermo, of the Volturno.
Who is doubtful of victory when, borne on the wings of
duty and conscience, he is impelled to meet danger and
death as though they were the kiss of his bride?

The Thousand stamp their rifle-butts on the rock like
the noble charger impatient for the battle. And whither
are they going to battle, so few of them, against

strong and veteran forces? Have they received a sovereign's orders to invade and conquer a poor unhappy population, which, ruined by the exactions of Government extortioners, has refused to pay? No; they hasten to Trinacria, where the Picciotti, intolerant of a tyrant's yoke, have risen and sworn to die rather than remain slaves. And who are the Picciotti? Though bearing this modest title, they are none other then the descendants of the mighty people of the Vespers, who in a single hour exterminated a whole army of tyrants, without leaving a trace.

The two steamers reached the roadstead of Quarto, and the Thousand were promptly embarked, all the boats necessary for the operation having been prepared beforehand.

CHAPTER III.

WHEN all were embarked and ready to proceed towards Sicily, a new incident made the most resolute shudder, and was within an ace of annihilating the whole enterprise. Two boats belonging to certain smugglers, and loaded with ammunition, percussion-caps, and small-arms, were to await us in the direction of Portofino mountain and the Genoa lighthouse; but, although we searched for several hours, it was impossible to find them.

The ammunition and percussion-caps were a serious loss to us; who would venture on an enterprise likely to involve fighting, without ammunition? Yet, after searching in every direction the whole forenoon, and having taken on board oil and tallow for the engine, at Camogli, the two steamers turned westward, trusting to the fortune of Italy.

To get ammunition, it was necessary to touch at some Tuscan port, and we chose Talamone for the purpose. I must commend all the authorities of Talamone and Orbetello for their cordial and generous welcome, but particularly Lieut.-Colonel Giorgini, the principal mil^t-

tary commandant, without whose help we certainly could not have made the necessary provision.

Not only did we find ammunition at Talamone and Orbetello, but coal and cannon, which greatly facilitated and encouraged our expedition.

As it was in Sicily we intended to act, I thought it not a bad idea for us to make a diversion into the Papal States, threatening these and the north frontier of the Bourbon kingdom, so that we might succeed in drawing off the attention of our enemy or enemies, for a few days at least, to that part of the peninsula, and thus deceiving them as to the real objective point of the expedition.

I proposed this to Zambianchi, who accepted eagerly, and would certainly have carried out the plan more effectually than he did, if I could have left him more men and means; as it was, he had to prepare for a task of great difficulty with about sixty men.

At last, having coaled at Santo Stefano, we weighed anchor direct for Sicily, with the vessel's head pointing to Marettimo, on the afternoon of May 9. The voyage was a successful one, in spite of two untoward incidents, both caused by the same man, an individual suffering from suicidal mania, who twice gave us a great deal of trouble without attaining his object. Having thrown himself overboard from the *Piemonte*, he was rescued, in spite of the swiftness of the steamer, by one of those acts of courage and skill which are so much to the honour of seamen. To stop the engines, lower a boat, jump into it in a twinkling, without calculating the danger, and row in the direction of the drowning man, as pointed out by those on board—all this was done in as short a time as it takes to describe. The Italian sailor is second to none at moments when great courage and activity are required.

The man, who had seemed so determined upon dying, .nevertheless changed his mind as soon as he felt the chill of the water and the reality of his danger. Once in the sea, he swam like a fish, and made every effort to reach his rescuers.

The same thing happened on board the *Lombardo*, and this time the folly of the would-be suicide was nearly fatal to the expedition. This man had made his first attempt on board the *Piemonte*, at Talamone. At that port, where we landed all the men during our stay, on account of the limited accommodation on board, he was sent on shore, under the idea that he was mad, and commended to the care of the commandant of Talamone. He contrived, however, to stow himself away on board the *Lombardo*, and afterwards, no one knows how, transferred himself again to the *Piemonte*, whence he jumped overboard, as above described. The boat which rescued him brought him back to the *Lombardo*, and from this vessel he made his last attempt to drown himself, on the evening of the 10th, the day before our landing in Sicily.

On that evening, in hopes of making the island of Marettimo, I had got up steam to the utmost possible speed on board the *Piemonte*, the swifter boat of the two. On this account, and because of the madman's leap overboard, the *Lombardo* remained behind out of sight.

Being unable to discover Marettimo, I suddenly thought of our consort, which I had some time before sighted to northward, just visible like a little cloud on the horizon. I was seized by a sense of dread and remorse, heightened by the approach of night, and ordered the vessel's head to be turned in the direction of the other steamer. With the deepening darkness, my alarm grew; every minute seemed an hour, and, being unaware of the occurrence which had caused the delay—the man overboard—I remained for a moment doubtful whether or not we had lost the *Lombardo*. I cannot describe what I suffered in that short time, or how I reproached myself for the foolish impatience which had driven me on to get the first sight of Marettimo. At last the *Lombardo* hove in sight; indeed, it was not likely we should miss her, as the one was steering straight for the other, but I had a terrible fright.

Now, to crown all, something still worse happened. At the point where night overtook us in the *Piemonte*, there were several unknown vessels in sight. Bixio had seen, and been unable to recognize them on account of the distance; so that, when he perceived us, instead of awaiting him as we had hitherto done, hastening towards him at full speed, he took us for a hostile vessel, and tried to escape by getting up steam and turning away in a south-westerly direction.

We were in despair. I perceived this mistake, and

had all sorts of signals made, prearranged or not, for, though we had agreed not to use lanterns for fear of awakening suspicion, we felt obliged to have recourse to them on this occasion. As this did not succeed, we hastened after our consort before she was lost in the darkness, and succeeded in coming up with her; when, in spite of the noise of the paddle-wheels, my voice was recognized, and everything set right. We kept close together for the rest of the night, and in the morning sighted Marettimo, and shaped our course for the south side of that island.

During the voyage the whole of the men had been divided into eight companies, the most distinguished officers of the expedition being placed at the head of each. Sirtori was appointed chief of staff; Acerbi, quarter-master; and Türr, staff-officer. The arms had been distributed, as also the few clothes we had been able to get together before our departure.

Our first idea was to land at Sciacca, but as the day was advanced, and we were afraid of meeting the enemy's cruisers, we resolved to put into the nearest port—that of Marsala (May 11, 1860).

As we approached the western coast of Sicily, we began to discover sailing-vessels and steamers. On the roadstead of Marsala two men-of-war were anchored, which turned out to be English. Having decided on landing at Marsala, we approached that port, and reached it about noon. On entering the harbour, we found it full of merchant vessels of different nations.

Fortune had indeed favoured us, and so guided our

expedition that we could not have arrived at a more propitious moment.

The Bourbon cruisers had left the harbour of Marsala that morning, sailing eastward, while we were arriving from the west; indeed, they were still in sight towards Cape San Marco, as we entered—so that, by the time they came within cannon-shot, we had already landed all the men out of the *Piemonte*, and were beginning to disembark those on board the *Lombardo*.

The presence of the two English men-of-war in some degree influenced the determination of the Bourbon commanders, who were naturally impatient to open fire on us, and this circumstance gave us time to get our whole force on shore. The noble English flag once more helped to prevent bloodshed, and I, the Benjamin of these lords of the ocean, was for the hundredth time protected by them.

The assertion, however, made by our enemies, that the English had directly favoured and assisted our landing at Marsala, was inaccurate. The British colours, flying from the two men-of-war and the English consulate, made the Bourbon mercenaries hesitate, and, I might even say, impressed them with a sense of shame at pouring the fire of their imposing batteries into a handful of men armed only with the kind of muskets usually supplied by Government to Italian volunteers.

Notwithstanding this, three-fourths of the volunteers were still on the quay when the Bourbons began firing on them with shells and grape-shot—happily, without injury to any one.

The *Piemonte*, abandoned by us, was carried off by the enemy, who left the *Lombardo*, which had grounded on a sand-bank.

The population of Marsala, thunderstruck at this unexpected event, received us pretty well, all things considered. The common people, indeed, were delighted; the magnates welcomed us under protest. I thought all this very natural. Those who are accustomed to calculate everything at so much per cent., are not likely to be reassured by the sight of a few desperadoes, who wish to ameliorate a corrupt society by eradicating from it the cancer of privilege and falsehood—especially when these desperadoes, few in number as they are, and with neither three-hundred-pounders nor ironclads, fling themselves against a power believed to be gigantic, like that of the Bourbon.

Men of high position—that is, the privileged class—before risking anything in an enterprise, wish to assure themselves which way the wind of fortune blows, and where the large battalions are; and then the victorious force may be certain of finding them compliant, cordial, and even enthusiastic, if need be. Is not this the history of human selfishness in every country?

The poor people, on the other hand, welcomed us with applause and with unmistakable tokens of affection. They thought of nothing but the sacredness of the sacrifice—the difficult and noble task undertaken by that handful of gallant young fellows, who had come from such a distance to the succour of their brethren.

We passed the remainder of the day and the following

night at Marsala, where I began to profit by the services of Crispi, an honest and capable Sicilian, who was of the greatest use to me in Government business, and in making all necessary arrangements which my want of local knowledge prevented my doing myself. A dictatorship was spoken of, and I accepted it without hesitation, having always believed it the plank of safety in urgent cases, amidst the breakers in which nations often find themselves.

On the morning of the 12th, the Thousand left for Salemi, but, the distance being too great for one *étape*, we stopped at the farm of Mistretta, where we passed the night. We did not find the proprietor at home, but a young man, his brother, did the honours with kindly and liberal hospitality. At Mistretta we formed a new company under Griziotti.

On the 13th, we marched to Salemi, where we were well received by the people, and were joined by the companies of Sant' Anna d'Alcamo, and some other volunteers of the island.

On the 14th, we occupied Vita, or San Vito, and on the 15th came in sight of the enemy, who, occupying Calatafimi, and knowing of our approach in that direction, had spread out the greater part of their forces on the heights called " Il Pianto dei Romani." *

* It is said that the Romans were destroyed by the natives in a great battle which took place at the time of the first Roman occupation of the island.

CHAPTER IV.

CALATAFIMI, MAY 15, 1860.

THE dawn of May 15 found us in good order on the heights of Vita ; and a little later, the enemy, whom I knew to be at Calatafimi, left the city in column, marching towards us.

The hills of Vita are fronted by the heights of the Pianto dei Romani, where the enemy deployed their columns. On the Calatafimi side these heights have a gentle slope, easily ascended by the enemy, who covered all the highest points, while on the Vita side they are steep and precipitous.

Occupying the opposite and southern heights, I had been able to perceive exactly all the positions held by the Bourbonists, while the latter could scarcely see the line of sharpshooters formed by the Genoese carbineers under Mosto, who covered our front, all the other companies being drawn up *en échelon* behind them. Our scanty artillery was stationed on our left, on the highroad, under Orsini, who succeeded, in spite of the poverty of his resources, in making a few good shots. In this way, both we and the enemy occupied strong positions, fronting each other, and separated by a wide space of undulating ground, broken by a few farm-steadings. Our advantage, therefore, clearly lay in awaiting the enemy in our own position. The Bourbon forces, to the number of about 2000, with some cannon, discovering a few of our men without distinguishing uniform, and mingled with peasants, boldly advanced a few lines of Bersaglieri, with sufficient support and two guns. Arrived within firing distance, they opened fire with carbines and cannon while continuing to advance on us.

The order given to the Thousand was to wait without firing for the enemy to come up, though the gallant Ligurians already had one man killed and several wounded. The clang of the bugles, sounding an American réveille, brought the enemy to a halt as if by magic. They understood that it was not the Picciotti alone they had to deal with, and their lines, with the artillery, gave the signal for a retrograde movement. This was the first time that the soldiers of despotism quailed before the filibusters—for such was the title with which our enemies honoured us.

The Thousand then sounded a charge—the Genoese carbineers in the van, followed by a chosen band of youths impatient to come to close quarters.

The intention of the charge was to put to flight the enemy's vanguard, and get possession of the two guns— a manœuvre which was executed with a spirit worthy of the champions of Italian liberty; but I had no intention of a front attack on a formidable position occupied by a strong force of Bourbon troops. But who could stop those fiery and impetuous volunteers in their rush on the foe ? In vain the trumpets sounded a halt; our men did not hear, or imitated Nelson's conduct at the battle of Copenhagen. They turned a deaf ear to the halt sounded by the trumpets, and with their bayonets drove the enemy's van back on their main body.

There was not a moment to be lost, or that gallant handful would have perished. Immediately a general charge was sounded, and the entire corps of the Thousand, accompanied by some courageous Sicilians and Calabrese, marched at a quick pace to the rescue.

The enemy had abandoned the plain, but, falling back on the heights where their reserve was, held firm, and defended their position with a dogged valour worthy of a better cause. The most dangerous part of the ground we had to cross was the level valley separating us from the enemy, where we had to face a storm of cannon and musket-balls, which wounded a good many of our men. Arrived at the foot of Monte Romano, we were almost sheltered from attack; and at this point the Thousand, somewhat diminished in number, closed up to the vanguard.

The situation was supreme; we were bound to win. In this determination, we began to ascend the first ledge of the mountain, under a hail of bullets. I do not remember how many, but there were certainly several terraces to be gained before reaching the crest of the heights, and every time we climbed from one terrace to the next—during which operation we were totally unprotected—it was under a tremendous fire. The orders given to our men to fire but few shots were well adapted to the wretched weapons presented to us by the Sardinian Government, which nearly always missed fire. On this occasion, too, great service was rendered by the gallant Genoese, who, being excellent shots, and armed with good carbines, sustained the honour of our cause. This ought to be an encouragement to all young Italians to exercise themselves in the use of arms, in the conviction that valour alone is not enough on modern battle-fields; great dexterity in the use of weapons is also necessary.

Calatafimi! the survivor of a hundred battles, if in my last moments my friends see me smile once more with pride, it will be at the recollection of that fight—for I remember none more glorious. The Thousand, clad just as at home—worthy representatives of the people —attacked, with heroic coolness, fighting their way from one formidable position to another, the soldiers of tyranny, brilliant in gaudily trimmed uniforms, gold lace, and epaulettes, and completely routed them. How can I forget that knot of youths who, fearing to see me wounded, surrounded me, pressing themselves closely together, and sheltering me with their bodies? If, while I write, I am deeply touched at the recollection, I have good reason. Is it not my duty at least to remind Italy of the names of those brave sons of hers who fell there?—Montanari, Schiaffino, Sertorio, Nullo, Vigo, Tükery, Taddei, and so many more, whose names I grieve to say I cannot remember.

As I have already said, the southern slope of Monte Romano, which we had to ascend, was formed of those ledges, or narrow terraces, used by the cultivators of the soil in mountainous countries. We made all possible haste to reach the bank of each terrace, driving the enemy before us, and then halting under cover of the bank to take breath and prepare for the attack. Proceeding thus, we gained one ledge after another, till we reached the top, where the Bourbon troops made a last effort, defending their position with great intrepidity : many of their chasseurs, who had come to the end of their ammunition, even throwing down stones on us. At last we gave the final charge. The bravest of the Thousand, massed together under the last bank, after taking breath and measuring with their eye the space yet to be traversed before crossing swords with the enemy, rushed on like lions, confident of victory and trusting in their sacred cause. The Bourbon force could not resist the terrible onset of men fighting for freedom; they fled, and never stopped till they reached the town of Calatafimi, several miles from the battle-field. We ceased our pursuit a short distance from the entrance to the town, which is very strongly situated. If one gives battle, one ought to be sure of victory; this axiom is very true under all circumstances, but especially at the beginning of a campaign.

The victory of Calatafimi, though of slight importance as regards acquisitions—for we only took one cannon, a few rifles, and a few prisoners—had an immeasurable moral result in encouraging the population and de-moralizing the hostile army.

The handful of filibusters, without gold lace or

epaulettes, who were spoken of with such solemn contempt, had routed several thousand of the Bourbon's best troops, artillery and all, commanded by one of those generals who, like Lucullus, are in the habit of spending the revenue of a province on one night's supper. One corps of citizens—not to say filibusters—animated by love of their country, can therefore gain a victory unaided by all this needless splendour.

The first important result was the enemy's retreat from Calatafimi, which town we occupied on the following morning, May 16, 1860. The second result, and one abundantly noteworthy, was the attack made by the population of Partinico, Borgetto, Montelepre, and other places, on the retreating army. In every place volunteer companies were formed, which speedily joined us, and the enthusiasm in the surrounding villages reached its height.

The disbanded troops of the enemy did not stop till they reached Palermo, where they brought terror to the Bourbon party, and confidence to the patriots. Our wounded, and those of the enemy, were brought in to Vita and Calatafimi. Among ours were some men who could ill be spared.

Montanari, my comrade at Rome and in Lombardy, was dangerously wounded, and died a few days after. He was one of those whom doctrinaires call demagogues, because they are impatient of servitude, love their country, and refuse to bow the knee to the caprices and vices of the great. Montanari was a Modenese. Schiaffino, a young Ligurian from Camogli, who had also served in the Cacciatori délle Alpi and in the Guides, was among the first to fall on the field, bereaving Italy of one of her best and bravest soldiers. He worked hard on the night of our start from Genoa, and greatly assisted Bixio in that delicate undertaking. De Amici, also of the Cacciatori and Guides, was another who fell at the beginning of the battle. Not a few of the chosen band of the Thousand fell at Calatafimi as our Roman forefathers fell—rushing on the enemy with cold steel, cut down in front without a complaint, without a cry, except that of "Viva l'Italia!"

I may have seen battles more desperate and more obstinately contested, but in none have I seen finer soldiers than my citizen filibusters of Calatafimi.

The victory of Calatafimi was indisputably the decisive battle in the brilliant campaign of 1860. It was absolutely necessary to begin the expedition with some striking engagement such as this, which so demoralized the enemy that their fervent southern imaginations even exaggerated the valour of the Thousand. There were some among them who declared they had seen the bullets of their carbines rebound from the breasts of the soldiers of liberty as if from a plate of bronze. Far more men were killed and wounded at Palermo, Milazzo, and the Volturno, but still I believe Calatafimi to have been the decisive battle. After a fight like that, our men knew they were bound to win; and the gallant Sicilians, whose courage had been previously shaken by the imposing numbers and superior equipment of the Bourbon force, were encouraged. When a battle begins with such prestige, with omens drawn from such a precedent, victory is sure.

Novara, Custoza, Lissa, and perhaps even Mentana, in spite of the disparity in troops and resources, were disasters for Italy, not so much on account of our losses in men and means, as through the insolent confidence acquired by our enemies, who are not, certainly, superior to the Italians, but who, if they ever have to fight us again, will look on us as an easy prey—as men who have to be driven forward with the butt-ends of muskets.

For Italy's future solemn trials a Fabius will be required, who knows how to delay when necessary. Indeed, the configuration of our country is such that we can carry on a war just as we like, accepting or refusing battle at pleasure, and, when position and circumstances are propitious, let loose our Italians, who will have become impatient for the fight, and are, happily, susceptible of a strong impetus. There will come a Zama, where Scipio, without asking the number of the enemy, will seek and put them to flight.

Even this subject I cannot consider without encountering the ever-present influence of the priesthood, who wish to make all the Italians into sacristans. And if Italy does not seek a remedy, it will be a serious business. Jesuitry can produce nothing but hypocrites, liars, and cowards. Let those who ought to do so think of it, and lay the matter well to heart, remembering, above all things, that, for marching and giving good bayonet-thrusts, we need strong men.

CHAPTER V.

CALATAFIMI, being evacuated by the enemy, was occupied by us on May 16, 1860. The greater number of our wounded had been taken to Vita. At Calatafimi, we found the most seriously wounded of the enemy, and treated them as brothers.

Did the ruling dynasties of Italy feel any compunction in urging on these unhappy populations, like fighting mastiffs, one against another? Compunction! What for? Has not their whole study been how to set them at variance, for the sake of purely personal or dynastic interests? Does not the "heap of dirt and blood," as Guerrazzi calls the Papacy, exist in Rome, at the heart of Italy, for the sake of selling her to the highest bidder, and keeping her permanently divided?

The history of all these petty lords would be long and tedious to narrate. To-day, fortunately for our country, they are nearly all beggars; and, if not that, still traitors to and corrupters of nations.

On the 17th, we reached Alcamo, an important town, where we were received with great enthusiasm. At Partinico the people were frantic. They had been subjected to the worst ill-treatment of the Bourbon soldiers before the battle of Calatafimi; and, when the latter returned as scattered fugitives, fell upon them, slaughtering as many as they could, and pursuing the rest towards Palermo. A sickening sight! we found the corpses of Bourbon soldiers lying along the roads, devoured by dogs. They were corpses of Italians—murdered Italians, who, had they grown up as free citizens, would have rendered active service to the cause of their oppressed country; instead of which they reaped the fruit of the hatred sown by their infatuated masters, and ended miserably—literally torn to pieces by their own fellow-countrymen, with a ferocious rage which would have made hyenas shudder.

From the beautiful plains of Alcamo and Partinico the column ascended by way of Borgetto to the plateau of Renne, which overlooks the Conca d'Oro * and the lovely city of Palermo. If Italy had half a dozen cities like Palermo, the stranger would long ago have ceased to tread underfoot this land of ours, and the present governments of spies and police-agents would assuredly have either to keep a straight course, or go to —— their own place.

Renne would be a formidable position if, while commanding the road from Palermo to Partinico, it were not itself commanded by the heights immediately adjacent on the north and south, which belong to the

---

* The valley in which Palermo is situated, abounding in fine orange-trees, whose golden masses of fruit, when ripe, give rise to its name (the Golden Shell).

irregular mountain system surrounding the rich valley of the capital. Renne is famous in the annals of the Thousand for two days of heavy rain, passed without the necessary shelter from the inclemency of the weather, during which the men were put to great inconvenience, but proved their willingness to face inglorious hardships as well as the horrors of battle.

CHAPTER VI.

ROSALINO PILO AND CORRAO.

BEFORE May 5, two young Sicilians had left Genoa for their native island. The one, very handsome, with dark brown hair, belonged to the family of the princes of Capace, and had that delicacy of form and feature which seems especially to belong to the wealthy classes. The other had the beauty of the southern plebeian, jet-black hair, regular but bronzed features, a sinewy and robust figure. ·He was unmistakably one of that class whom fortune has condemned to subsist by the labour of their hands—a class where sometimes one man or another, stimulated by ambition, throws himself out of his orbit, and, if helped by genius, is seen to rise from the lowest of human positions to the upper ranks. Such men were Cincinnatus, Marius, and Columbus. For the rest, both of them, Rosalino Pilo and Corrao, had the hearts of lions. They preceded the Thousand to Sicily, and, landing after a dangerous voyage, at once set themselves to spread the doctrines of emancipation, calling on the brave sons of Etna to rise, in hopes of prompt succour from the mainland of Italy.

Two men, and no more, they landed, proscribed and

under sentence of death, and passed over the whole island, fulfilling their sacred mission, as safe as if they had been in a city of refuge. Hear it, tyrants, and learn that this is not a country of spies! You have wasted your time in lavishing every kind of bribe. Here on the lava of the father of volcanoes, your power, defiled as it is with blood and shame, is but the thing of a day. Throw off your regulation mask, in which no one believes now, and appear under the hideous aspect of Heliogabalus or Caracalla. Here it is nothing but a question of time—of years, perhaps of days. If these wrangling descendants of discord and greatness succeed. in coming to an understanding and acting in concert, in a few hours—as at the time of the Vespers—not a trace will remain of the Maniscalchi and suchlike refuse.

Rosalino Pilo fell in a skirmish with the Bourbon troops, with whom the Thousand exchanged a few shots in the neighbourhood of Renne. He was struck by an enemy's bullet while preparing to write to me from the heights of San Martino, and dropped dead. Italy lost in him one of the bravest of that gallant band whose noble bearing makes her forget, or at least feel less acutely, her degradation and misery.

Corrao, less fortunate than Rosalino, after having fought bravely in every battle of 1860, died by an Italian bullet in a private quarrel.

Sicily will certainly never forget these two heroic sons of hers, worthy harbingers of the Thousand.

CHAPTER VII.

CALATAFIMI TO PALERMO—*Continued.*

AFTER having passed two days of heavy rain at Renne, without shelter and almost without firewood, so that we were forced to burn even the telegraph-poles, we descended as far as the village of Pioppo, above Monreale. This position, however, proved unsuitable, on account of the smallness of our force.

About the 21st, a reconnaissance undertaken by the enemy, in the course of which a few shots were exchanged, determined me to take up a stronger position above the meeting-point of the roads which converge at Renne, thus keeping open the communication along the Partinico road, by which we had come, and also by way of San Giuseppe, further south.

The above-named was a convenient strategic position, and we might have awaited the enemy there with advantage. But I thought the road from Palermo to Corleone better suited for us, for a double reason— besides offering a much wider field of action, it placed us in contact with numerous bands in the direction of Misilmeri, Mezzoiuso, and Corleone, whither I had sent Lamasa to collect them.

I therefore decided to cross over by night, from the road we were occupying, to Parco on the Corleone road.

The march began before nightfall, but the difficulty of the path, along which cannon and all supplies had to be carried on men's shoulders, and the heavy rain, which lasted all night long, with thick fog, rendered this march the most disagreeable I ever performed; and it was already broad day when the head of the column reached Parco by twos and threes. The last of the cannon, indeed, had scarcely arrived by the evening— and that only by dint of tremendous exertions.

The same rain and thick fog prevented the enemy's knowing of our march till long after our arrival at Parco. The latter place is commanded by strong positions, which we seized, erecting on them some works of defence, on which we mounted our cannon. These positions, however, are commanded by lofty mountains, and can therefore easily be turned.

On May 24, the enemy marched out of Palermo with a considerable force, divided into two columns. The first came along the high-road which leads from the capital to Corleone and into the interior of the island, passing by Parco. The second, after following the Monreale road for some distance, crossed the valley and threatened our rear, flanking us on the left, and approaching the pass of Piana dei Greci.

I should not have feared a front attack, though the enemy's force was far superior to ours; but the movement in our rear, along the mountains which overlooked us, made me arrange for a retreat before the enemy's arrival. I therefore ordered the artillery and baggage to start immediately along the high-road, while I, with a handful of Picciotti and the Cairoli company, marched through the pass to meet the second column, which was attempting to cut off our retreat.

Our movement was a complete success. I reached the heights before they had been seized by the enemy, and with a few shots brought the latter to a halt, so that I found myself with my whole force at Piana, having, by the Corleone road, free access to the whole interior of the island, and being able to move whichever way I pleased.

The people of Piana and Parco helped us greatly as auxiliary forces, and as guides, especially a Baron Peta of the first-named place.

At Piana dei Greci we passed the remainder of the day, letting the men rest. That day we had to mourn the loss of young Mosto, brother of the major commanding the Genoese carbineers, who with their usual bravery had retarded the march of the Bourbon troops.

Here, moreover, I resolved to get rid of the cannon and baggage, so as to be less embarrassed in my operations on Palermo, by effecting a junction with the troops of Lamasa, just then at Gibilrossa.

At nightfall, therefore, I ordered the baggage and artillery to follow along the Corleone road, under Orsini, while I with my men, having followed the same road for a time, turned off to the left in the direction of Misilmeri by a not very difficult path through the woods.

The movement of the artillery along the Corleone

road deceived the enemy, as I had hoped it would. They continued their march towards that town on the 25th, in the belief that they were pursuing our whole force, when in fact there was only Orsini, with scarcely any men.

I passed with the column through the wood of Cianeto, where we slept, reaching Misilmeri, where the population received us with great enthusiasm, on the following day. On the 26th, we were at Gibilrossa, already occupied, with several companies, by our friend Lamasa.

After conference with Lamasa and the other Sicilian chiefs, inside and outside of Palermo, it was resolved to attack the enemy in the Sicilian capital. That day several foreigners came to our camp, especially English and Americans, who showed much sympathy for the noble Italian cause. One young American officer took his revolver from his belt, and offered it to me with kindly courtesy, as a pledge of the interest he took in us.

Von Meckel and Bosco were in command of the Bourbon column which was pursuing our artillery towards Corleone, in ignorance of our movement on Gibilrossa. It must be confessed, to the honour of the brave Sicilian people, that only in Sicily could this have been done. Yes, not till two days after our entrance into Palermo, did those chiefs of the enemy know that we had given them the slip, and reached the capital while they thought us at Corleone.

On the evening of the 26th, as night came on, we began our march on Palermo, descending by a covered

path of considerable difficulty, which leads from Gibilrossa to the road outside Porta Termini.

Several incidents happened during the night, which
somewhat retarded our march. The column, consisting
of about 3000 men, being forced to follow a narrow and
difficult path, formed a greatly extended line, while for
the same reasons it was impossible to pass along it to
front and rear, to secure greater compactness. A horse
which had broken loose gave occasion for a few shots,
quite sufficient to alarm the whole force. Lastly, the
front of the column having taken the wrong road, we
were obliged to stop to get the men back into the
proper path, so that by the time we reached the
enemy's outposts outside Porta Termini it was broad
daylight.

CHAPTER VIII.

THE ATTACK ON PALERMO, MAY 27, 1860.

A SMALL band of brave men under Tükery and Missori formed our vanguard, which included Nullo, Enrico Cairoli, Vico Pellizzari, Taddei, Poggi, Scopini, Uziel, Perla, Gnecco, and other gallant fellows, whose names, to my great grief, I cannot recall.*   This band, chosen from among the Thousand, never thought of reckoning the troops, the barricades, the cannon, with which the Bourbon mercenaries had hedged the road outside Porta Termini.   They routed the enemy's advanced posts at the Ammiraglio bridge in a headlong charge, and hastened on.

The barricades at the Termini gate were crossed with a rush, and the columns of the Thousand, with the companies of the Picciotti, followed close on the track of the glorious vanguard, vying with them in heroism.

The vigorous resistance of numerous enemies at all points did not avail, nor the thunder of artillery from sea and land, nor a battalion of Cacciatori stationed in

* Being unable to remember the names of those who formed part of that sacred band, I resolved to note down the above-mentioned martyrs of the Thousand, as I remembered them, though they did not all belong to the vanguard.

the convent of Sant' Antonio, which commanded the assailants' left flank at a distance of half a carbine-shot. It was no use—victory smiled on courage and justice, and in a short time the centre of Palermo was invaded by the soldiers of Italian freedom.

As the population of the capital were completely unarmed, they could not at first expose themselves to the tremendous firing which was taking place in the streets, not only from the artillery of the troops and that in the forts, but from the Bourbon fleet, which, raking the principal streets, swept them with heavy projectiles. Every one knows that when a poor city can be bombarded with impunity, the savage ferocity of such assailants as these is excited to its highest pitch.

Very soon, however, the Palermitans flocked to the erection of those civic bulwarks which strike such terror into the hirelings of tyranny—the barricades. Colonel Acerbi, of the Thousand, a brave soldier in all Italy's battles, distinguished himself in directing this work.

The populace, armed with any weapon they could get, from knives to hatchets, presented on the following days an imposing mass of the kind which no troops of any sort, however well organized, can resist.

From Porta Termini I reached Fiera Vecchia, and thence went on to Piazza Bologna, where, seeing how difficult it was to concentrate our men—scattered as they were through that great capital—in a strong body, I dismounted, and took up my station in a gateway.

As I was laying down my mare Marsala's saddle, with the pistol-holsters, one of the pistols struck against the ground and went off; the ball grazed my right foot, carrying away a piece of the lower part of my trousers. "Good fortune never comes singly," I said to myself.

With the zealous patriots of the Palermo Revolutionary Committee, I resolved to establish my head-quarters at the Palazzo Pretorio, the central point of the city.

We did not obtain any great contingent of armed men from the city of Palermo, the Bourbon party having taken care to remove all weapons from it. But it must be acknowledged that the enthusiasm of these honest citizens never failed, either in the murderous street-fighting, or the furious bombardment by the enemy's fleet, the fort of Castellamare, and the Royal Palace. On the contrary, many presented themselves to us, armed, in the absence of muskets, with daggers, knives, spits, and iron instruments of any kind. The Picciotti * of the volunteer companies, too, fought courageously, and filled up the gaps in the decimated ranks of the Thousand. Even the women were sublime in their patriotic impulse; in the midst of that hell of bombs and rifle-bullets, they cheered on our men with look, voice, and gesture. They flung down from the windows chairs, mattresses, furniture of every kind, as material for the barricades, and many were even seen coming down into the street to help in building them. The people had at first been overcome by surprise at our daring entry, but when the first moments of astonishment were over, their courage and intrepidity

* A name given to the Sicilians from the country.

increased from day to day. The barricades rose from the ground as if by magic, and Palermo was quite hedged in with them. Perhaps their number was excessive; but there can be no doubt that they had a great influence in encouraging the people and spreading alarm among the Bourbon troops. Besides, the continual work supplied occupation for all the people, and kept up their enthusiasm.

One of the greatest difficulties of the situation was our want of ammunition. Powder-mills, however, were set up, and people kept at work night and day making cartridges; but the quantity was insufficient for the incessant fighting against the numerous Bourbon troops, occupying the principal points of vantage in the city. The soldiers, therefore, especially the Picciotti, who wasted a great deal of shot, were continually in want of ammunition, and worried me to death to get it. In spite of all this, the Bourbons were at last reduced to the fort at Castellamare, the Palazzo di Finanze, and the Royal Palace, with a few adjacent houses, leaving us masters of the entire city outside these limits.

The strongest body of the enemy was stationed in the Royal Palace under Lanza, the commander-in-chief; but these were cut off from communication with the sea and their other positions.

Several of our companies occupied the openings which led from the city into the country, so that the troops at the Royal Palace, with their commander-in-chief, found themselves absolutely isolated, and after a few days began to be aware of a scarcity of victuals, and a lack of accommodation for the wounded. This induced Lanza to make proposals for a truce, with the immediate object of burying the corpses, already beginning to putrefy, and transporting the wounded on board the fleet, to be conveyed to Naples. This required an armistice of twenty-four hours; and Heaven knows whether we needed it, obliged as we were to manufacture powder and cartridges, and fire them off as soon as made.

Here I must remark that no help in arms or ammunition reached us from the men-of-war at anchor in the harbour and the roadstead—including an Italian frigate—in those momentous days, when we would have paid for a few rounds of cartridges with their weight in blood. If I remember rightly, we bought an old iron cannon from a Greek vessel. The appearance of the columns under Von Meckel and Bosco, returning to the capital after proceeding towards Corleone in search of us, was very near making the Bourbon general change his mind. In fact, the advent of these two chiefs, at the head of five or six thousand picked troops, was an event of the greatest importance, and might have been fatal to us. Disappointed in the hope of surprising and dispersing us, and informed, on the contrary, of our entry into Palermo, they arrived, boiling over with mortification, and made a determined attack on Porta Termini. My small force, spread out over the whole area of the city, could with difficulty present a sufficient contingent to oppose the enemy's irruption. Nevertheless, the few men of ours near Porta Termini defended themselves bravely, and the ground, though yielded as far as Fiera Vecchia, was contested inch by inch.

Warned of the enemy's progress in that direction, I collected a few companies and hastened thither. On the way I received information that General Lanza wished to continue negotiations on board the English flag-ship, anchored in the Palermo roadstead, under the command of Admiral Mundy.

Leaving General Sirtori, my chief of staff, in command of the city, I repaired to the vessel aforesaid, where I found Generals Letizia and Chrétien, who had come to treat with me on behalf of the commander-in-chief of the Bourbon army.

I have not now before me a copy of the proposals made to me by General Letizia, but I remember very well that they included the exchange of prisoners; the embarkation of the wounded on board the fleet; permission to introduce supplies into the Royal Palace, and to concentrate the enemy's force at Quattro Venti, a position with extensive buildings abutting on the sea; and, lastly, the presentation of a declaration of respect and obedience on behalf of the city of Palermo to his Majesty Francis II.

I listened with patience to the reading of the first articles of the proposed treaty; but when the reader came to the one so humiliating to the city of Palermo, I rose indignantly, and told General Letizia that he knew very well that he had to deal with men who could fight; and that I had no other answer.

He asked for a truce of twenty-four hours in order

to embark his wounded, which I granted, and thus the conference ended.

Here, it is worth noting, in passing, that the leader of the Thousand, treated as a freebooter up to this point, suddenly became "His Excellency"—a title with which he was annoyed in all subsequent negotiations, and which he has always heartily despised. Such is the baseness of the powerful ones of the earth, when once overtaken by misfortune.

However, the situation was anything but satisfactory. Palermo was in want of arms and ammunition; the shells had dismantled part of the city; the enemy's best troops were inside it, while the rest occupied the strongest positions; and the artillery of the fleet was raking the streets, while the cannon of the Royal Palace and Castellamare aided in the work of destruction.

I returned to the Palazzo Pretorio, where I found the principal citizens awaiting me, and trying, with the keen glance of southerners, to read in my eyes my impression as to the result of the conference. I frankly explained the conditions proposed by the enemy, and did not find them inclined to despond. They asked me to speak to the people assembled under the balconies, which I did.

I confess that, though not discouraged, as I have not been in circumstances perhaps still more difficult, yet, considering the numbers and power of the enemy, and the scantiness of our means, I felt somewhat undecided as to the course we should take—that is, whether we ought to continue the defence of the city, or collect all our forces and take to the country again.

This last idea weighed upon my mind like a nightmare, but I put it indignantly from me; it would have meant giving up the city of Palermo to the devastation of an unbridled soldiery. I therefore appeared, angry, as it were with myself, before the brave nation of the Vespers, and told them of my assent to all the terms demanded by the enemy, except the last. When I came to this, I said that I had rejected it with scorn. A roar of indignation and approval broke with one voice from that true-hearted crowd—a cry which was decisive for the liberty of the two peoples and the fall of a tyrant. It calmed me again, and from that moment every symptom of fear, hesitation, or indecision vanished; soldiers and citizens vied with each other in activity and resolution. Barricades were multiplied; every balcony, every bit of rising ground, was covered with mattresses for the defence, and heaped with stones and projectiles of every kind to throw down on the enemy. The manufacture of powder and cartridges also went on with feverish haste; a few old cannon, unearthed I know not where, made their appearance, were mounted and placed in suitable positions; and others were bought from merchant vessels. Women of every class showed themselves in the streets to encourage the workers and those preparing for battle.

The English and American officers from the vessels in the roads made our men presents of revolvers and fowling-pieces. A few Sardinian officers, too, showed some sympathy for the sacred cause of the people; while the sailors of the Italian frigate were on fire with eagerness to share the dangers of their brethren, and threatened to desert. Those whose allegiance was given to the cold and calculating Turin ministry were the only ones untouched by the sight; they remained impassive witnesses of the impending destruction of one of the noblest of Italian cities—waiting for orders. Or, more probably, they already had orders to give us the ass's kick if we lost, and treat us with the greatest friendliness if we won.

A young Sicilian of a respectable family, sent by me on board the Sardinian frigate—which he only reached at considerable risk to himself—was told, "You may be a spy for aught we know to the contrary," and was refused a small quantity of ammunition, which I had sent him to ask for.

However, the enemy became aware of our determination, and that of the townsfolk—for a people resolved to fight to the death are not to be challenged with impunity. Moreover, despots make a great mistake in pampering their proconsuls, who naturally find it very hard to endanger their persons among the barricades of the "mob."

Before the twenty-four hours' armistice was over General Letizia was announced, and asked me for three days' truce—twenty-four hours not being a sufficient time to get the wounded on board. I granted the three days as well, and meanwhile lost not a second in the manufacture of gunpowder and cartridges, while the work at the barricades also continued. The volunteer companies from the neighbourhood of the capital swelled our forces, and threatened the enemy's rear. Orsini also, had, arrived with the remaining cannon, and with him other companies. Our condition improved every day, and diminished the enemy's inclination to attack us.

In a fresh conference with General Letizia, the retreat of the troops now in the Royal Palace and at Porta Termini, with a view to their concentration at Quattro Venti and on the Molo, was brought under discussion. This measure was a clear gain to us.

The suspension of hostilities, and the retreat of the Bourbon forces towards the sea, again inspired the people with confidence and daring; so much so, that we were obliged to station red-shirts * at the advanced posts, to prevent the collisions between the Sicilians and the Bourbon troops which would have ensued from the intense hatred of the former for the latter. The final departure of the troops—as they certainly could not remain many days in the confined positions they occupied—and the complete evacuation of the city and forts, were at last negotiated.

Great bravery was shown by the Thousand, as well as by the defenders of Palermo in general, whose courage had not given way for a moment; in fact, the whole population were quite ready to bury themselves under

---

* The red shirts, few in number at the beginning of the expedition, had acquired great importance, inspiring our friends with confidence and respect, and our enemies with terror. The Bourbon deputations asked for red shirts as a protection in passing along the streets of Palermo. I had ordered as many as possible to be made and distributed, in order to increase the influence of the colour.

the ruins of their beautiful capital—and it must be confessed that the result was fully what might have been expected.

When those twenty thousand soldiers of despotism were seen to capitulate before a handful of citizens, self-devoted to suffering, and, if need were, to martyrdom, it seemed like a portent—for, after all, they were splendid troops, and fought well. Rejoice, all of you, men, women, and children, who helped in your country's deliverance! Palermo free, and the tyrants expelled! It is quite a matter for joy and exultation. The glorious capital of the Vespers, like her volcanoes, sends her shocks to a great distance, and at her fearless voice the unstable thrones of falsehood and tyranny totter and fall.

We lost at Palermo, among others, the gallant Hungarian, Tükery. Among our wounded were Bixio, the two Cairoli—Benedetto and Ernesto—Cucchi, Canzio, Carini, Bezzi.

CHAPTER IX.

MILAZZO.

THE departure of the Bourbon troops from Palermo was a perfect national festival; the more so as, in accordance with the stipulated conditions, they left behind them all the liberated political prisoners — men of the principal families—who had been detained in the fort of Castellamare.

The sight of the men who had suffered so much in the horrible dungeons, filled the whole population with rejoicing, and the welcome given to the noble captives was intensely touching.

I had established my head-quarters in a pavilion attached to the Royal Palace, which commanded on one side a view of the whole Via Toledo, and on the other, of its continuation, as far as Monreale. Here I could enjoy the spectacle presented by the emotion of a great and enthusiastic people. The freed prisoners were carried in triumph towards my abode by an immense crowd, frantic with joy for the liberation of their dear ones. I was overwhelmed with gratitude by them, and could not restrain my own tears.

Then began an interval of rest, which we all needed,

especially the Thousand. [Poor young fellows! the choicest part of the population from all regions of Italy, unaccustomed to hardship and privation, the greater number of them university men—all, with few exceptions, were devoted to a heroic martyrdom for the deliverance of this land of ours, afflicted by strangers, and perhaps deserving of slavery, because once mistress of the world. Indeed, this conquest of the whole known world was a guilty act, which entailed, as necessary consequences, the robbery and reduction to servitude of the conquered, and universal hatred on their part towards the conqueror.]

The Thousand, the majority of whom were no sailors, had quitted the discomforts of the sea to plunge into the destruction of battle, and by almost impracticable paths had reached Palermo; then, driving before them an army of 20,000 of the best Bourbon troops, with the help of the people, in twenty days they freed the whole of Sicily.

The enemy, though leaving us, were doing so in order to prepare for new battles, and we had to place ourselves in a condition to meet them again. Enlistment commissions were therefore opened at Palermo, and in every part of the island evacuated by the Bourbons; we entered on contracts for arms from abroad; a foundry was established in the capital, and the manufacture of powder and cartridges indefatigably pursued. Palermo, the drill-ground of despotism, became in a few days a seed-plot of fighters for liberty. It was a fine sight, in the cool hours of the day, to see those active young Sicilians at their military exercises, showing a dash and heartiness which were a real comfort to the veteran whose whole life's dream had been the deliverance of Italy. And Italy's deliverance might have been fully accomplished by this time, had not the inertia of some, and the malice of others, combined to stifle national heroism at that glorious time.

Our stay at Palermo, after the enemy's departure, was employed in useful works. A great number of boys running wild about the streets—for the most part, a school of corruption to them—were gathered together, placed in suitable establishments, and trained to the life of honest citizens and soldiers. The condition of charitable establishments was ameliorated, and all the indigent part of the population, as well as those who had been sufferers by the bombardment, and the war in general, were supplied with provisions. The organization of the dictatorial government was also effected, with the help of several excellent Sicilian patriots, chief among them being the illustrious lawyer, Francesco Crispi, one of the Thousand.

The national forces, being arranged in three divisions, took the name of the Southern Army, and afterwards marched eastward in fulfilment of their task of emancipation.

During the fighting at Palermo, a small Italian steamer called the *Utile* had arrived with a hundred or so of our men, who, having landed in safety at Marsala, reached the capital in time to take part in the last skirmishes.

The Medici expedition, with three steamers and about 2000 men, arrived at Castellamare—a few miles west of Palermo—before the Bourbon troops had all embarked. Other contingents followed, from all the Italian provinces, so that in a short time we were in first-rate condition, and able to detach expeditionary columns to different parts of the island, in order to get the new government recognized—an easy matter, our coming having already been hailed with universal acclamations—or to seek the enemy, where they were still to be found. One division, under General Türr, marched for the centre of the island. The right wing, commanded by Bixio, started for the south coast, and the left, under Medici, for the north coast, with orders to collect as many volunteers as presented themselves, and finally to concentrate the whole force on the Strait of Messina.

General Cosenz also arrived at Palermo with 2000 men, followed by others despatched by various committees " for furnishing assistance to Sicily," which had been formed in the different provinces, the head committee being at Genoa, under the direction of Dr. Bertani.

The Cosenz column also went on to Messina, to support Medici, then threatened by a strong Bourbon force under Bosco, who was marching from that city in search of us by way of Spadafora.

Bosco had left Messina at the head of 4000 excellent troops, with artillery, in order to keep up communication with Milazzo, and attempt a surprise on Medici's corps, which occupied Barcellona, Santa Lucia, and some of the surrounding villages. He did, in fact, attack Medici, and, being repulsed, fell back on Milazzo, occupying the plains south of it, and annoying the whole neighbourhood. We had to rid ourselves of this hostile force, the only one still in the country.

Warned by General Medici of the movements and the strength of the enemy, I took advantage of Colonel Corti's arrival at Palermo with about 2000 men, and, without allowing them to land, transferred part of them to the steamer *City of Aberdeen*, on board which I myself embarked. We reached Patti on the following day, and, having joined Medici and Cosenz—the brigade which was to march by land had not yet arrived—resolved to attack the Bourbon forces at dawn on the day after my arrival.

CHAPTER X.

THE FIGHT AT MILAZZO.

It was only malice and a want of truthfulness that could characterize as "easy victories" the battles won in 1860 by the few Italians over the Bourbon troops. I have seen a good many battles in my time, and must confess that those of Calatafimi, Palermo, Milazzo, and the Volturno do honour to the volunteers and soldiers who took part in them. The fact that out of six or seven thousand men who fought at Milazzo, about a thousand were killed or disabled, proves that the victory was not such an easy one after all.

General Medici, as has been said, had marched along the northern coast towards the Strait of Messina, with his division; and the Bourbon general Bosco, with a chosen corps, superior in number to our own, and comprising cavalry, infantry, and artillery, was intercepting the principal road to Messina, using the town and fortress of Milazzo as a base of operations. Already a few small skirmishes had taken place between the two armies, in which our men had behaved with their usual gallantry, being opposed to Bosco's chasseurs—a fine corps armed with excellent carbines.

The dawn of July 20 found the sons of Italian liberty engaged with the Bourbon troops south of Milazzo, the advantage being greatly on the side of the mercenaries, whose position was much stronger. Being well acquainted with the ground, the enemy had with much sagacity profited by every natural or artificial obstacle to be found. Their right, écheloned in front of the formidable fortress of Milazzo, was protected by the heavy artillery of the latter, and covered in front by several hedges of cactus, forming excellent entrenchments, behind which Bosco's chasseurs with their good carbines could pour a hailstorm of bullets into our badly armed ranks.

The centre, with its own reserves, on the road leading along the shore to Milazzo, had its front covered by a strong boundary-wall, in which many loopholes had been cut. The front of this wall, again, was protected by a piece of ground thickly overgrown with canes, which made a front attack well-nigh impracticable. So that the enemy, being thoroughly sheltered and well armed, could see and shoot down our men at their leisure, through the treacherous covert of the cane-ground.

The Bourbon left, occupying a line of houses east of Milazzo, formed a right angle with the last-named position, and was therefore able to pour a murderous flanking fire into any force attacking the centre.

Our ignorance of the ground on which the fight was being carried on was the principal cause of the considerable loss on our side, and many of our charges on the enemy's centre might have been spared.

My first idea had been to attack the enemy before daylight, breaking his centre with a strongly massed column, so as to separate his left from the rest of the force—capture it, if possible, and thus diminish his superiority in cavalry and artillery. This plan, however, proved impracticable, as it was a long time before our scattered corps could be gathered together; and the general engagement did not begin till broad daylight.

My principal object, however, having been to shut up the enemy's centre and right in Milazzo, where so large a number, in addition to the garrison of the place, could not have held out long, I concentrated the greater part of our force on the enemy's centre and left, where a vigorous attack was made.

The battle-field being a perfectly level plain, covered with trees, vines, and cane-grounds, the enemy's positions could not be discovered. I had mounted to the roof of a house to try and see something, and had ordered a charge along the high-road with the same object; both measures were in vain. Many of our poor fellows were killed and wounded in our charges on the centre, and the rest driven back without even seeing the enemy, whose murderous fire from behind the loop-holed parapet mowed them down. We went on with this unequal but obstinate battle till the afternoon. By noon our left had fallen back a few miles, and remained unprotected; our right and centre, united in the common danger, were holding out, though with difficulty and at considerable loss.

Yet we felt that we *must* win, and this thought was

the mainspring of that stupendous campaign, where, in the most serious fights, such as those at Milazzo and the Volturno, the tide of battle was against us for more than half the day; and where, by sheer force of dogged endurance and determination never to give in, we succeeded in routing an enemy superior in every respect. May these so-called easy victories serve as examples to our sons when, in their turn, they have to maintain the honour of Italy on the battle-field !

We had to win! Our losses were greater than in any other action in South Italy, and the men were tired out; while the enemy had lost few or none in comparison—his soldiers were fresh, and their ranks unbroken, his positions formidable. Yet we knew we had to win. Italians must ever be animated by the same feeling, as long as the smallest part of their country is crushed beneath the heel of the stranger—as long as the native places of the Trentine Bronzetti and the Roman Monti are not ours.

As I have already said, all the conditions of the battle were in favour of the enemy till the afternoon, and our gallant fellows, so far from advancing a single step, had lost ground, especially on our left.

"Try to hold out as long as you can," I said to Medici, who commanded the contre. "I will collect some scattered detachments and try to make a diversion on the enemy's left wing." This resolution was the turning-point of the day.

The enemy, attacked in flank behind their entrenchments, began to waver; we charged boldly in, and carried off a cannon, which had done us great damage by ricochet-firing with grape-shot along the road. The Bourbon cavalry supporting the gun we had now captured made a brilliant charge, and drove our men back for some distance, so that I was passed by the charging horsemen, and obliged to throw myself into a ditch at the side of the road, where I defended myself sword in hand.

This reverse did not last long. Colonel Missori, with his usual bravery, appearing at the head of those detachments which had previously carried off the gun, relieved me with his revolver of my mounted antagonist.

The detachments aforesaid were, as far as I can remember, Bronzetti's company, and the newly enrolled Sicilians commanded by the gallant Colonel Dunne ; the rest I have forgotten.

The enemy, hard pressed by these troops, wavered for the last time, and broke into a headlong flight towards Milazzo, closely pursued by our whole attacking line.

The victory was complete. The heavy artillery of the place in vain attempted to cover the Bourbon retreat; our soldiers, caring nothing for the hail of grape and musket-balls, attacked Milazzo, and by nightfall were masters of the town, had surrounded the fort on all sides, and raised barricades in the streets exposed to the fire of the fortress.

The triumph of Milazzo was dearly bought, our killed and wounded being far more numerous than those of the enemy. And here I take occasion to remark once more on the wretched weapons our poor volunteers have always had to fight with.*

This action, if not one of the most brilliant, was certainly one of the most murderous. The Bourbon troops fought, and held their ground gallantly, for several hours.

The fate of the Bourbon was sealed. The results of the victory were tremendous. The troops shut up in Milazzo were almost immediately obliged to retreat into the citadel, where, surrounded by our barricades, and finding themselves crowded into a very insufficient space, they were obliged to capitulate, July 24, 1860, surrendering the fortress, with all artillery and ammunition, and a number of mules for the transport of the guns.

Having thus occupied Milazzo, we were in possession of the whole island, with the exception of the fortresses of Messina, Agosta, and Syracuse, and immediately transferred our forces to the shores of the Strait. Medici, having occupied Messina without resistance, began to fortify the point of Faro, so that our steamers could ply without hindrance between Palermo and our positions on the coast. Since the occupation of Palermo, other merchant steamers had come into our hands, and after

---

* Among those killed in this glorious fight are counted Poggi, an officer in the Genoese carbineers, and one of the Thousand—the same who had so greatly distinguished himself at Calatafimi ; and Migliavacca, of Medici's corps, also a gallant soldier. Cosenz and Corti were wounded.

the acquisition of the *Velocc*,* a Bourbon war-steamer brought over to us by the brave Commandant Anguissola, we found ourselves possessed of a small fleet which served admirably for all our needs.

We therefore occupied the Strait of Messina, from that city to the Faro; and in the meanwhile Bixio's and Eber's † columns joined us by way of Girgenti and Caltanissetta, and a fourth division was formed under Cosenz; so that we soon had a force which to us, accustomed as we were to small numbers, seemed of imposing dimensions.

* Which we re-named the *Tükery*, after the gallant leader of our vanguard, who died a hero's death when we entered Palermo.

† General Türr had crossed to the continent for the sake of his health, leaving the command of the brigade to Eber.

CHAPTER XI.

IN THE STRAIT OF MESSINA.

HAVING reached the strait, it became necessary to cross
it. To have reinstated Sicily in the great Italian
family was certainly a glorious achievement. But what
then ? Were we, in compliance with diplomacy, to leave
our country incomplete and maimed ? What of the
two Calabrias, and Naples, awaiting us with open arms ?
And the rest of Italy still enslaved by the foreigner
and the priest ?. We were clearly bound to pass the
strait, despite the utmost vigilance of the Bourbons
and their adherents. One day we found an opportunity
to open a communication—through a Calabrese liberal—
with some soldiers of the garrison of Alta Fiumara, an
important fortress on the eastern side of the strait. I
ordered Colonels Missori and Musolino to cross by night
with 200 men, and try to seize this fort. But, whether
for want of concerted action, from fear on the part of
the guides, or for other reasons, the enterprise failed.
The men, on landing, met a patrol of the enemy, who,
though defeated, gave the alarm, so that our men were
obliged to take to the mountains.

This was not a favourable prelude to our enterprise, and we had to give up our plan of crossing the strait at Faro, and try to effect the passage elsewhere. About the same time Dr. Bertani arrived from Genoa, bringing me news that about 5000 of our friends were to assemble at Aranci, on the east coast of Sardinia, having been collected and sent off by him at Genoa, previous to his departure. This determination of collecting the force at Aranci originated with those men who, like Mazzini, Bertani, Nicotera, and others, without disapproving of our expeditions into Southern Italy, were of opinion that we ought to make diversions on the Papal States or Naples, or perhaps were still unwilling to submit to a dictatorship.

In order not to clash entirely with the strategic ideas of these gentlemen, it struck me that I might join these 5000 men myself, and with them attempt a landing in Naples. I therefore embarked, with Agostino Bertani, on board the *Washington*, for the Gulf of Aranci. Arrived at that port, we found only part of the expedition there, the greater number being already *en route* for Palermo. This circumstance made me change my mind about the Neapolitan plan. We took some of the men on board the *Washington*, so as to give the rest more room in their own vessels, and passed on to Maddalena to take in coal; thence in turn to Cagliari, Palermo, and Milazzo; and finally back to Punta di Faro, where General Sirtori had two of our steamers, the *Torino* and the *Franklin*, in readiness to make the circuit of Sicily from the north-westward, coming round at last to Taormina on the eastern coast of the island.

This was a wise and fortunate resolution. The two steamers reached Giardini, the port of Taormina, took Bixio's division on board, and carried it safely across to Melito, in Calabria.

Knowing that the two steamers, with Bixio's division, were to start from Giardini, I left Faro for Messina on the very day of my arrival, hired a carriage there, and arrived in time to embark on board the *Franklin* and cross over to Calabria with the rest.

Here it may not be out of place to narrate a curious incident which occurred at Giardini previous to our departure. When I reached that point on the eastern coast of Sicily, I found Bixio occupied in embarking part of his own men and the Eberard brigade in the two steamers, *Torino* and *Franklin*. The splendid *Torino* already had a large number on board, and was in excellent condition. The *Franklin*, on the other hand, seemed to be sinking; she was nearly full of water, and the engineer declared that she could not possibly make the voyage in that state. Bixio was greatly annoyed by this, and was preparing to start with only the *Torino*. However, being myself on board the *Franklin*, I ordered nearly all the officers on board to jump into the sea, dive, and try whether they could find the leak ; while at the same time I sent on shore for a quantity of farm-yard manure, in order to make what is called *purina*.*

---

* A kind of plaster, made by mixing chopped straw with the ingredient above mentioned, lumps of which are thrust under the

In this way we contrived to stop the leak to some extent; the engineer was pacified; and, it being known that I was going to cross by the *Franklin* myself, the rest of the men began to come on board, so that by 10 p.m. we were under way for the Calabrian coast, which we reached in safety.

ship, on the end of a pole, in the direction of the supposed leak. The water, rushing into the opening, naturally carries with it some of the straw, etc., and thus the leak is stopped, at any rate partially.

CHAPTER XII.

ON THE MAINLAND OF NAPLES.

TOWARDS the end of August, 1860, and about 3 a.m. on a lovely morning, we landed on the shore at Melito. By dawn all the men were landed, with arms and baggage; and if the *Torino* had not run aground, defying all the efforts made by the *Franklin* to get her off, we might have gone on to Reggio the same day.

At 3 p.m. three Bourbon steamers hove in sight, led by the *Fulminante*, and began to bombard men, vessels, and all. They also tried to float the *Torino*, but, being unable to do so, they set her on fire. The *Franklin*, which had already left, was safe.

About 3 a.m. on the following day the landing took place, and we started for Reggio. We passed Capo dell' Armi by the high-road, and made our noonday halt near a village situated between that cape and the beautiful sister city of Messina, the enemy's squadron keeping watch on our movements the whole time.

Towards evening we resumed our march on Reggio, and, having arrived within a certain distance of the city, turned off to the left along by-paths, avoiding the enemy's outposts awaiting us on the main road.

Colonel Antonino Plutino and several Reggian patriots accompanied us and served as guides.

We made several halts during the night, so as to let the men rest and get together all stragglers, and at 2 a.m. attacked Reggio.

CHAPTER XIII.

THE ATTACK ON REGGIO.

THE attack on Reggio was made from the hills, that is, from the east, where we found little resistance, not being expected in that direction.

The Bourbon troops shut themselves up in the forts, after discharging their arms at us, wounding General Bixio, Colonel Plutino, and a few other officers and men. The enemy's outposts were cut down, and some of them made prisoners.

On that night one of those accidents took place which ought to serve as a warning to young soldiers, and should be scrupulously avoided. In night-operations, I always recommend the men not to fire—a piece of advice I did not fail to repeat several times that very night, before the beginning and during the course of the march. But in spite of my admonitions, while my young comrades were drawn up in the principal square of Reggio, after having driven the enemy into the forts, a shot from the ranks—some say from a window—perhaps purely accidental, induced the whole column, consisting of about 2000 men, to fire, though not a single enemy was in sight. Being on horseback, in the midst of that tempestuous square (the men were drawn up in that order), I flung myself down, and only had my hat struck by a single bullet.

It was not the first time I had seen such a panic— a truly disgraceful thing among soldiers, who ought always to combine presence of mind with courage. However, such panics, unless followed by flight, are not irremediable, and so it turned out in this case. But when the confusion is complicated by flight, and, as sometimes happens, by the action of downright cowards, the matter becomes scandalous, and one to be punished, not by shooting, but by flogging. "Cavalry! cavalry!" I have heard the rabble cry, and seen this cry cause the flight of hundreds of young untrained soldiers, often dragging those who who had seen service along with them. Men liable to such disgrace must naturally desire their cowardice to be hidden by night, for if such actions took place by day they would be exposed to the scorn and derision of the vilest of human beings. But, fools that they are! if there really were cavalry, which is not generally the case in these panics, arising for the most part from the slightest causes, would it not be better to receive them at the bayonet's point, cavalry being only really formidable to a flying force. I can understand that, in a cavalry charge through the streets or squares of a city, a score of men on horseback may disperse thousands of people; but one man on foot with his rifle, standing aside in a doorway, or behind a pillar, can aim at any horseman he may choose, and carry off the tip of his nose, if he does not wish to knock him out of the saddle. In any case, panics—to which the southerners are more especially subject—are a disgrace to any class of soldiers, and the only effectual remedy is absolutely to prohibit any firing at night, and only to allow it very sparingly by day.

Having occupied the city, I said, at break of day, to General Bixio, "I will climb the heights to take observations, and leave you here." My object in this was twofold—to find out if there remained any hostile forces outside Reggio; and to look out for Eberard's column, which had been left behind, and was to arrive in the morning.

Scarcely had I reached the heights overlooking Reggio, when I perceived a column of the enemy, about 2000 strong, coming from the north, and advancing towards my position. In starting from Reggio, I had taken with me a small company of infantry, and was also accompanied by three members of my staff, Bezzi, Basso, and Canzio, who were all obliged to multiply themselves that day, on account of the smallness of our number compared to that of the enemy. I had stationed my small force on the highest peak of the hills, near the hut of a peasant, whom, foreseeing a fight, I ordered to retire. I was not mistaken; the column under General Ghio, commander-in-chief of the forces at Reggio, was in fact advancing, and now very near. I placed my company in a position of defence, and sent into the town for reinforcements.

The situation was a delicate one. The enemy were

many, and my men few, and if the Bourbon troops, instead of following their favourite tactics of firing during their advance, had charged us outright, resistance would have been impossible, and the issue of the conflict extremely doubtful; for, the town of Reggio, being on the sea-shore, is overlooked on three sides by the surrounding hills, and if the Bourbon troops succeeded in seizing these commanding heights and the forts, a reverse for us was almost inevitable. But once more victory smiled on us. The reinforcements sent by Bixio—small indeed, but welcome—arriving, we held the high positions occupied at first; and, our numbers being sufficiently increased, charged the enemy, who abandoned the field and began to retreat northward.

The results of the fighting at Reggio were of the highest importance. The forts surrendered after a feeble resistance, and we remained masters of an enormous mass of provisions and ammunition, while acquiring a place on the continent as our base of operations—the main point with us.

In the morning we followed up Ghio's corps, which capitulated the day after, leaving in our hands a quantity of small-arms and several field-batteries. All the forts commanding the Strait of Messina also surrendered, including Scilla, near which Cosenz had landed his division, and, in conjunction with Bixio's, had helped to bring about Ghio's capitulation.

Here I must mention a loss acutely felt by democrats all the world over—that of Deflotte, a representative of the people at Paris in the time of the Republic, who, proscribed by Bonaparte, had joined the Thousand in Sicily, and crossed the strait with Cosenz's division.

The Bourbon troops, on hearing of the landing of this division, marched down to the shore to attack it, but contented themselves with annoying it by slight skirmishes. In one of these, Deflotte, who had behaved with admirable courage and coolness, was mortally wounded by a Bourbon bullet.

Our march through the Calabrian provinces was truly a triumphal one. We made a quick progress among a martial and enthusiastic population, great numbers of whom were already in arms against the Bourbon oppressor.

At Soveria, Vial's division, about 8000 strong, laid down their arms, furnishing us with an ample supply of cannon, muskets, and ammunition. Caldarelli's brigade capitulated, with Morelli's Calabrian column, at Cosenza. At last, after a hurried journey of a few days from Reggio, always keeping ahead of my column, which could not come up with me, though proceeding by forced marches, I reached the beautiful city of Parthenope.

CHAPTER XIV.

OUR entry into the great capital sounds more imposing than it was in reality. Accompanied by a small staff, I passed through the midst of the Bourbon troops still in occupation, who presented arms far more obsequiously than they did at that time to their own generals.

September 7, 1860 !—which of the sons of Parthenope will not remember that glorious day ? On September 7 fell the abhorred dynasty which a great English statesman had called " The curse of God," and on its ruins rose the sovereignty of the people, which,. by some unhappy fatality, never lasts long.

On September 7, a son of the people, accompanied by a few of his friends, who acted as his staff,* entered the splendid capital of the fiery courser,† acclaimed and supported by its 500,000 inhabitants, whose fervid and irresistible will, paralyzing an entire army, urged them to the demolition of a tyranny, and the vindication of their sacred rights. That shock might well have moved the whole of Italy, impelling it

* Missori, Nullo, Basso, Mario, Stagnetti, Canzio.
† The emblem of Naples.

forward on the path of duty ; that roar would suffice to tame the insolent and insatiable rulers, and overthrow them in the dust.

Though the Bourbon army was still in possession of the forts and the principal points of the city, whence they could easily have destroyed it, yet the applause and the impressive conduct of this great populace sufficed to ensure their harmlessness on September 7, 1860.

I entered Naples with the whole of the southern army as yet a long way off in the direction of the Straits of Messina, the King of Naples having, on the previous day, quitted his palace to retire to Capua.

The royal nest, still warm, was occupied by the emancipators of the people, and the rich carpets of the royal palace were trodden by the heavy boots of the plebeian. These warnings ought to be of some use even to the governments falsely styling themselves " restorative," and should induce them to ameliorate, at least in some degree, the condition of mankind. That they have not been thus useful is due to the selfishness, ostentation, and obstinacy of the privileged classes, who do not even amend their faults when the lion of the people, driven to desperation, roars at their gates, ready to tear them limb from limb in his wrath, which, though savage, is well-deserved, and springs naturally enough from the seed of hatred sown by tyranny.

At Naples, as in all places we had passed through since crossing the strait, the populace were sublime in their enthusiastic patriotism, and the resolute tone assumed by them certainly had no small share in the brilliant results obtained.

Another circumstance very favourable to the national cause was the tacit consent of the Bourbon navy, which, had it been entirely hostile, could have greatly retarded our progress towards the capital. In fact, our steamers transported the divisions of the southern army along the whole Neapolitan coast without let or hindrance, which could not have been done in the face of any decided opposition on the part of the navy.

In Naples, the efforts of the Cavourist party had been more indefatigable than at Palermo, so that I met with considerable obstacles. Encouraged, after a while, by the news that the Sardinian army was invading the Papal States, they became insolent. This party, founded on corruption, had left no means untried. They had at first flattered themselves they were going to keep us on the other side of the strait, and confine our action to Sicilian soil. For this purpose they had called in the help of their magnanimous patron, and a French man-of-war had already appeared in the Faro; but we derived immense advantage from the veto of Lord John Russell, who, in the name of Britain, prohibited any interference in our affairs on the part of the French ruler.

What shocked me most, in the intrigues of this party, was that I found traces of their influence in men who were dear to me, and whom I had never thought of doubting. Men who could not be bribed were overcome by the hypocritical but terrible pretext of necessity.

The necessity of being cowards! The necessity of grovelling in the mud before an image of transitory power, and being deaf and blind to the forcible, weighty, and masculine will of a people who, determined at any cost to acquire a real existence, prepare to break down these images, and scatter their fragments in the dust-heap whence they came!

This party, composed of hired journalists, pampered proconsuls, and parasites of every description, always ready to debase themselves to any extent in the service of any one who pays them to betray their master when he shows signs of falling,—this party, I say, always makes me think of worms on a corpse, their number showing the stage of corruption reached. The corruption of a people may be estimated by the number of these wretches. I had to put up with insults from those gentlemen who, after our victories, posed as our protectors, and who, if we had been defeated, would have hastened to give the ass's kick to the fallen, as they did to Francis II.—insults which I certainly would not have borne, had anything but the sacred cause of Italy been at stake.

For instance, two battalions of the Sardinian army arrived without my having asked for them, their real object being to secure the rich spoils of the city of Naples; though, ostensibly, they were sent to place themselves under my orders, should I wish it. I did express such a wish, and was told that I must obtain the sanction of the ambassador, who, when consulted, replied that I must get the necessary permission from

Turin. Meanwhile my gallant comrades were gaining victories on the Volturno, not only without the help of a single soldier of the regular army, but deprived of the contingents which the noble youth of all Italy wished to send us, and which were being detained or even imprisoned by Cavour and Farini.

The few days I spent in Naples, following the generous welcome given me by the people, were more productive of disgust than anything else, just on account of the intrigues and petty persecutions of those sycophants of monarchy—immoral and ridiculous aspirants, using the most ignoble expedients to ruin that poor wretch of a Francis, whose only guilt was that he had been born on the steps of a throne, and to put a substitute in his place, in the way we all know.

Every one knows the plot of an attempted insurrection which was to have taken place before the arrival of the Thousand, in order to rob them of the chance of driving out the Bourbon, and secure the credit of that exploit with little trouble or merit. This plan could easily have been executed were monarchies able to endow their agents, not only with heavy salaries, but with a little more courage, and a little less anxiety for the safety of their own skins.

The partisans of the House of Savoy had not the courage for a revolution on their own account, but it was very easy for them to build on the foundations laid by others, skilled as they are in this kind of appropriation. They had plenty of men to plot, intrigue, and overthrow public order; and, whereas they themselves had taken no part in the glorious expedition, when the completion of the work was easy, and but little remained to be done, they swaggered as our protectors and allies, landing Sardinian troops at Naples (to secure the spoil, of course), and arrived at such a point of patronage as to send us two companies of the same army on October 2, the day after the battle of the Volturno. They showed themselves adepts in the noble task of kicking the Bourbon now he was down.

They wanted to overthrow a monarchy only to put another in its place, without the power or the will to improve the condition of the unfortunate people. It was a fine thing to see those magnates of all despotisms exercising every kind of evil influence ; corrupting army, navy, court, and ministers ; making use of the crookedest means to obtain their unworthy ends. Yes, it was fine to see the manœuvring of all these satellites, who had acted the part of allies to the King of Naples, advising him, trying to induce him to adopt *fraternal* measures, and surrounding him with snares and treachery. And afterwards, if they had been less afraid of incurring any personal risk, they might have shown themselves off as liberators of Italy. It would have been a glorious result, could they have made fools of the Thousand and all Italian democrats. It would have been a choice morsel to the palate of the liveried liberators of Italy.

At Palermo, too, as was only natural, the partisans of Cavour were laying their plots, and sowing distrust of the Thousand broadcast among the populace, whom they instigated to a premature annexation. They obliged me to leave the army on the Volturno, on the very eve of a battle, in order to repair to Palermo and pacify the people excited by them. This absence of mine cost the southern army the battle of Caiazzo, the only defeat of that glorious campaign.

CHAPTER XV.

PRELIMINARIES OF THE BATTLE OF THE VOLTURNO, OCTOBER 1, 1860.

BEING obliged to leave the army on the Volturno and return to Palermo, I had recommended General Sirtori, my worthy chief of staff, to send out some detachments and cut off the enemy's communications. This was done, but it would seem that those entrusted with the task thought themselves capable of doing something more serious, and, remembering the prestige of previous victories, never doubted the feasibility of any enterprise on the part of our gallant soldiers.

The occupation of Caiazzo, a village to the east of Capua, on the right bank of the Volturno, was therefore resolved on. This fairly defensible position, however, was only a few miles distant from the main body of the Bourbon army, encamped east of Capua, which consisted of about 40,000 men, and was increasing from day to day.

In order to occupy Caiazzo, they made a demonstration on the left bank of the Volturno, in which we lost several good men, chiefly through the superiority of the Bourbon carbines, and because our forces had no cover. The operation took place on September 19; Caiazzo was occupied, and I arrived from Palermo on the same day, in time to be present at the deplorable spectacle of the sacrifice of our men, who, having made a rush, after the manner of volunteers, towards the river-bank, and finding no protection there against the hail of bullets from the other side, were obliged to retreat, while the enemy poured their volleys into the flying mass. This was the result of the demonstration on the river, intended to divert the enemy's attention while we were occupying Caiazzo. On the following day, Caiazzo being attacked by an overwhelming Bourbon force, our few men were forced to evacuate it, and effect a hasty retreat on the Volturno, in which we lost a great many, shot down and drowned in crossing the river.

The Caiazzo operation was more than an imprudence —it was a tactical failure on the part of its director. We lost, among others, the brave Colonel Tito Cattabene, who was taken prisoner, covered with wounds; and the gallant Bosi, son of Major Bosi, also wounded and taken prisoner. There were others whose names I do not remember.

While this unfortunate enterprise was in progress, our forces were somewhat demoralized by the equally disastrous result of another operation near Isernia, and the revival of clerical influence in the districts north of the Volturno (a movement which gained strength in direct ratio to the concentration of the Bourbon army at Capua, and the increase in its numbers), together with the cunning wiles of the Cavourians, who were working away to a man to bring us into discredit. All this likewise raised the spirits of the enemy, and seemed to them to promise well for the contemplated great battle which took place shortly after, on October 1 and 2.

The Bourbon army, crushed by so many losses in Sicily, in Calabria, and at Naples, had retired behind the Volturno, having its centre at Capua, which was being fortified. The foremost columns of the southern army, as soon as they reached the neighbourhood of Naples, were despatched towards Avellino and Ariano, to quiet some reactionary movements excited by the priests and Bourbonists. General Türr was entrusted with this commission, which he executed to perfection.

As soon as the disturbances at Avellino were quieted, Türr had orders to occupy Caserta and Santa Maria with his division, while the other corps were sent in the same direction, one after another, as they arrived from Naples, being left in that capital as short a time as possible.

Bixio's division occupied Maddaloni, covering the high road to Campobasso and the Abruzzi, and formed the right wing of our small army. Medici's division occupied Monte Sant' Angelo, which overlooks Capua and the Volturno, and was afterwards reinforced by some newly raised corps under General Avezzana. A brigade of Medici's division, under General Sacchi, occupied the northern declivity of Monte Tifata—a height overlooking the plains of Capua, and sloping towards the Volturno. All these forces formed our centre, while Türr's division occupied Santa Maria, on our left. The reserves, under the orders of General Sirtori, the chief of staff, were stationed at Caserta.

CHAPTER XVI.

THE 1st of October, in the plains of the ancient capital of Campania, dawned upon a hideous tumult—a fratricidal conflict. On the side of the Bourbons, it is true, foreign mercenaries were numerous—Bavarians, Swiss, and others belonging to the nations who for centuries have been accustomed to look upon this Italy of ours as their pleasure-ground. This crew, under the guidance and with the blessing of the priest, have always been accustomed, by sheer right of the strongest, to cut the throats of Italians, trained from childhood by the priest to bow the knee to them. But only too truly were the greater number of the men who fought on the slopes of Tifata, sons of this unhappy country, driven to butcher one another, one side led by a young king, the child of crime, the other fighting for the sacred cause of their country.

From the days of Hannibal, the conqueror of the haughty Roman legions, to our own, the plains of Campania had surely never beheld a fiercer conflict, and the peasant, driving his plough over those fertile clods, will strike his share for many a day to come against the skulls sown by human passions in the soil.

After my return from Palermo, having every day visited the dominant position of Sant' Angelo, whence I had a good view of the enemy's camp, east of the city of Capua, and on the right bank of the Volturno, I conjectured that the Bourbon troops were making ready for a battle. They were preparing to assume the offensive, having increased their numbers as far as they could, and acquired some confidence through a few partial victories gained over us.

On our side, we threw up some works of defence, of which we soon found the value, at Maddaloni, at Sant' Angelo, and above all at Santa Maria, which stood most in need of them, being in a greatly exposed situation on the plain, with no natural obstacles to the enemy's advance. Our line of battle was defective, being extended too far between Maddaloni and Santa Maria. The enemy's centre, practically their strongest point, was at Capua, whence, at any hour of the night, they might make a descent on our left wing and crush it at a blow, before the other divisions or the reserve could come up. Sant' Angelo, the centre of our line, though a naturally strong position, would have required more time to construct the necessary works, and more men to defend its vast extent. Besides, it is overlooked by the lofty heights of Tifata, which, in the hands of the enemy, would entirely command it.

The important position of Maddaloni had also to be held by the whole of Bixio's division, as the enemy might, by crossing the upper Volturno with a strong force, and taking the road to Naples, *via* Maddaloni, have reached the capital in a few hours, leaving us behind on the Volturno near Capua.

The reserves stationed at Caserta were by no means numerous, as we had to occupy so extended a line; besides which, we were obliged to retain some detachments to keep up communications in front, between Monte Sant' Angelo and Caserta on the Volturno, and at San Leucio, so as to prevent the enemy from throwing themselves between our wings. Santa Maria was our least tenable position, being on the plain, defended only by the works we had been able to throw up in the course of a few days, and offering a favourable point of attack to the enemy's numerous cavalry, and their even more efficient artillery. We had only occupied this place out of consideration for its inhabitants, who, having manifested liberal proclivities on the retreat of the Bourbon army, trembled at the thought of seeing their former masters back again.

If our force at Santa Maria had been stationed instead on the slopes of Tifata, as a reserve to Monte Sant' Angelo, our line would have been much stronger.

Having occupied Santa Maria, we had also to occupy San Tammaro as an outpost on the left, and station a force along the road from Santa Maria to Monte Sant' Angelo, to keep open the communication between the two points. All this weakened our position; and I advise all my young countrymen who may find themselves similarly circumstanced, not to risk the safety of their army out of consideration for any danger to the neighbourhood, whose inhabitants can, after all, retire to a place of safety.

In fact, the weakness of our line disturbed me quite as much as the necessary preparations for an immediate battle, for which the Bourbon army—more numerous and in every way better supplied than our own—was evidently making ready.

About 3 a.m. on October 1, I started by rail from Caserta, where I had my head-quarters, and reached Santa Maria before daybreak. Just as I was getting into a carriage, to proceed to Sant' Angelo, I heard firing on our left. General Milbitz, who commanded the forces stationed there, came to me, and said, "We are attacked in the direction of San Tammaro, and I am going to see what has happened." I ordered the driver to go on as fast as he could.

The noise of the firing grew louder, and gradually extended along our whole front as far as Sant' Angelo. With the first daylight, I reached the road to the left of our forces at Sant' Angelo, which were already engaged, and was saluted, on my arrival, by a hail of bullets. My coachman was killed, the carriage riddled with balls, and my staff and myself were obliged to alight and draw our sabres to cut our way through. I soon found myself, however, in the midst of Mosto's Genoese and Simonetta's Lombards, so that personal defence became no longer necessary. These gallant fellows, seeing us in danger, charged the Bourbon troops with such impetus as to drive them back a considerable distance, and facilitate our progress to Sant' Angelo.

The fact of the enemy's penetrating within our lines and getting in our rear—a movement which, though

taking place by night, was well and skilfully executed—
of course proved them to be well acquainted with the
country. Among the roads leading from Tifata and
Monte Sant' Angelo in the direction of Capua there are
some hollowed out to a depth of several mètres in the
soil overlying the volcanic tufa of the district.

Such roads were, perhaps, formed in ancient times, as
military routes, and the rain-water, running down from
the surrounding mountains, has no doubt helped to
scoop them out more deeply, As matters stand, a considerable force, even including cavalry and artillery; can
pass along one of these lanes and remain completely
invisible.

The Bourbon generals, in their carefully-thought-out
plan of battle, had skilfully taken advantage of these
lanes to send several battalions into our rear, and
station them, during the night, on the formidable
heights of Tifata.

Getting free from the confusion in which I had for a
moment been involved, I proceeded with my staff
towards Sant' Angelo, under the impression that the
enemy were only on our left; but, going on towards the
heights, I soon perceived that they had seized these, and
were in the rear of our line. In fact, there were the
Bourbon battalions, who, marching by night along the
hollow lanes I have already mentioned, had broken
through our line and seized the heights behind us.
Without losing a moment, I collected all the soldiers
at hand, and, taking the mountain-paths, attempted
to turn the enemy's position from above. At the

same time, I sent a Milanese company to occupy the summit of Tifata, or San Niccola, which commands all the hills of Monte Sant' Angelo.

These troops, with two companies of Sacchi's brigade which I had asked for, and which appeared just at the right moment, checked and dispersed the enemy, of whom a great number were taken prisoners; and this allowed me to ascend Monte Sant' Angelo, whence I saw the battle raging all along the line from Santa Maria to Sant' Angelo—sometimes in our favour, while at others our men wavered before the impetus of the enemy's masses. For some days past, from Monte Sant' Angelo, which commanded a view of the whole of the enemy's camp, many indications had given warning of an attack; and for this reason I had not let myself be deceived by the various diversions made by them on our right and left wings, the principal motive of which was to force us to remove part of our troops from the centre, against which they intended to direct their main efforts.

And I had guessed quite rightly, for the Bourbons employed against us on October 1 all the force at their disposal in the field and in the fortresses, and, as luck would have it, they made a simultaneous attack all along our line.

The fighting was going on in all directions, but most obstinately between Maddaloni and Santa Maria. At Maddaloni, after various changes of fortune, Bixio had victoriously repulsed the enemy. At Santa Maria they were also repulsed, and at both places left prisoners

and guns in our hands. On our side, General Milbitz was
wounded.

At Sant' Angelo the same result took place, after a
fight of over six hours, but the enemy's forces, being
very considerable at that point, had remained with a
strong column in possession of the communications
between it and Santa Maria, so that, to reach the reserves
which I had demanded of General Sirtori, and which
were to arrive by rail from Caserta, I was obliged to
make a circuit eastward from the road, and only reached
Santa Maria after 2 p.m.

The reserves from Caserta arrived at the same time,
and I had them drawn up in an attacking column on
the Sant' Angelo road—the Milan brigade in front was
supported by Eberard's, part of Assanti's forming the
reserve. I also sent on to the attack Pace's gallant
Calabrians, whom I found among the trees on my right,
and who also fought splendidly.

Scarcely had the head of the column left the shelter
of the woods which protect the road in the neighbourhood of Santa Maria, when it was discovered about
3 p.m. by the enemy, who began firing shells, and
caused some confusion among our men; but only for a
moment, for the young Milanese bersaglieri of the vanguard rushed on the enemy as soon as the trumpet
sounded the charge.

The skirmishing columns of the Milanese bersaglieri
were soon followed by a battalion of the same brigade,
which fearlessly charged the enemy, according to orders,
without firing a shot.

The road from Santa Maria to Sant' Angelo is to the right of that from Santa Maria to Capua, and forms with the latter an angle of about forty degrees, so that, as our column marched along the road, it always had to deploy, when it did so, on the left, where the enemy were in great numbers, sheltered behind natural ramparts.

As soon as the Milanese and Calabrians were engaged, I pushed forward Eberard's brigade on the right of the former. It was a fine thing to see the veterans of Hungary,* with their comrades of the Thousand, marching under fire with the same calm and coolness as at a review, and in the same order. Assanti's brigade followed up their forward movement, and in a short time the enemy were seen retreating on Capua.

The movement of this attacking column on the enemy's centre was followed almost instantaneously on the right by Medici's and Avezzana's divisions, and on the left by the remainder of Türr's on the Capuan road.

The enemy, after an obstinate combat, were routed all along the line, and retired in disorder within the walls of Capua about 5 p.m., their retreat being covered by the guns of that fortress. About the same time Bixio announced to me the victory of his right wing over the Bourbon troops; so that I was able to telegraph to Naples, "Victory all along the line."

The engagement of October 1, on the Volturno, was

---

* Türr, Tükery, Eberard, and Dungorr were Hungarians ; and in the same brigade we had many gallant comrades of that nationality, both mounted and on foot.

a regular pitched battle. I have already said that our line was defective, being irregular and stretched out too far. Fortunately for us, the Bourbon general's plan of action was likewise defective. They engaged us in direct order, instead of adopting an oblique formation, as they might have done, and thus have rendered our defensive works useless, while themselves obtaining an immense advantage. They attacked us in force at six different points along the whole line—at Maddaloni, Castel Morone, Sant' Angelo, Santa Maria, San Tammaro, and San Leucio. They thus gave battle in parallel order, throwing their full weight against positions and forces quite prepared to receive them.

Had they, instead of this, chosen an oblique order (which, being the attacking party, they might easily have done, with an additional advantage in the strong position of Capua, commanding, as it does, the bridges over the Volturno), threatening, by means of night skirmishes, five out of the six points aforesaid, and in the same night bringing a force of 40,000 men between our left and San Tammaro, I have no hesitation in affirming that they might have reached Naples with very little loss.

It is true that the southern army need not in this case have been ruined; but there is no doubt that such a course of operation would have proved disastrous to us, especially placed as we were among the impressionable Neapolitan population. Another circumstance which contributed to the defeat of the Bourbon troops was their habit of firing while advancing. This, the favourite

method of our opponents, was fatal to them in all
encounters with our volunteers, who, on the other hand,
always gained the victory by charging home without
firing a shot.

It may be objected that this plan of ours may be
injurious with the new improved firearms; but it is
my firm conviction that these only make it more
necessary than ever. Let us suppose the battle-field
to be a level plain, entirely free from obstacles. Two
lines of riflemen are face to face with one another—one
marching and firing on the other, which stands firm,
replying to the enemy's shots. I say that the advantage
is with the stationary line, the men in which can
load and fire with more coolness and less waste of
strength. The soldier, moreover, is better able to place
himself sideways, so as to offer less surface to the
enemy's projectiles, while the advancing line must of
necessity be more agitated, and consequently less
accurate in their firing; and, above all, it is impossible
for them to advance without exposing themselves more
than those do who are standing still to await them.

With the arms in use to-day, if a line of riflemen have
coolness enough to await a line of the enemy, firing
as they come up, the former will, indeed, lose many
men, but not one of the enemy will reach them un-
injured. Besides, there are few places and few
occasions where some, at least, of a line of riflemen
who have to await the enemy in position cannot find
some cover. In this latter case, the numbers being equal,
not a single soldier of the marching line will reach

those waiting in position. The enemy's position should not be charged at all, unless with a force strong enough to throw him into confusion. Any other course than this will involve the loss of many lives, without attaining the desired end.

Another of our great advantages at the battle of the Volturno was the gallantry of our officers. When a commander has officers like Avezzana, Medici, Bixio, Simonetta, Türr, Sirtori, Eberard, Sacchi, Milbitz, Missori, Nullo, and others, it is very improbable that victory will desert the side of liberty and justice.

CHAPTER XVII.

BRONZETTI AT CASTEL MORONE, OCTOBER 1, 1860.

BESIDES the immortal families of the Cairoli and
Debenedetti, and many others for whom all Italy
mourns, all honour is due to the Bronzetti.

The elder brother had fallen fighting against the
Austrians at Seriate; the second died no less heroically
at Castel Morone. A third has been spared to his aged
parents, and this one too is ready, with the full consent
of that noble pair, to give his life at any time for Italy.
Such men and women may well serve as heroic examples
to future generations.

While the battle was raging on the plains of Capua,
Major Bronzetti, at the head of about 200 men, stood
firm against the onset of 4000 Bourbon troops, and
drove them back, time and again, from the positions
he occupied.

In vain the enemy, astonished at such valour, called
on him, over and over again, to surrender, on any terms
he pleased. In vain! The gallant Lombard had
resolved to die with his comrades, not to surrender.

After ten attacks, but few of his little band were
left; most of them lay dead or dying on the field of

slaughter. Yet the survivors, entrenched on the height
where the ruined castle stands, and animated by the
example of their gallant .leader, would hear of no
surrender.

"Surrender, lads!" cried the Bourbon officers.
"Surrender! not a hair of your heads shall be hurt;
and you have already done enough for honour!"

"Surrender?" cried those gallant and glorious sons
of Italy. "Come on, if you are brave enough!"

Having fired away their last cartridge, they met the
final rush, with the bayonet, and fell every one! Only
a few, severely wounded, were carried into Capua.

And where rest the bones of those heroes—of the
noble Bronzetti? Will Italy, the land of monuments,
be able to remember the spot?

CHAPTER XVIII.

BATTLE OF CASERTA VECCHIA, OCTOBER 2, 1860.

RETURNING to Sant' Angelo, on the evening of the 1st, tired and hungry—having had no food all day—I was fortunate enough to find my gallant Genoese carbineers there, in the house of the parish priest. After a capital dinner, followed by coffee, I stretched myself out deliciously to sleep, I do not remember where.

But not even that night was I destined to enjoy any repose. Scarcely had I lain down, when I heard that a column of the enemy, between 4000 and 5000 strong, was at Caserta Vecchia, threatening a descent on Caserta. This was intelligence not to be despised; and I gave the carbineers orders to be ready by 2 a.m., with 350 men of Spangaro's corps, and sixty or so of the mountaineers of Vesuvius. With this force I marched on Caserta at the hour aforesaid, by the mountain path to San Leucio. Before reaching Caserta, Colonel Missori, whom I had commissioned, with some of his gallant Guides, to observe the enemy, brought me word that the latter were drawn up on the heights of Caserta Vecchia, extending towards Caserta—information which I was shortly afterwards enabled to verify.

I repaired to Caserta, to consult with Sirtori as to the mode of attacking the enemy, whom I did not credit with daring enough to attack our head-quarters; but I was mistaken in this opinion, as will soon be seen.

I arranged with Sirtori to collect all the forces at hand and march on the enemy's right flank, that is, attack them from the heights of the park of Caserta, and thus place them between us, Sacchi's brigade at San Leucio, and Bixio's division, to whom I had sent orders to attack the enemy from Maddaloni.

The Bourbons, seeing from the heights only a few men in Caserta, proposed to seize that place, being probably unaware of the result of the battle on the previous day; and to that end flung half their forces in a vigorous attack on the town. In this way, while I was marching under cover, to turn their right flank, 2000 of them were descending the heights just above our head-quarters, which they would have seized if Sirtori, who was there in command of a mere handful of troops, had not, with his usual gallantry, repulsed them. Meanwhile I was proceeding, with General Stocco's Calabrians, four companies of the regular Italian army,* and some fragments of a few other corps, towards the enemy's right. We found them drawn up on the height, ready for battle, and acting as reserves to those attacking Caserta, our unexpected appearance, no doubt, taking them quite by surprise.

* The major in command of these gallant fellows offered to accompany me—an offer I willingly accepted.

The Bourbon troops, taken unawares, offered but little resistance, and were driven back almost at a run, hotly pursued by the brave Calabrians, as far as Caserta Vecchia. A few of them held this village for a short time, firing from the windows and from behind the cover afforded by some ruined walls; but these were quickly surrounded and made prisoners. Those who fled southward fell into the hands of Bixio's corps, which, after having bravely fought and won at Maddaloni on the 1st, had reached the new battle-field at lightning speed. Those who took a northerly direction capitulated to General Sacchi, whom I had ordered to follow the movements of my column; so that of the whole corps which had, and with some reason, alarmed us only a few men were able to escape. This corps was the same that had attacked and destroyed Major Bronzetti's little band at Castel Morone, and had been detained there by their heroic defence through the greater part of the 1st. Who knows whether the sacrifice of those 200 martyrs did not secure the safety of our army?

As has been seen from my account of the battle of the Volturno, it was decided by the reserves, which reached the battle-field about 3 p.m. Had these been detained at Caserta by a hostile corps, the battle would at the very least have been a drawn one. This also shows that the arrangements made by the Bourbon generals were not so bad, and that the calculations of strategists are apt to prove unsuccessful without the assistance of fortune or of transcendent genius.

Sacchi's corps had no small share in detaining the

above-mentioned hostile column on the other side of the park of Caserta, during the engagement on the first day, repulsing its charges with the utmost valour.

With the victory of Caserta Vecchia, October 2, the glorious period of our campaign of 1860 closes. The Italian army of the north, sent by Farini and company to combat the "revolution personified"* in us, found us brothers; and to this army fell the task of completing the annihilation of Bourbonism in the Two Sicilies. In order to regulate the position of my gallant fellow-soldiers, I asked for the recognition of the army of the south as part of the national army; and it was a piece of injustice not to grant my request. They resolved to enjoy the fruits of conquest while banishing the conquerors.

When I understood this, I handed over to Victor Emmanuel† the dictatorship conferred on me by the people, proclaiming him King of Italy. To him I recommended my gallant comrades, the thought of whom was the only painful element in my departure, eager as I was to return to my solitude.

I was leaving those noble young fellows who had crossed the Mediterranean, trusting in me, and who, heedless of every difficulty, hardship, and danger, had

* Alluding to Farini's letter to Bonaparte.

† At another time a Constituent Assembly might have been convened; at that epoch such a step was impossible, and would have resulted in nothing but loss of time and an absurd complication of the question. Annexations by *plébiscite* were then in fashion; the people, deceived by political "rings," hoped everything from the reforming action of Government.

faced death in ten hard-fought battles, hoping for no reward but that already won in Lombardy and in Central Italy—the approval of their own pure conscience, and the applause of a world the witness of their glorious deeds.

With such comrades, to whose valour I owe the greater part of my successes, I would willingly attempt any enterprise, however arduous.

FOURTH PERIOD.

1860–1870.

CHAPTER I.

THE ASPROMONTE CAMPAIGN, 1862.

THE value of a plant is in direct ratio to its productiveness; and in the same way, the value of the
individual is determined by the degree of his beneficial
productiveness in relation to his fellow-creatures. To
be born, live, eat and drink, and finally die, is an insect's
privilege as much as our own.

In an epoch such as was that of 1860 in Southern
Italy, a man truly lives; he lives a life that is useful
to the multitude. This is the true life of the soul.

"Let it be done by those whom it concerns!" was the
general motto of those who, having both hands in the
public pocket, were disposed either to do nothing or to
work mischief. In consequence of this theory, the
Savoyard monarchy three times levelled its veto against
the expedition of the Thousand—the first time, we were
not to start for Sicily; the second, we were not to pass
the Faro; the third, we were to draw the line at the
Volturno.

We started for Sicily; we passed both Faro and the Volturno; and the Italian cause was none the worse.

"You ought to have proclaimed the republic!" was and is still the cry of the Mazzinians—as if those learned academics accustomed to legislate for the world from their studies could be better acquainted with the moral and material condition of the people than ourselves, who have had the happy lot of leading them in battle and guiding them to victory.

It is a self-evident fact that monarchies, like the priesthood, give bitter proof every day that nothing good can be expected of them; but that we ought to have proclaimed the republic at Palermo and Naples in 1860, is *false.* And those who try to convince us of the contrary, only do it out of that party spite which they have, since 1848, taken every opportunity of showing, and not because they are certain of the truth of their own assertions.

We had the veto of the monarchy in 1860, and again in 1862. I think that overthrowing the Papacy was a work at least as necessary as that of overthrowing the Bourbons. And in 1862 the task proposed to themselves by the usual red-shirts was that of knocking over the Papacy (assuredly the most inveterate and most dangerous enemy to Italy), and winning our natural capital—without any other aim, without any other ambition, than the good of our country.

The mission was sacred, the conditions the same, and the noble Sicilians, with the exception of a few already comfortably seated at the table prepared by us in 1860, replied, with their wonted enthusiasm to the cry of "Rome or Death!" proclaimed by us at Marsala.

Here it is as well to repeat what I have already said on other occasions, "If Italy had possessed two such cities as Palermo, we might have reached Rome without let or hindrance."

The venerated martyr of the Spielberg, Pallavicino, was Governor of Palermo. It certainly went against my inclination to cause any trouble to this old friend of mine. I was, however, convinced that the *laissez-faire* spirit was in itself a crime, sure that nothing would be attempted if those who were themselves unwilling to remain useless refrained from giving the impulse.

Hence the cry of "Rome or Death!" raised at Marsala, answered by the gathering of my gallant followers at Ficuzza, a farmhouse of the Selva, a few miles from Palermo, where a goodly band of the young men of that city and the provinces was assembled.

Corrao, the brave companion of Rosalino Pilo, and other staunch friends procured arms; Bagnasco, Capello, and other illustrious patriots formed a committee of supply.

In this way, by the help of my inseparable comrades during the continental campaign—Nullo, Missori, Cairoli, Manci, Piccinini, and others—a new Thousand were soon in the field, ready, like the first, to face that sacerdotal tyranny which is assuredly more noxious than even that of the Bourbons. But in the eyes of the monarchy, we were guilty of the crime of winning ten victories, the insult of having doubled its civil list—matters which kings never forgive. A large number of those who in 1860 shouted for the unification of their country, being now satisfied, and in office, either blamed our enterprise or kept themselves apart, so as not to be contaminated by contact with such insatiable and restless revolutionists.

However, thanks to the resolute attitude assumed by Palermo, and the quick sympathies of all Sicily, we were able to pass through the island and reach Catania without meeting any serious opposition. The honest population of this city were equally favourable to our cause, and their behaviour kept those who certainly wished to put a stop to our enterprise to the policy of inaction.

Two steamers which happened to put into the harbour of Catania—one of them French, the other belonging to the Florio Company—furnished us with the means of transport. Several frigates of the Italian Navy, cruising about outside the harbour, might have prevented both our embarkation and our passage. No doubt they had orders to do so, but, to the honour of their commanders be it said, no hostility was manifested on their part. I take this opportunity of applauding the conduct of those commanders; and being, as I think, fully acquainted with the laws of military honour, I say, in all sincerity, that in such a case a man of honour should break his sword in pieces.

Our passage across the Straits of Messina was attended with some danger, the boats being greatly overloaded, though, as it was, we had been forced to

leave many men behind for want of room. During my
life at sea I have often seen vessels heavily laden, but
never so excessively as in this case. The greater
number of the soldiers being new arrivals, not yet
enrolled in their companies, or personally known to
the officers, crowded on board those unfortunate
steamers in such numbers that I fully expected to see
them sink. It was useless to entreat them to leave the
boats—they scorned the bare idea. We were hastening into desperate danger—perhaps to destruction. It
was a terrible perplexity and responsibility, and indeed,
for a time, I was doubtful whether we ought to start
in this fashion. Who could tell how our country's
destiny might be affected by that moment's resolution?
It was no use giving orders while every man on board
the steamers found it impossible to move from his place
or even to turn round. The darkness was already
coming on, and we had to decide whether to start, or
remain in our intolerable situation, packed like sardines,
and waiting for the morning to rise upon our failure.

We started, and fortune once more took the side of
right and justice. The wind and sea were exactly
suited to the state of the vessels. There was—as in
our first passage in 1860—only a slight breeze on the
strait, and the sea was extremely smooth. About
daybreak, having successfully crossed the strait, we
anchored off Melito, and landed all the men. As in
1860, we took the coast road towards Capo dell'
Arma, in the direction of Reggio. At that time our
adversaries had been the Bourbons, whom we were

.seeking in order to give them battle; to-day we were opposed by the Italian Army, which we wished to avoid at any cost, but which was determined, at all risks, to find and annihilate us.

Hostilities were begun by an Italian ironclad, which, coasting along the shore in a direction parallel with our own, bestowed some shots on us, obliging us to place the men under shelter. Some detachments, sent from Reggio to oppose us, attacked a few men marching in our van. In vain the latter signified their determination not to fight; they were summoned to surrender, and, on their refusal, fired at, and compelled by fratricidal volleys to retreat.

This being so, in order to prevent useless bloodshed, I gave directions to turn to the right, and take the path to Aspromonte. The hostility of the Italian Army towards us had the natural effect of frightening the people, and made the procuring of supplies a matter of great difficulty. My poor volunteers were in want of everything—even of necessary food; and when, for a wonder, we succeeded in meeting with a stray shepherd and his flock, he refused, with greater obstinacy than if we had been brigands, to have any dealings with us. In short, we were looked upon as outlaws and excommunicated men, the priests and reactionaries having little difficulty in getting these kindly but uncultured people to take that view of us.

Yet we were the same men as in 1860, and our object as noble, although we were less favoured by fortune; but it was not the first time that I had seen the Italian people inert and indifferent towards those who wished to redeem them.

It was otherwise with Sicily, as one must in justice confess; for that generous people were as enthusiastic in 1862 as before. They gave us the best of their young men, and, among other veterans, the venerable Baron Avizzani of Castrogiovanni, who bore the hardships and privations of the campaign like a man in the full vigour of his youth.

These hardships were no trifles. I know that, for my own part, I suffered from hunger, and I fancy that many of my comrades suffered far more than I. At last, after disastrous marches over all but impassable paths, the dawn of August 29, 1862, found us, wearied out and starving, on the plateau of Aspromonte. Some unripe potatoes were collected, and served as food, raw at first—afterwards, when the first pangs of hunger were so far alleviated as to enable us to wait long enough, we ate them baked.

Here I must do justice to the kindly mountaineers who inhabit that part of Calabria. They did not at once appear, on account of the steepness of the paths and the difficulties of communication, but, in the course of the afternoon, they arrived with abundant supplies of fruit, bread, and other things. The imminent catastrophe, however, allowed us but little time to profit by their kindness.

About 3 p.m. we began to discover, at a distance of some miles to westward, the head of Pallavicini's column on its way to attack us. Thinking that the level ground where we had been resting during the day was too weak a position, and too easily surrounded, I ordered a change of camp towards the mountain. We reached the verge of the magnificent pine-forest which crowns the heights of Aspromonte, and encamped there, fronting our assailants, and with our back to the woods.

It is true that in 1860 we had already been threatened with an attack from the Sardinian army, and had required a great deal of patriotism to keep us from entering on a fratricidal war; but in 1862, the Italian army, being much stronger than before, while we were weaker, devoted us to destruction, and rushed upon us with as much alacrity as if we had been brigands—perhaps with more. There was no warning whatever; our adversaries arrived, and charged us offhand with surprising ease and assurance. Such, certainly, were the orders. Our extermination had been decided on; and as it was to be feared that, between sons of the same mother, some hesitation might arise, it was no doubt thought undesirable to give any time for reflection. Arrived within long-range rifle-shot, the Pallavicini corps formed in skirmishing order, advanced resolutely, and began the usual fire while marching—a method which I have already described as faulty when adopted by the Bourbon troops. We did not reply. That moment was a terrible one for me, forced as I was to choose whether we should lay down our arms like sheep, or stain ourselves with the blood of our brothers. The soldiers of the monarchy, or, to speak more accurately, their leaders, were certainly troubled by no such scruples. Can it be that they reckoned on my horror of civil war? Even this is probable, and, as a matter of fact, they marched up to us with a confidence that made it seem so.

I ordered my men not to fire, and the order was obeyed, except by a few fiery young fellows under Menotti, on our right, who, seeing themselves charged somewhat insolently, charged in their turn, and repulsed the attacking line. Our position on the height, with the forest in our rear, was one of those which can be held by ten men against a hundred. But what was the use? If we did not defend ourselves, it was very certain that our assailants would soon reach us. And, as it always happens that the attacking party gains confidence in inverse ratio to the resistance met with, the bersaglieri who were marching on us increased their fire to a murderous extent; and, as I was standing between the two lines, to prevent bloodshed as far as possible, I received two carbine-balls to my own share —one in the left hip, and the other on the inside of the right ankle. Menotti, too, was wounded at the same time. At the order not to fire, nearly all our men had retired into the forest, but all my brave officers remained near me, and among them our three surgeons—Ripari, Basile, and Albanese, to whose care and kindness I certainly owe my life.

It is hateful to me to relate the miseries I had to endure. But enough were inflicted on me on that occasion to have created disgust even in the mind of a scavenger.

There were men who rubbed their hands with satisfaction at the, for them, happy news of my wounds, which were believed to be mortal. There were others who denied their friendship with me, and others yet, who said they had been mistaken in singing my praises. Yet, to the honour of mankind, I must confess that there were good men, too, who tended me with a mother's care, who could not have watched me with greater love and tenderness had they been my sons. First among these I must ever remember my dear friend, Cencio Cattabene, too soon lost to Italy.

The Sardinian Government had won the great prize, and won it just as they desired—that is to say, in a condition which allowed them to hope that, in all probability, the devil would soon take possession of his own.

It is true that they used those commonplace courtesies which are customary even towards great criminals when led to the scaffold; but, for instance, instead of leaving me in a hospital at Reggio or Messina, I was placed on board a frigate and taken to Varignano, thus being forced to sail the whole length of the Tyrrhene sea, with the greatest torture to the wound in my right foot, which, though not mortal, was assuredly one of a most painful character. But they wanted their prey safe and close at hand. I repeat, it is hateful to me to recount these miseries, and I shrink from disgusting those who may have patience enough to read me, with descriptions of wounds, hospitals, prisons, and the caresses of the royal vultures.

Enough, that I was taken to Varignano, in the Gulf of Spezia, to Pisa, and at last to Caprera. My sufferings were great, and great also the kind care of my friends. It was the illustrious Professor Zannetti, the *doyen* of Italian surgeons, who successfully achieved the operation of extracting the ball.

At last, after thirteen months, the wound in my right foot healed, and from that time till 1866 I led an inactive and useless life.

CHAPTER II.

THE CAMPAIGN IN THE TYROL.

ABOUT four years had passed since the day when I was struck down by a bullet at Aspromonte. I soon forget injuries; and, moreover the opportunists—those who are guided by the expediency rather than the morality of a measure—were well aware of the fact. For some time already the cry of an alliance with Prussia against Austria had been raised, and on June 10, 1866, my friend General Fabrizi came to Caprera to invite me, in the name of the Government and of our own party, to take command of the volunteers, who were mustering in great numbers from all parts of Italy. On the same day we left by steamer for the mainland, and repaired to Como, where the greatest concentration of the volunteers was to take place.

They had, in fact, assembled in great numbers—the usual fine, enthusiastic young fellows, always ready to fight for Italy, asking for no reward. The brave veterans of a hundred fights were also present, to act as their leaders.

Nevertheless, there was no word of cannon—the volunteers were to get them as they could; and the arms furnished were the usual wretched muskets, instead of the excellent carbines supplied to the army. The same miserable parsimony was shown in the clothing department, so that many men had to march to battle in civilian garments; in short, we found the usual annoyances with which the supporters of monarchy have already familiarized our volunteers.

The auspices under which the campaign of 1866 was initiated promised Italy a brilliant result. As a matter of fact, the result was wretched and disgraceful.

It is the worst of systems under which this country is governed, where the public money serves to corrupt that part of the nation which ought to be incorruptible —that is, the members of Parliament, the military, and officials of every description; all of them, unhappily, men who require but slight inducements to make them worship at the shrine of self-interest. The corruption introduced by Napoleon III., and multiplied in France by his distribution of sausages and wine to the troops, whose help he required for the *coup d'état*, has extended into our poor country, whose miserable fate it has ever been to ape her neighbours.

Certainly there was no want of corruption in Italy, and the corruptors were as skilful here as elsewhere. But, taking the empire as its model—an empire which, starting with a proclamation of peace while its habitual policy was a continual encouragement of war (knowing that, without war, it could not exist for a moment), and devoting its whole strength to the destruction of liberty, and the substitution for it of despotism, was a lie from the beginning—taking, I say, this empire as its model, it was no wonder that Italian society should become corrupted in its innermost recesses, or that our army, whose destiny it is to be one of the best in the world, should not have escaped the contagion. The degrading picture was completed by the state of the peasant element, the strongest in our army, kept by the clergy in the state of ignorance and hatred of the national cause which have had the same effect in Italy as in France, as we have seen in the famous defeats of Novara and Custoza.

For the moment we were withdrawn from the ignominious patronage of Bonaparte, but, ever unable to act on our own account, threw ourselves into another alliance, less objectionable at any rate—that with Prussia, whose estimate of us was undeservedly high.

However that may be, the campaign of 1866 opened with the most brilliant prospects. The nation, though its resources had been exhausted by a rapacious government, showed itself rich in enthusiasm and self-sacrifice. The numerous fleet was to measure its strength against an enemy inferior in numbers, and looked upon as already defeated; while our army—nearly double that of the Austrians in Italy—saw under its banners for the first time all the sons of the Peninsula, from Marsala to Mont Cenis, hastening, in eager emulation, to battle with the foe of centuries. It was only the insolent ignorance and incapacity of its leaders that could have brought about the disaster of Custoza.

The volunteers, who under a moderately good government might have amounted to a hundred thousand, were, on account of the usual fear, limited to a third of that number, and treated in the usual way as regards arms and clothing. And when the catastrophe of Custoza took place, only a few thousands were at Salò, Lonato, and Lago di Garda, while the regiments which ought to have followed them were still in South Italy, waiting for supplies.

There was every promise of a brilliant campaign, in spite of all obstacles—one to rank our nation with the first in Europe, to renew her youth, and bring back to her the ancient times of Roman glory. But it was not to be; the war into which she was led by Jesuitism was to end in her humiliation. The Government, yielding to public opinion, but still hostile to the volunteers, whom it feared and distrusted as representing the rights and liberties of Italy, armed a few of them; but their arming, their organization, and the way in which their wants were supplied, all showed the influence of the antipathy and ill-will felt towards them.

Nevertheless, they were sent on towards the frontier, where, in two days more, the battle was to rage. The eagerness with which the army's movements were hastened, and the unfortunate events which followed, favoured the concentration of the volunteers. For the higher ring had intended, as a consequence of the usual Jesuit intrigues, to prevent the massing of so many volunteers together by dividing them into two bodies, and leaving half in the south. The reasons they published by way of masking the game were the merest pretexts.

Here I must do the King the justice to say that from the first moments when he communicated to me, through Dr. Albanese, his intention of placing me in command of the volunteers, he imparted to me the idea of sending me to make a descent on the Dalmatian coast, which I was to have done in concert with Admiral Persano. It was said that this determination met with unqualified opposition from his generals, and more particularly from Lamarmora.

This resolution of sending us towards the Adriatic pleased me so much that I complimented Victor Emmanuel on a conception at once admirable in itself and likely to meet with success. In fact, the conception was too fine to be appreciated by certain members of the Italian Privy Council, and I was soon convinced that the detention of five regiments in the south had no other motive than distrust, and a wish to keep them away from me; in fact, to do pretty much what had been done with the Apennine regiments in 1859. I therefore had my field of action assigned to me on the shores of the Lake of Garda—contrary to the first proposals made, according to which the choice of operations was to have been left entirely to me.

What a splendid prospect was opening before us in the east!

Thirty thousand men on the Dalmatian coast would have been quite enough to overthrow the Austrian monarchy; and we had plenty of sympathetic elements and many friends in that part of Eastern Europe, from Greece to Hungary—all warlike populations, hostile to

Austria and Turkey, and needing little persuasion to rise against their conquerors. We should certainly have kept the enemy in play to such purpose as to force him to send a powerful army against us, and diminish his armaments in the west and north, without which he could not prevent our penetrating into the heart of Austria, and throwing the firebrand of insurrection among the ten nationalities composing that heterogeneous and monstrous body politic.

Knowing that I was to operate on the Lake of Garda, I requested that the flotilla at Salò might be put under my command, which was granted without hesitation. But, considering the wretched state in which that flotilla then was, it will easily be seen that it was nothing but a hindrance to me; and I had no little trouble in saving it from the more numerous and better organized force of the enemy. The crews of the vessels, and the garrisons of the lake-shore, especially the former, were principally furnished by the volunteers, particularly after the defeat of our army on the ill-omened field of Custoza. A whole regiment had to remain at Salò, for the sole purpose of keeping a look-out on that post and the adjacent shore, as well as on the forts gradually being built to guard it.

General Avezzana, with a sufficient number of officers, and a strong detachment of naval volunteers from Ancona, Livorno, and other seaports, had also to remain at Salò for the same purpose.

The Austrian flotilla on the Lake of Garda comprised eight war-steamers, armed with forty-eight cannon, fully manned, and furnished with all needful supplies. The Italian flotilla, when I arrived at Salò, had nothing ready for use but a single gunboat with one gun; of the other five vessels—also steamers, and armed in the same way—one was ashore, useless, and the engines of the other four out of order. It is true that we set to work at once to get them in motion; but by the end of the war, the five gunboats, with a twenty-four-pounder a-piece, were only just ready. That is to say, we had five twenty-four-pounders; while the enemy reckoned forty-eight guns of a calibre from eighty pounds downwards.

We also worked at the construction and arming of rafts, which might have proved of considerable service; but the want of necessaries and the slow progress of the work prevented us from ever having a single one fit to be towed across the lake.

CHAPTER III.

ALL our regiments being summoned to the western shore of the Lake of Garda, and having orders to carry on operations in the Tyrol, I pushed on the second regiment and the second rifles towards Caffaro, to seize that bridge and the strong position of Monte Suello, a manœuvre which was both promptly and gallantly carried out, the Austrians being driven from the ground in a brilliant skirmish.

This was a good beginning to our campaign, and, with the rest of the regiments at my disposal, I was preparing to follow up our gallant vanguard into the Tyrol, when the fatal battle of June 24 took place. The unfortunate result of that engagement having been communicated to me by General Lamarmora, along with orders to cover Brescia, and not to count on the support of the army, which was retiring behind the Oglio—I recalled the vanguard from the Tyrol, and began at once to think of concentrating all available forces on Lonato; a point which, besides covering the two positions of Brescia and Salò, might also, I thought, be useful in collecting the scattered men and supplies of the army—as, in fact, it turned out.

Our gallant volunteers, rich only in patriotism and enthusiasm, came forward at my orders, by forced marches, towards Lonato; but, armed as they were with inferior muskets, and in want of the principal items of a soldier's outfit, with which they had to provide themselves on the march, it was difficult for them to make the journey quickly, especially the regiments from the south.

In the days which followed the disastrous 24th of June, we occupied Lonato and Desenzano, with advanced posts at Rivoltella, first with one regiment, afterwards with several, which took up their positions ready for battle immediately on arriving, as it seemed very probable that the Austrians would not remain inactive after the retreat of our army. However, the regiments from the south, in spite of every effort they made to advance, would not have arrived in time to help us had the enemy made use of their advantages and attacked us; and it seems to me that, on or about the 26th (the probable day of their appearance), we could not have opposed to them more than 8000 men, with one mountain battery, and one twenty-four-pounder from the flotilla, mounted on the height above Lonato. From all this it may be inferred that the resolution of holding Lonato against the victorious Austrian army, should the latter advance, was somewhat risky; yet, nevertheless, it was productive of much advantage. The Italian volunteers may well be proud of it, and I hope my younger readers will deduce from it the lesson not to retreat before an enemy, however strong, without having first seen and carefully examined his numbers, and coolly calculated the injury and disgrace which may result from an over-hasty retreat.

Holding Lonato, Desenzano, our outposts at Rivoltella, and the country to the right of our front as far as Pozzolengo, we were, in fact, as we had been ordered, covering Brescia, as well as Salò, with its arsenal, the depôts, and the flotilla; and were enabled, to our great satisfaction, to collect the stragglers of the army and some of the baggage-trains.

I am sorry to seem to kick those who are down, and should not wish my opinion on the devotion of the army to be set down to vindictiveness. Yet it must be confessed that, when every one expected brilliant results from a brilliant army double the number of the enemy's force, with immense resources, the first artillery in the world, great enthusiasm among the troops, and great courage,—it must be confessed, I repeat, that it was a terrible blow to find all these hopes disappointed in a moment, and that splendid army retreating in confusion, without being pursued by the enemy, behind a river thirty miles off, and leaving almost the whole of Lombardy unprotected.

The main army retreated from the Mincio to the Oglio, and that after having fought a battle. But why did the army on the right, the army of the Po, retreat? With 90,000 men, and a river like the Po right in front, that army retreated—pursued by whom? The enemy had 80,000 men on the Mincio, and though victorious, those 80,000 must, after an engagement with a superior force, at the very least be tired and have lost some of their number. And why fall back from the Po on the Apennines? I. cannot give a reason for it.

I do not know the Austrian general who commanded our enemy in 1866, but he must be a military genius, having defeated an army twice as numerous as his own, and composed of soldiers who, individually, were at least equal to his men.

The Prussian victories in the north certainly had some influence in checking his course; but with a little more determination, he might easily have shattered my force of 8000 men and no artillery, and have come to take his pleasure in the country, in the heart of Lombardy and Piedmont, with a strong probability of obtaining peace on very favourable terms.

Among the volunteers, however, there was neither confusion, nor fear, nor lack of concert. All grieved over that national disaster, but not one was troubled by any feeling of distrust in the destiny of his country, and the same enthusiasm which had stimulated those brave young fellows to leave their homes, not only lasted, but increased in our delicate and precarious position. War, fighting—that was what they all demanded; and if they could have had at least a month of organization and drill, and had been decently armed, they would have worked miracles. Thinking quietly over the causes of our overthrow, and leaving entirely out of the question the incapacity of certain commanders, and the disaffection of the peasant element towards the national cause, one may, with the impartiality of history, lay it down boldly as an established fact that the plan of campaign adopted from the beginning was defective. Its weak point consisted in always trying to beat the enemy's whole force with the half of our own, while the Austrian general defeated half our army with the whole of his own—a system which generally ensures victory for the side adopting it, and of which there are many examples in military history.

The Italian army was divided into two sections—one of 120,000 men on the Mincio; the other of 90,000 on the Po—both, as will be seen, superior to the Austrian army, which numbered barely 80,000 men outside its fortresses.

The first blunder made by our commander-in-chief seems to me to be his threatening various points with divisions, or at most with army corps, and then, with only a body of about 80,000 men, dealing the decisive blow at the full strength of the hostile army.

The mouths of the Po would, I think, have been the most suitable point for the passage of our large army, as we could then have procured all the steamers and boats required, and, once in possession of both banks of the great river, could have brought up, in a short time, our whole force with supplies. By this means, when the Austrians approached to give battle, they would at least have been deprived of the support of the terrible Quadrilateral.

The Austrian general, profiting by our errors wisely

concentrated as large a force as he could in the environs of Verona, and fell upon the half of our army stationed on the Mincio, which took the initiative.

Not very many years before, Napoleon I. had manœuvred in a similar manner, and, leaving the siege of Mantua, had defeated the two halves of the Austrian army, one after the other, on either shore of the Lake of Garda. They had made the mistake of separating in order to attack him, putting the lake between them; the great captain anticipated their intention, and crushed them both.

After the great battle of Custoza, we held the positions of Lonato and Desenzano, till we received orders from head-quarters to recommence operations in the Tyrol, the army being once more in a state to assume the offensive.

Leaving the second regiment to cover Salò, the flotilla, and the most important points on the lake as far as Gargnano—the whole under the orders of General Avezzana—and having completed the batteries which were to defend the western shore, we once more marched towards the Caffaro, with the first and third regiments and the first battalion of bersaglieri.

The enemy, meanwhile, encouraged by the victory at Custoza, had, after our abandonment of the Caffaro, strongly garrisoned this position and Monte Suello. I resolved to dislodge them by a *coup de main*, in order to open the way into the Tyrol. Leaving Salò at dawn on July 3, I reached Rocca d'Anfo about noon, and there found Colonel Corte, at that time in command of the van (consisting of the three corps aforesaid), who had already made his arrangements for driving the enemy from our frontier.

He had sent Major Mosto, with 500 men, towards Bagolino by the mountain road and through the commanding valleys of Rocca d'Anfo, with the object of making a division on the right, and in the rear, of the Austrians.

Discovering, from Rocca d'Anfo, an Austrian outpost at Sant' Antonio, about a cannon-shot from the fortress, we tried to turn that also, by sending a detachment of the first bersaglieri, under Captain Bezzi, over the mountains.

Neither of the two detachments succeeded in making a diversion, owing to the difficulty of the roads and the heavy rain which was falling. Perhaps I reckoned too confidently on the pluck of the gallant volunteers, and ought to have deferred the attack till next day, the soldiers being worn out and wet through, and their arms and ammunition in a deplorable state. But, counting on the effect of a brisk, unexpected attack, and above all on the enthusiasm of men whom I had known to overcome far greater obstacles, I decided on fighting.

About 3 p.m. I perceived Captain Bezzi's signal, he having reached the point agreed upon, over the mountains to the left, and gave orders for the attacking column, which had till then remained under cover of the fortress, to march forward at the quick pace, and fall upon the enemy. Colonel Corte, marching at the head of the column with his staff, arranged the attack, with that coolness which distinguishes him, in good order, and with a dash worthy of Italian volunteers.

For a while all went well, and the enemy began to fall back; but they were soon reinforced by the reserves which covered the heights of Monte Suello, while our men, finding the ground more and more difficult, were at last checked in their rush; and a large number of wounded, returning along the road, supported by their comrades, threw the column into some confusion. We lost one of our best officers, Captain Bottino, and many other brave men. Our wounded were certainly more numerous than those of the enemy—the usual privilege reserved for Italian volunteers by the usual privy council, which forces them to fight with inferior against improved weapons. Here, moreover, it was a question of Tyrolese carbines, the enemy's corps being entirely composed of those mountaineers. There was not, strictly speaking, a flight—fear did not seize upon our young soldiers; but they were worn out by the fatigues of previous marches and the difficult ground over which they had to advance to the attack. The greater number—especially the third regiment, who were unprovided with cartridge-pouches—had not a single dry cartridge about them, to say nothing of the wretched muskets, which would not go off, or, if they did so, failed to reach the enemy, who, armed with magnificent carbines, poured never-ceasing volleys into us.

In short, the day remained undecided, and we continued to occupy our former positions under Monte

Suello. Being wounded in the left thigh, I was obliged to retire, leaving the command to Colonel Corte, who held his ground bravely all the rest of the day, with the gallant co-operation of Colonel Bruzzesi, of the third, in the positions we had gained.

At dawn, on the 4th, the enemy having retired from Monte Suello, we occupied that position with Cairoli's battalion of the ninth regiment, which I had picked up on the Barghe road on the preceding day, and ordered to march forward. On the same day we occupied Bagolino and the Caffaro. The rest of the volunteer corps, still unprovided with necessaries, were advancing towards the Tyrol, but slowly, being obliged to supply themselves on the march.

Lodrone and Dazio were occupied after a slight resistance, and finally Ponte Dazio and Storo, where I established my head-quarters. Storo, a small village at the junction of the two valleys of Giudicaria and Ampola, might be of importance to us; but in order to make it so in reality, we had to occupy the heights above it, especially Rocca Pagana, a lofty peak overhanging Storo with an almost vertical cliff.

Besides this, to penetrate into the valley of Giudicaria, it was absolutely necessary first to seize the fort of Ampola, which commands the valley of the same name, while looking into the Val di Ledro, whence the enemy might issue forth, and, seizing Storo and Ponte Dazio, cut us off from Brescia, our base of operations.

Having covered our left by the occupation of Condino and the western heights, our whole care was now devoted to surrounding the fort of Ampola by scaling the heights above it.

About the same time we were joined by the famous eighteenth brigade, under Major Dogliotti, with fifteen splendid twelve-pounders. Judging from the action of these guns, I was enabled to form an exact idea of the value in general of our Italian artillery, which I esteem with pride as second to none in the world. On July 16, the enemy attempted to dislodge us from Condino. Our men had, contrary to my orders, pushed on from Condino to Cimego, and occupied the bridge over the Chiese at the latter place, without posting any troops on the heights—an indispensable precaution in that mountainous country, to protect all forces in the valleys.

The enemy, with a force in every respect superior, repulsed our men from Cimego, and had it not been for a few of our excellent guns, lately arrived, the engagement would have cost us dear. Fortunately our losses, though greater than those of the enemy, were not heavy. Here, as elsewhere, they were caused by the inferiority of our weapons. Major Lombardi, one of the heroes of all Italian battles, and one of my best officers, fell that day on the field. On the same day, as I was driving back from Condino to Storo, an Austrian ambuscade on Rocca Pagana fired at us for a time, but without wounding any one. Colonel Guastalla distinguished himself greatly that day at Condino, while the gallant General Haug and Major Dogliotti, who were entrusted with the siege of the fort of Ampola, soon brought it to a successful conclusion. The volunteers, clambering up the steep mountains which overlook the fort, pressed the besieged so hard that they could not show their faces anywhere, and at last completely surrounded it. The guns, carried up on the shoulders of the men, or dragged up the precipices with ropes, soon knocked into heaps of stones, not the casemates, which were of great solidity, but the houses adjacent to them. Many shells fired by our brave gunners reached those of the fort, and diminished their numbers. One of our guns, stationed on the road by the gallant Lieutenant Alasia, who lost his life in the exploit, did a great deal towards disconcerting the enemy. At last, after a few days' siege, with cannonading and musketry fire, this small but, to us, exceedingly important stronghold surrendered.

War in the Tyrol, as in all mountainous countries, can only be carried on by keeping possession of the heights. It would be vain to attempt, even with great odds in one's favour, to pursue the enemy in the valleys. The latter, with excellent sharpshooters on the peaks and slopes of the mountains, would always make havoc of the troops advancing along the valley roads. For this reason—except at Monte Suello, where, perhaps through impatience, we did not observe the rule—all operations during our advance were preceded by the occupation of the surrounding heights; and however skilled the Tyrolese *jäger* may be in this kind of war, and brave soldiers as they undoubtedly are—armed, moreover, with excellent carbines, which they handle with surpassing dexterity—they do not know how to resist when an enemy succeeds in gaining the heights above them. Our obstinacy in pressing on was always rewarded by success, though alloyed with considerable losses, and this success was especially owing to our occupation of the heights. "Acting the eagle" was therefore the prevailing watchword of the volunteers, who were always particularly recommended to scale the heights before attempting a forward march through the valleys. This maxim ought also to be observed in retreating, when the ground and other circumstances permit. The surrender of the fort of Ampola, and the occupation of the chain of mountains stretching from Rocca Pagana to the summits of Burelli, Giovio, and Cadré, dominating the two valleys of Ledro and Giudicaria, opened an easy way into Val di Ledro, and allowed us to push on the head of our right-hand column as far as Tiarno and Bezzecca.

Our movement on the right in Val di Ledro was all the more important as it was on this side that we had to protect the junction of the second regiment, which had advanced by Monte Nota towards Pieve, Molina, and the Lake of Garda—contrary to my orders, which directed it to march through Val Lorina, to assist in the siege of Ampola. This regiment had insubordinately chosen a route too far to the right, running the risk of being entirely destroyed by the enemy; though the companies which composed it had, singly, fought with great bravery against superior forces of the enemy.

I have already said that I left the second at Salò,

to protect the flotilla, arsenal, and forts. The tenth had then taken the place of the second, which received orders to march through Val Tostina on our right, scale the mountain ridge, and descend through Val Lorina on Ampola. Many fatigues and hardships were suffered by the second on this march, and not a few blunders committed. If the surrender of Ampola had taken place one day later, or if we had delayed to occupy Bezzecca, this regiment would certainly have been lost, as will appear from the sequel.

As I was anxious about the occupation of Val di Ledro, principally for the sake of securing the junction of the second regiment, I had ordered General Haug to leave the siege of Ampola to Major Dogliotti, and transfer himself, with as many men as could be spared from the siege, into that valley. It was a difficult undertaking, so long as the fort still held out; and, in fact, was found to be impossible of execution. It is true that, Haug's brigade being composed of the third regiment and part of the second, and the men of the former nearly all occupied in the siege works, while of the latter only a few companies were at Ampola, it was certainly not easy to obey my orders.

However, I was anxious about the fate of the second, and lost not a moment, after the surrender, in sending to Val di Ledro the fifth regiment, the only one remaining in reserve, with some companies of the various regiments which had contributed to bring about the capitulation of Ampola, and two battalions of the ninth, then occupying the heights of Monte Giovio.

It was high time that a movement should be made on Val di Ledro, for the enemy, having assembled 6000 of their best soldiers, were descending the valley of Conzei to Bezzecca, with the intention of cutting off from us, and annihilating, the detachments of the second regiment. The valley of Conzei, running from north to south, joins the Val di Ledro at Bezzecca, forming a right angle with it.

On the 20th, the road to Ampola being open after the surrender of the fort, the head of our right column occupied that village, and during the night a battalion of the fifth, under Commander Martinelli, was sent to reconnoitre on the eastern heights.

This battalion—through whose fault I do not know; it may have been by accident—found itself at dawn surrounded by a considerable Austrian force. Its remnants, pursued by the enemy, fell back on the main column, occupying Bezzecca and the adjacent villages to the north; and here a serious combat began.

CHAPTER IV.

THE enemy, elated with their first successes, drew near with a daring to which we were little accustomed, and dislodged us, bit by bit, from the whole valley of Conzei. In vain we had stationed in front of Bezzecca a battery of eight pieces, which fired on them for a time; in vain our officers, heedless of the personal risk, attempted to check their advance by charging at the head of their men. All our positions as far as Bezzecca were gained by the enemy, who not only occupied that village, but pushed further on, and threw out a detachment on our right, south of the Val di Ledro, to attack us in flank.

I had left Storo at dawn, in a carriage, being still disabled by my wound of June 3. From information received I did not expect to find my men engaged in so fierce a conflict. However, on leaving Storo, I had given the ninth regiment and first bersaglieri orders to march, in the same direction as myself, at 3 p.m. Arrived in the neighbourhood of Bezzecca, the sound of firing apprised me of the battle that was going on. I sent for Haug, to make inquiries of him, and gathered from his answers that a serious affair was on hand.

We agreed to have the heights on the left occupied by the battalions of the ninth regiment, which were beginning to arrive. It was well we did so, for the first advantage gained during the day was derived from the occupation of these positions by the brave fellows of that regiment, led—I say it with pride—by my son Menotti. The two battalions of the ninth were commanded by Cossovich and Vico Pellizzari, both of the Thousand, and quite worthy of the distinction.

In the centre and on our right, the volunteers were retreating along with the above-mentioned battery, keeping up their fire while doing so, and on the whole behaving gallantly. In this battery, the horses belonging to one piece were killed, and its gunners killed or wounded, all but one. This gallant fellow, after sending his last projectile at the enemy, mounted astride his gun, as coolly as if he had been at a review. Meanwhile Major Dogliotti informed me that there was a fresh battery in the rear. "Forward!" I cried, and in a few minutes the brave fellows arrived at a gallop, turned to the right, mounted their six guns on a piece of gently rising ground, and opened fire on the enemy with shots that followed one another so quickly that they seemed to proceed from musketry rather than cannon.

Of the six pieces in retreat three were added to the fresh battery, which formed a total of nine formidable pieces of ordnance.

All the officers of my staff, and as many more as happened to come within earshot, had orders from me to pick up men where they could and push them forward.

Canzio, Ricciotti, Cariolati, Damiani, Ravini, and others, rushed forward at the head of a little band of heroes, and, supported on the left by the intrepid ninth, put the enemy, whose ranks were already broken by our artillery practice, to flight, driving them beyond Bezzecca and the adjacent villages. The Austrians could do no more, and entered upon a complete retreat, abandoning all the positions they had gained, a long way up the valley of Conzei, and in the mountains to the east.

This fight of July 21, the most serious and murderous of the whole campaign, cost us heavy losses in killed and wounded. Among the first to fall was the heroic Colonel Chiassi, at the head of his regiment. Among the wounded were the gallant Majors Pessina, Tanara, Martinelli; Captains Bezzi, Pastore, Antongina; and many more of our best officers. The enemy, too, sustained such losses that from that day forward they gave up all idea of defending the Italian Tyrol, and made arrangements for retiring to the German territory.

On the 22nd, I drove as far as Pieve di Ledro, where I found Colonel Spinazzi with part of his regiment, the second. It must be remembered that Pieve is only a rifle-shot distant from Bezzecca. I asked the colonel how long he had been in that position, and he replied, three days. I was perfectly thunderstruck, and asked him why he had not taken part in the fight on the preceding day. He told me it was for want of ammunition. I left him, and ordered General Haug to arrest him, so soon as he should have assembled his regiment. It seems that Spinazzi's behaviour showed symptoms of insanity. His preceding conduct, so far as I knew, had not been that of a coward; and besides, however cowardly a man may be, it would be impossible for him, accompanied as he was by part of a regiment which had been fighting valiantly, to remain neutral within a kilomètre of Bezzecca, when the battle lasted from daybreak till two in the afternoon, the cannon thundering away for nine hours on end, and some 12,000 men fighting furiously on both sides.

At his trial, however, it came out that he was not at Pieve di Ledro at all on the 21st, but on Monte Nota, which overlooks that village on the south—a circumstance which confirms my opinion of the unfortunate officer's madness—and that, on Monte Nota, he held a council of his officers, who resolved to march towards the battle-field, where, not making sufficient haste, they at last arrived too late. If the second regiment had had an active leader, it might have played a glorious part that day. It was just in the enemy's rear when the latter occupied Bezzecca, and, by seizing the heights east of that village, could have completed a triumph which might have cost the Austrians their artillery and a great number of prisoners (as any one may see who cares to examine the locality); whereas that fine regiment, for whose safety so much blood was being shed at Bezzecca, remained inactive, and was not the slightest use to us.

Let this incident serve as a warning to all young officers. When you hear firing, and it is known that your comrades are engaged with the enemy, nothing excuses you from marching to join them. If you are in want of ammunition, the dead and wounded will be able to supply you. I repeat you ought to march to the scene of action, unless you are sent elsewhere, or have express orders to the contrary.

I will not describe the partial skirmishing carried on in the mountains; there were some very creditable actions, besides those in which I took part in person. I will only say that on the 21st, the enemy, to mask their serious movements on Bezzecca, had made a feint, with a respectable force, on Condino, where the brave General Fabrizi, chief of staff, repulsed them with Nicotera's and Corte's brigades, and a few guns.

At Molina, too, in the direction of the Lake of Garda. two engagements of doubtful result took place, in which some companies of the second made a gallant fight. After the 21st the enemy did not again appear; and having sent Colonel Missori, with his guides, to reconnoitre beyond Condino, I heard that they had evacuated the whole valley as far as the forts of Lardaro.

The object of the operations on our left through the Giudicaria valley was to effect a junction with Cadolini's column, which, leaving Valcamonica, was marching towards us through the valleys of Fumo and Daone.

At the same time with the fights at Bezzecca and Condino, another took place in the mountains on our left, where Major Erba—I think with some detachments of the first regiment—held his ground against a superior force of the enemy, which shows how numerous the

Austrians were on our front. The Giudicaria valley being clear of the enemy, the junction with Cadolini was easy ; and, having reconnoitred the forts of Lardaro, I resolved on a movement of our right towards Riva and Arco. We were already making arrangements to reinforce Haug when the order of August 25 for the suspension of hostilities took us by surprise. The campaign of 1866 is marked all through by unfortunate events, which I know not whether to attribute to fatality or to the malevolence of those at the head of affairs. The fact is that, after having laboured so hard, and shed so much precious blood in order to command the valleys of the Tyrol, we were arrested in our victorious course just when about to reap the fruit of our efforts. This assertion will not be thought exaggerated when it is known that on August 25, the day on which we were ordered to cease hostilities, there were no Austrians left on this side of Trento ; that Riva was abandoned and the cannon thrown into the lake ; that for two days the Austrian general, to whom we had to communicate the suspension of hostilities, was not to be found ; that our ninth regiment was already descending the mountains in the rear of the fort of Lardaro without opposition, the whole garrison of these forts consisting of less than one company ; and, lastly, that General Kuhn, commander-in-chief of the Austrian forces in the Tyrol, announced in one of his orders for the day, that, being unable to defend the Italian Tyrol, he was going to fall back on the German Tyrol.

On the same day, General Medici, after his brilliant

achievements in Val Sugana, had arrived within a few kilomètres of Trento. General Cosenz was following with his division, and in two days, at the outside, we should have effected our junction at the Tyrolese capital, with 50,000 men. Encouraged by our advantages, and reinforced by the numerous bands being mustered at Cadore, Friuli, and other places, what might we not have attempted? Instead of this, here I am, soiling paper, in order that those to come may hear what we went through. An order from the chief command of the army intimated to me that I was to retreat and evacuate the Tyrol; my reply was, " I obey "—a word which afterwards gave rise to the same cavillings and complaints as ever on the part of the Mazzinians, who, as usual, wanted me to proclaim the republic, and march either on Vienna or Florence.

Throughout the campaign of 1866 I was greatly assisted by my superior officers, being forced to travel in a carriage, and therefore unable to superintend all movements and strategic operations as it was my habit to do. Chiassi, Lombardi, Castellini, and the many other brave men who fell in this campaign, have ransomed with their noble blood our enslaved brethren, whom Italy will surely not again abandon to the foreigner—no, not though he were the devil himself!

This time, too, some good firearms reached us after the war was ended: I say no more.

From the Tyrol we retired on Brescia, where the volunteers were disbanded, and whence I again retired to Caprera.

I must take this opportunity of recalling to the grateful memory of my countrymen the devoted services rendered by Jessie White Mario, who was always, but especially in the French campaign, a true providence to our wounded.

CHAPTER V.

AGRO ROMANO.

THE short expedition of 1867 into the Roman territory was prepared for, on my part, by a trip to the Italian mainland and Switzerland, where I was present at a congress of the League of Peace and Liberty. I must therefore assume the greater part of the responsibility. A general of the Roman Republic, and invested by that Government (the most legitimate that ever existed in Italy) with extraordinary powers, living in an idleness which I have ever believed to be culpable so long as anything remains to be done for our country, I had good grounds for imagining that the time had come to give the final push to the tottering shanty of the Papacy, and win for Italy her own illustrious capital.

To wait till the initiative was taken by those whom it concerned was to indulge in a hope akin to that inscribed on the gates of the Inferno. The French emperor's troops were no longer at Rome; were a few thousand mercenaries, the offscourings of Europe, to keep a great nation at bay and prevent it from exercising its most sacred rights?

I prepared for the crusade, first at Venice, and afterwards in our other provinces nearer to Rome. The governments of Paris and Florence, with their agents, were watching me, as was only to be expected; and though I had the support of many honest men in the enterprise, there were others who spared no pains to thwart me, especially the Mazzinians, who proclaim themselves, without the shadow of a reason, the party of action, and will allow no one else to take the initiative, if they can help it.

At last, having travelled hither and thither all over Italy, I thought, after my return from Switzerland, that it was unadvisable to delay any longer. I resolved on immediate action towards the month of September.

At the same time that we were preparing for a movement in the north, we asked the help of our friends in Southern Italy for a concentrated operation on Rome. I had, however, reckoned without my host; and one fine night, having arrived at Sinalunga, where I was kindly received and entertained, I was arrested by order of the Italian Government, and taken to the fortress of Alessandria.

From Alessandria, where they detained me some days, I was conducted to Genoa, and thence to Caprera, the island being then surrounded by men-of-war. I was thus a prisoner in my own dwelling, visibly, and indeed very closely, guarded by ironclads, with smaller steamers and some merchant vessels, which the Government had chartered for the purpose.

The impulse thus given to the continental movement,

though, for obvious reasons, I was unable to superintend it, stimulated the action of our friends, who did not allow themselves to be discouraged by my detention.

General Fabrizi, my chief of staff, with other enthusiastic workers, formed a committee of supply at Florence. General Acerbi entered the Viterbo territory with a volunteer column; while Menotti, with another, penetrated into the Papal States by way of Corese; and the heroic Enrico Cairoli, with his brother Giovanni and about seventy brave fellows, carried arms to the Romans, who stood in great need of them, by boat along the Tiber.

Inside Rome, again, the brave Major Cucchi, with a handful of men who had entered at the risk of their lives, was organizing an internal revolution, which, in conjunction with the revolution from without, was to work the final overthrow of that monstrous power of the Papacy, so long fixed like a cancer in the heart of our unhappy land. I could not, in my prison at Caprera, gain exact information of all that was going on, but could guess the development of affairs from the state in which I had left them; besides which, I gathered something from the newspapers and from rumour, so that I knew for certain that my sons and friends were on Roman soil, engaged in conflict with the mercenaries of the Church.

I leave it to be imagined whether I could remain idle while those dear ones, at my own instigation, were fighting for the liberation of Rome, my whole life's ideal. The vigilance of those commissioned to guard me was great, and the ships and other resources at their disposal many; but greater still was my desire to fulfil my duty, by joining those brave hearts who were fighting for Italian freedom.

At 6 p.m. on October 14, 1867, I left my house, directing my steps towards the north shore of the island. On the beach I found the *Beccaccino*, a small dingey purchased on the Arno, and capable of holding two persons only.

The *Beccaccino* happened to be a few yards from the water's edge, to the eastward of a small boat-house which stood there. In the same place was a lentisk tree, which concealed the tiny skiff almost entirely from view, so that my royal guardians had not discovered it.

Giovanni, a young Sardinian, whose business it was to look after the schooner (the gift of my generous English friends), which was anchored in the port of Stagnatello, was waiting for me on the beach, and helped me to launch the *Beccaccino* and get on board her. He then rowed away in the schooner's boat, singing; while I turned to the left and followed the shore of Caprera, making less noise than a duck, and getting out into the open sea round the point of Arcaccio, where Froscianti, another faithful friend, and Barberini, a Caprera engineer, had explored the ground for fear of some ambuscade.

My guardians were many. They occupied the small islands in the harbour of Stagnatello, where they had a gunboat and some smaller vessels cruising all night long, in every direction but the one I had chosen to escape their clutches.

The moon was full—a circumstance which rendered my undertaking much more difficult—and, according to my calculations, would rise above the Teggiolone mountain (the highest peak in Caprera) about an hour after sunset. I had, therefore, to take advantage of this hour in order to cross to Maddalena; it would be useless to attempt it either sooner or later, as in the first case the sun would have betrayed me; in the second, the moon. An unexpected circumstance, which greatly favoured me, was the following. Maurizio, my orderly, had gone to Maddalena the same day, and was returning to Caprera about the time of my departure. Being perhaps slightly excited, he did not attend to the challenge of the gunboats cruising in the channel of Moneta, which separates Maddalena from Caprera, and was accordingly fired at several times, but fortunately without being hit. By a curious coincidence, this happened just while I was crossing.. I was, moreover, favoured by the south wind, the small waves raised by which completely hid the *Beccaccino*, whose sides scarcely rose more than a few inches above the surface of the water. My experience acquired in the American rivers with Indian canoes managed only with a paddle, here stood me in good stead. I had an oar or paddle about a mètre in length, with which I was able to propel myself along as noiselessly as do water-birds.

While, therefore, the majority of my guards were

rushing on Maurizio, I was quietly crossing the channel of La Moneta, and landing on that small island separated from Maddalena only by a fordable channel.

Reaching the north-east side of the islet, I landed among the numerous reefs which surround it just as the edge of the moon's disc appeared above Teggiolone. I hauled the *Beccaccino* ashore and hid her in the bushes, and then turned southward, in order to ford the channel and make for Mrs. Collins's house.

Major Basso and my friend Captain Cunco, who had expected me to pass by this channel, had been waiting for me at the ford; but Maurizio's mishap, and the number of shots (which they thought had been fired at me), convinced them that the affair was over, and that I had been killed or at least made prisoner. They therefore decided on retiring to the Maddalena.

Weakened as I was by age and infirmities, I was not very active among the boulders and bushes of the island of Maddalena. Fortunately, I had the moon to light my way, and, much as I had feared her on the sea, I was very thankful for her light on that rough ground, which was all the more difficult because, having kept my boots on to cross the channel, which was full of sharp-pointed granite rocks, I had them full of water, and this made walking very difficult. In this state I arrived, after taking all possible precautions, at the house of Mrs. Collins, who received me most cordially.

CHAPTER VI.

FROM SARDINIA TO THE MAINLAND.

I REMAINED at the house of Mrs. Collins, where I received the kindest and most cordial hospitality, till 7 p.m. on October 15, 1867, when my friend Pietro Suzini arrived there with his horse. I mounted, and, under his experienced guidance, crossed the island to Calla Francese, on the western side, where Basso and Captain Cuneo were awaiting me with a skiff and a boatman.

I embarked, and then the six of us crossed the strait between Maddalena and Sardinia. Sending back the boat, we passed the rest of the night in a cave * near the *stazzo* (grazing-farm) of Domenico N——. About 6 p.m., on the 16th, having procured three horses, we set out—half of us at first on foot, afterwards all on horseback—crossed the hills of Gallura, passing the gulf and village of Terranova, and at dawn on the 17th found ourselves on the heights above the port of San Paolo.

Not finding the vessel which Canzio and Vigiani

* The Sardinians frequently pass the night in these caves in the granite rocks (locally called *conca*), which often afford shelter to bandits.

were to have had ready at that port, we passed the morning at the farm of a certain Nicola, while Captain Cuneo, tired as he was after fifteen hours on horseback, pushed on southward to Porto Prandinga, where our friends were awaiting us, having arrived in safety after many adventures with the fishing-vessel *San Francesco.*

Before quitting the subject of Sardinia, I owe a word of grateful acknowledgment to the kindness of the friends who facilitated my escape.

Giuseppe Cuneo and Pietro Suzini set to work to help me in a most devoted way. With the greatest kindness, skill, and courage, they served us with guidance and advice, faced hardships, fatigue, and danger in our company, and refused to leave us till they had seen us on board the *San Francesco.*

Domenico N——, at the first farm we came to, took the only mattress he possessed from the bed where his sick wife was lying, and carried it to the cave, to make my sleeping-quarters a little more comfortable—such is Sardinian hospitality. He also took a great deal of trouble in procuring us all the necessary horses, without which it would have been almost impossible for us to cross the mountains of Gallura. Nicola, of the farm at Porto San Paolo, as soon as he had recognized me—in spite of my disguise, and my dyed hair and beard— welcomed me with that frank goodwill which cha- racterizes the rough but high-spirited and generous Sardinian shepherd. I am a great admirer of the Sardinian people in general, in spite of the faults attributed to them, and am certain that, under a good government, willing to occupy itself in earnest with the prosperity and progress of that fine but miserably poor population, the latter might, brave and intelligent as they are, become one of the first in the world.

An extensive and fertile country, Sardinia might be made into a perfect Eden ; whereas at present it is a desert where want, squalor, and malaria are legibly written on the characteristic features of the inhabitants. The Government which, unfortunately for every one, rules the Peninsula, scarcely knows whether the island of Sardinia is in existence, so occupied is it in preparing a nauseous reaction, and spending the riches of Italy in hiring spies, police agents, priests, and similar rabble, demoralizing and ruining the army, in order to work the wicked will of Bonaparte. In fact, it is at this date (1867) only a miserable *préfecture* of the French empire.

On October 17, 1867, I embraced Canzio and Vigiani on board the *San Francesco*. They had performed a most difficult task, and faced many risks and hardships in order to liberate me.

At 3 p.m. on the same day we weighed anchor, with a light southerly breeze, and, after tacking a little, the vessel sailed out of Tavolara, with her head north by east. On the 18th, about noon, we sighted Monte Cristo, and on the same night entered the Strait of Piombino. The 19th broke threateningly enough, with heavy rain, and gales from the south and south-west. These circumstances favoured our touching at Vada, between the channel of Piombino and Livorno. The rest of the 19th was passed near Vada, waiting for the night to enable us to land. About 7 p.m. we landed on the weed-covered beach south of Vada, five of us—Canzio, Vigiani, Basso, Maurizio, and I. We had to wander about for some time before finding the road, the shore being very marshy; but, helped in the more difficult places by my companions, I was able to keep up with them, and reach the village of Vada, where, Canzio and Vigiani fortunately finding two light carts, we started at once for Livorno. Arrived there, we went to Sgarallino's house, and found at home only the women-folk, who received us with great kindness. To this house came Lemmi, who had been expecting us for several days, with a carriage to take us to Florence. We started, and reached the capital towards morning, being received with the kindest hospitality by Lemmi's family.

At Florence, on the 20th, I was welcomed by my friends, and the population—from whom my arrival could not be kept secret—with demonstrations of joy, though the business in hand was to make Rome the capital of Italy, and take away that position from lovely Florence. This was a real and striking manifestation of patriotic feeling on the part of the noble Florentine people, of which Italy, as when Turin acted in like manner, ought to take account.

My greatest desire was to rejoin my brothers-in-arms, and my sons, who were already in the field and in presence of the enemy. My stay in the capital was therefore short. I spent the rest of the 20th and the whole of the 21st at Florence. On the 22nd, I started for the Roman frontier, travelling by special train as far as Terni, and thence in a carriage to Menotti's camp, coming up with him on the 23rd at the Pass of Corese.

The position of Corese being scarcely suited for defence by troops in the worst of condition—as our poor volunteers then were—we marched on Monte Maggiore, and from this position, during the night of the 23rd, threw ourselves in several columns on Monterotondo, where there were known to be about 400 of the enemy with two guns. The column commanded by Majors Caldesi and Valsania was to begin its movement at 8 p.m. on the 23rd, reach Monterotondo about midnight, and attempt to penetrate into the town by means of an attack on the western side, which was believed to be, and in fact was, the weakest part, the ruined walls having had their place supplied by houses, with outer doors to them, and therefore not difficult of access. The right-hand column, composed for the most part of courageous Romagnoles, owing to the deficiencies inevitable with a badly organized and ill-supplied corps, tired out, and possessing no guides acquainted with the country, reached Monterotondo by day; hence the night-attack became impossible.

The state of craven fear and imbecility to which the clergy have reduced those descendants of the ancient legions of Marius and Scipio is perfectly incredible. I had already experienced it during my retreat from Rome in 1849, when it was impossible to get a guide for love or money; and the same thing happened in 1867.

To think that in an Italian town like Monterotondo, with house-doors on the western side outside the walls, it was not possible to find a single individual able or willing to give us any information as to what there was within!—when we ourselves—by Heaven!—were Italians, fighting for the freedom of our country, while within the walls was the vilest crew of foreign mercenaries in the service of imposture! . . . " A free Church in a free State," was the saying of a great but crafty statesman. Yes, leave them free, this plague of nations, and you will have the same results as may be seen in France and Spain, fallen this day, through the agency of the priests, to the lowest place in the civilized world.

The left-hand column, commanded by Frigezy, arrived under Monterotondo on the east, occupied the Capuchin convent, with its adjacent positions, about 10 a.m., and threw out some companies on its left, to support our corps on the right, which was impossible all through the 24th, on account of the tremendous fire kept up by the enemy in that direction. The central column, under Menotti, with which I was for the moment, having marched from Monte Maggiore directly on the objective point, was stopped on the way by the difficult parts of the Noletta road ; but, nevertheless, at dawn it was the first to reach the foot of the heights surrounding Monterotondo on the north.

I ordered this column (commanded by Menotti, and composed for the most part of Mosto's and Burlando's gallant Genoese bersaglieri) to occupy the strong northern positions already alluded to, but not to attack, thinking that I could arrange the attack in conjunction with the other columns, about to arrive. But the impetuosity of the volunteers could not be controlled, and instead of limiting themselves to the occupation of the aforesaid positions, they rushed to the attack of Porta San Rocco, meeting a murderous fire poured on them from all the windows on that side of the town.

Having gone away from the central column to a little distance on the left, in order to try and discover Frigezy's, which was to arrive in that direction, I saw with pain and astonishment the difficulty into which the Genoese riflemen had ventured through excess of courage. This premature attack cost us a number of dead and wounded. It succeeded, however, in establishing in the houses adjacent to Porta San Rocco, a few hundred volunteers, who later on, with the co-operation of fresh companies from other corps, were able to set the gate on fire, and secured us the entrance into the town. The whole of October 24, therefore, was spent in surrounding Monterotondo with our forces; while the garrison—consisting of Papal Zouaves, armed for the most part with excellent carbines, and possessing two cannon—blazed away at us with a very inadequate reply on our part, our muskets being of the usual stamp, and the enemy so well sheltered that we could not discover a single one to take aim at.

On the crest of Monterotondo is the palace of the princes of Piombino, and a young man of this family was fighting in our ranks. This palace, or rather castle, is very extensive, and strongly fortified. The enemy had turned it into a fortress, with loopholes all round, and a parapet on the eastern platform, where they had mounted two guns, one nine and one twelve-pounder. Among our losses in the attack on Porta San Rocco were the gallant Major Mosto, severely, and Captain Uziel mortally wounded; while my dear, good Vigiani—to whom I owed, in great part, my escape from Caprera, not to speak of other kindnesses—was killed, and many other brave men with him.

I will try and record the names of those who fell, bravely fighting for the liberation of Rome in 1867; but, as I cannot remember them all for certain, I leave it to my staff to complete this sacred duty.

Dead.—Majors Achille Cantoni, Vico Pellizzari, Martino Franchi, Martinelli, Luigi Testori, Defranchis, De Benedetti; Captain Uziel; First Lieutenant Antonio Vigiani; Gironimo Bortolucci, Sante Lenari, Ettore Giordano, John Scoley of London (found wounded at the station of Monterotondo, and massacred by the Papal Zouaves); Ercole Latini; Achille Borghi; Antonio Annighini; Pio Lombardi; Giuseppe Fermi; Count Bolis di Lugo; Lieutenant Silvio Andreuzzi; Ettore Morasini; Bovi, son of the major of the same name.

Wounded.—Majors Egisto Bezzi, Antonio Mosto, Luigi Stallo; Vincenzo Gavitani; Giacomo Galliani; Domenico Manara; Antonio Sgarbi; Mayer, of Livorno; Pasquale Sgarallino; Paolo Capuani.

CHAPTER VII.

THE ATTACK ON MONTEROTONDO.

THIS attack is a sufficient proof that the *morale* of the men under my command was quite above the influence of the Mazzinian propaganda, which called upon the volunteers to return home in order to proclaim the Republic.

We spent October 24, as I have said, in surrounding Monterotondo, preparing fascines and brimstone for burning the gate of San Rocco, and making all possible arrangements for an attack.

The three columns commanded by Salomone, Caldesi, and Valsania, with Menotti, were massed (with the exception of some scouting-parties sent out towards the Roman road, by which reinforcements might reach the enemy) for the decisive attack on Porta San Rocco. Frigezy was to attack the town simultaneously on the eastern side, and, if possible, also to set the gate of the castle on fire.

The attack was fixed for 4 a.m. on the 25th. Our poor volunteers, starving, half-naked, and with their few clothes wet through, had stretched themselves out at the edge of the road, which the heavy rains of the preceding days had turned into all but impassable sloughs of mud. I confess that I almost despaired of being able to get the poor fellows up again at the hour for the attack, and, seated among them, shared their miserable situation till about 3 a.m. At that hour the friends who were about me begged me to enter the convent of Santa Maria, a short distance off—at least for a little while, so as to get some shelter from the wet. They took me to the only seat that was to be found, a confessional, where I remained a few minutes. I had scarcely sat down and leaned my shoulders, aching with long standing, against the wall, when a noise like that of an approaching storm, an awful cry from a band of our men rushing towards the burning gate, made me start up and run as fast as I could towards the scene of action, shouting with the rest " Forward ! "

The whole of the gate, having been set on fire, and battered in with two little cannon of ours, which seemed scarcely bigger than telescopes, was now only a heap of burning ruins. While we were waiting for the fire to go out, the enemy tried to barricade the gateway afresh, and began to bring carts, planks, and other things for the purpose. This did not precisely meet the views of our men, who had spent so much time and labour in firing it. The first article pushed into the gateway by the Zouaves was a cart ; but they had no time to put it in its place. An electric spark of heroism spread like lightning through the ranks of the patriots, who threw themselves like men possessed into the burning gateway.

Weary, exhausted, starved—what did that matter? Had I not already seen those young Italians perform impossibilities? It was a crime to distrust them—a thought worthy of decrepit and doting old age.

Neither the cart that blocked the entrance, nor the burning fragments heaped on the ground, nor the hail of bullets poured into them on all sides, was able to stay their progress. They seemed to me like a torrent, which, breaking through banks and dykes, spreads over the country.

In a few minutes our men had overrun the town, and the garrison was shut up in the castle. At 6 p.m. the attack on the castle began. Our men, being already masters of the openings of all the streets leading to it, barricaded them, and set fire to the stables by means of fascines, straw, carts, and all the combustibles to be found on the spot.

At 10 a.m., we repulsed with a few shots about 2000 men advancing from Rome to the assistance of the besieged. At 11, the garrison, suffocated with smoke, and fearing that the fire would reach the powder, which was stored underground, hoisted a white flag and surrendered at discretion.

The gallant Major Testori, a short time before this, had shown himself in the open with a white flag, in order to summon them to surrender, but, in violation of every law of war, they fired several shots at him, and left him dead. I had the greatest difficulty, after so many and such atrocious acts of barbarity, in saving the lives of these agents of the Inquisition from the resentment of our men. I had to see them out of Monterotondo myself, and then have them escorted to the Pass of Corese by forty men under Major Marrani.

There happened at Monterotondo what one might expect to happen in a town taken by assault, which had deserved little sympathy on account of the passive and indifferent, almost hostile, attitude previously assumed towards us, and I must confess that there was no lack of disorder. This disorder was also a hindrance to the proper organization of our forces, for which reason little could be done in that direction during the few days of our stay.

In the hope of better organizing the men, once outside the town and in motion, putting an end to the riotous scenes enacted there, and approaching Rome, we marched out of Monterotondo on October 28, and occupied the hills of Santa Colomba. Frigezy occupied Marcigliano with the vanguard, and pushed his outposts as far forward as Castel Giubileo and Villa Spada.

On the evening of the 29th, while I was at Castel Giubileo, a messager arrived from Rome, who, having some of his relatives in the column, was known to us; he assured me that the Romans had decided on making an attempt at insurrection that very night. This somewhat embarrassed me, the men not being all at hand; yet I resolved to push forward myself at dawn on the 30th, with two battalions of Genoese bersaglieri, as far as the Casino dei Pazzi, a short distance from Ponte Nomentano.

One of our guides and an officer, who were the first
to arrive at the main building of the Casino, met with
a picket of the enemy, and a few revolver-shots were
exchanged. The guide was wounded in the chest; and,
being outnumbered by the enemy, our men retreated,
warning me, by other shots, of the presence of the
Papal soldiers. All this, however, they did like
brave men, and with the greatest presence of mind.
We fell back from that point, to meet the two battalions on the march, and, as soon as they arrived, occupied the Casino dei Pazzi, the houses of La Cecchina,
a grazing-farm, at the distance of a long carbine-shot to
northward of the former, and the road, flanked by a
stone wall, leading from the Casino to the farm-buildings. We remained in that position during the whole
of the 30th, waiting to hear of some movement in Rome,
or to receive some communication from our friends
within the walls, but in vain.

About 10 a.m., two Papal columns marched out to
reconnoitre, one from Ponte Nomentano, and the other,
some time later, from Ponte Mammolo. The papal
soldiers on our right, advancing in skirmishing order
till they were within carbine-shot, kept firing on us all
day long; but our men, obedient to orders, made no
reply—which would, indeed, have been useless with our
wretched weapons, the Genoese being unprovided with
their good carbines. Only when the Zouaves, over-con-
fident, or irritated by our silence, advanced still nearer,
our men, ambushed in the Casino dei Pazzi, killed four
of them, and wounded several.

Our position, within a short distance of Rome, where the whole papal army was concentrated, was a risky one—so much so, that when I saw the two columns, whose numbers it was impossible to estimate precisely, marching out, I asked Menotti, who was in the rear, to support us with some battalions, which accordingly he immediately brought forward himself.

Persuaded that nothing was doing at Rome, and that it was still less likely that anything would be done after the arrival of the French—which was already announced, and took place shortly afterwards—I prepared for a retreat on Monterotondo, leaving many fires burning in all positions occupied by us, in order to deceive the enemy.

Here the Mazzinians profited by their opportunity to turn sulky and scatter discontent among the volunteers. " If you are not going to Rome," they said, " it is better to return home." And indeed, at home, one can eat well, drink better, and sleep warmly, and feel much safer into the bargain.

The positions we had occupied, Castel dei Pazzi, Cecchina, Castel Giubileo, and the rest, were too near Rome, and untenable against a superior force; we therefore required stronger positions further off. Monterotondo fulfilled these conditions; and, moreover, the victualling there was easier.

CHAPTER VIII.

MENTANA, NOVEMBER 3, 1867.

ON October 31, the whole of the volunteer force had re-entered Montcrotondo, where we remained till November 3. All this time was spent in clothing a few of the neediest of the soldiers, providing them with shoes and weapons, and organizing them as best we could.

The strong positions of Sant' Angelo, Monticelli, and Palombara were occupied by three battalions under Colonel Paggi, Tivoli by Colonel Pianciani with one battalion, Viterbo by General Acerbi with 1000 men, and Velletri by General Nicotera with another thousand. Major Andreuzzi was to operate on the right bank of the Tiber with two hundred men.

Before October 31, many volunteers flocked to swell the columns under Menotti's command, so that these had already reached the number of about 6000 men.

The situation of the volunteer corps, therefore, if not brilliant, would not have been altogether deplorable, had we been able, by the help of the country people, to supply our poor soldiers with arms, clothes, and other necessaries.

The Papal army was completely demoralized. We had defeated part of it at Monterotondo, and the rest had concentrated itself in Rome, whence it had not since ventured out, though challenged by us. The Roman people, oppressed and, after their attempts at insurrection, massacred, were crying out for vengeance, and preparing, with renewed courage—under the leadership of Cucchi and other brave men, to co-operate with their deliverers outside the walls, and make an end of the sway of priests and mercenaries. All, in short, promised well for the fall of the priest, the enemy of the whole human race.

But the genius of evil was still watching over the preservation of his principal adherent—the pontiff of falsehood. From the banks of the Seine—where, to the sorrow of France and the world, he still rules—he threatened us on the Arno, accused the timid of cowardice, and roused the courage of fear and treachery. At the word of their master, the men who so unworthily govern Italy, covering their faces with the usual mask of patriotism, cheated the nation, invaded the Roman territory, and said, "Here we are! we have kept our word! At the first shots fired in Rome, see how we hasten to the help of our brothers."

Lies! lies! You hastened indeed, but for the destruction of your brothers, in case they had achieved the final victory; and you hastened when you were sure that the Roman patriots were scattered and slain.

Lies! lies! You and your magnanimous ally occupied the city and territory of Rome, in order to set the Pope's entire host of mercenaries—completely recovered after its defeats—free to fall, with the full weight of its more numerous, well-armed, and well-supplied forces, on a handful of volunteers, wretchedly armed, and in want of the chief necessaries of life, with the deliberate purpose of devoting the latter to destruction. And in case the Papal army should not suffice—as it did not—there were all Bonaparte's soldiers ready, and (I shudder to think of it) also those who are unhappy enough to obey *you*.

Were they not marching on us in 1860 with the intention of fighting ? (See Farini's despatch to Bonaparte.)—Why should they not do the same in 1867 ? The hills of Mentana were covered with the corpses of the gallant sons of Italy, mingled with those of foreign mercenaries, as the hills of Capua had been, seven years before. And the cause for which those men fought, whom I had the honour of commanding in the south, was as sacred as that which had spurred us to battle under the walls of the ancient capital of the world.

Here I must record with pain another cause of the disaster at Mentana. I have already said that the Mazzinians had begun their propaganda of dispersion with the commencement of our retreat from Casino dei Pazzi, and this conduct on their part had no sort of justification. Any man with the smallest stock of common sense can easily understand that our position under the walls of Rome must have become untenable when the French arrived. We had no artillery or

cavalry.   If the Papal troops alone had made a sortie
in good earnest, we could not have made head against
them; and had they attacked us, we had not rations
enough to have held out for two days.   Masters, on
the other hand, of Monterotondo, which is within sight
of !Rome, we were at the central point of our small
resources, in a commanding position, and able to descry
the enemy at a considerable distance, in case of attack.

All these things, however, only served as pretexts for
the Mazzinians to turn against us.   The treacherous and
obstinate opposition of the Government, the power of the
priesthood, and the support given to it by Bonaparte, were
not enough; they too must come, as usual, to give the
ass's kick to men whose sole ambition was the deliverance
of their enslaved countrymen.   "We shall do better,"
the men of that party—who are this day partisans of
the monarchy—said to me at Lugano, in 1848.   It will
be seen that the war of pin-pricks carried on against
me by the Mazzinians dates from a long while back.
"Let us go home, to proclaim the republic and build
barricades," they said to my soldiers in the Agro
Romano, in 1867.   And, indeed, it was much easier for
those poor lads who followed me to return home than
to stay with me in November, without food or necessary
clothes to cover them, and with the Italian army, as
well as the Papalini and the French to fight against.

These Mazzinian intrigues resulted in the desertion
of about 3000 men during our retreat from Casino de
Pazzi to Mentana; and when, in a force of 6000, half
the men deliberately desert—and they made no secret

of it—it may well be imagined what amount of courage and discipline, and confidence in the successful completion of our enterprise, was to be found among the remaining half.

This party has, from first to last, caused me unspeakable injury, which I would willingly forget had it been inflicted on me personally, but it was on the national cause. And how can I forget it? how can I refrain from pointing it out to those, the noblest of our young men, who were led astray by them? Mazzini, indeed, was better than his followers, and, in a letter addressed to me, under date February 11, 1870, with regard to the affair at Mentana, he wrote, "You know that I had no confidence in our success, and was convinced that it was better to concentrate all our forces on a strong movement in Rome itself" (a plan entirely disapproved of by our Roman friends) "than to make an attempt on the province; but, the undertaking once begun, I helped it as much as I could."

I do not doubt Mazzini's assertion, but the mischief was done. Either he was not in time to advise his supporters, or else they persisted in their course of action in spite of him. Ricciotti could not get the assistance we had hoped for in England, as the catchword circulated among our friends there was this, " Why should we overthrow the Papacy, to put a worse government in its place?"

In the Agro Romano, his followers, as I have already said, spread discontent among my soldiers, and caused the wholesale desertion already mentioned, which, no doubt, was the principal cause of the defeat at Mentana. From the tower of the Piombino palace at Monterotondo, where I passed the greater part of the day, watching Rome, the drill of our men on the level ground, and every movement on the campagna, I saw that procession marching towards Passo di Corese, that is, going away to their own homes. To the comrades who called my attention to the fact, I only said, " Nonsense! those are not our men going away; they will be peasants going to or coming from their work." But in my heart I felt the bitterness of the cruel act, though I tried to hide it, or at any rate make light of it to the bystanders—one's usual resource in critical circumstances.

In consequence of this state of mind on the part of my men, and as the northern frontier was hermetically sealed against us by a detachment of the Italian army, and it was therefore impossible to procure the necessary supplies in that quarter, we had to seek another scene of action and base of operations, to enable us to live, hold our ground, and await the events that were to bring about the final solution of the Roman question. For all these reasons it was decided to march along the river to the left, towards Tivoli, in order to get the Apennines in our rear, and approach the southern provinces.

The march was fixed for the morning of November 3, but a distribution of shoes delayed us so long that we could not be ready to start before noon. We left Monterotondo by the Tivoli road, the order of march being pretty nearly as follows :—Menotti's column were to march in good order, with a vanguard of bersaglieri at a distance varying from 1000 to 2000 paces in front of them. In advance of the vanguard scouts on foot were to march, preceded by guides on horseback. On all the roads coming from Rome on our right, scouts on foot and on horseback were to be thrown out as far as possible towards Rome; and on the heights which commanded a view of the country, vedettes were to be posted, to warn us in time of any movement on the part of the enemy. A rearguard was to urge on the stragglers, and leave none behind. The artillery was to march in the centre of the columns, and their respective baggage in the rear of each.

In this order, more or less, we began our march from Monterotondo for Tivoli. Unhappily, however, it seems that our mounted scouts, who were very few in number, fell into the hands of the enemy, so that the Papal troops, marching along the Via Nomentana, nearly surprised our van, which they engaged.

Having passed the village of Mentana, the firing warned me of the presence of the enemy. A' retreat in such a contingency, when the enemy had already engaged us, was the same thing as a flight, and there was no other resource but to accept the combat, occupying the strong positions which we found at hand. I therefore sent Menotti, who was marching with the vanguard, orders to occupy these positions and assume the defensive. I then sent forward the rest of the columns in succession, making them deploy right and left in support of the first, while several companies remained in column as a reserve on the right.

The road from Mentana to Monterotondo, our line of operation that day, is a good one, but low, with high banks on either side. I was therefore obliged to seek, on our right, a position suited for mounting the two guns we had taken from the enemy on October 25. This was done with great difficulty, for want of men and trained horses, and because the ground, cut up with hedges and vineyards, was very uneven.

Meanwhile a murderous conflict was raging all along the line. We occupied positions as good as those of the enemy, or better, as the latter could not show their artillery during the day; and maintained them for a time, in spite of the superiority of our adversaries both in arms and numbers.

I must acknowledge, however, that the volunteers, demoralized by the great number of desertions, did not that day show themselves worthy of their reputation. Some distinguished officers, and a handful of gallant fellows who followed them, shed their blood without yielding a handbreadth of ground; but the majority had lost their old daring and endurance. They gave up splendid positions without the resistance I might reasonably have expected.

The fight began about 1 p.m., and by 3 p.m. the enemy had driven us from position to position, about 1000 mètres backward, to the village of Mentana. At 3 p.m., we were able to place our guns in an advantageous position on our right, and they opened fire with great effect on the enemy.

A bayonet-charge executed by the whole line, and the short-range fire of our men posted at the windows of the houses in Mentana, had strewn the ground with Papalini corpses. We were victorious; the enemy were in retreat, the lost positions were being regained, and till 4 p.m. victory smiled on the champions of Italian liberty, and we were masters of the field. But, I repeat, a fatal demoralization had crept into our ranks. Our troops were victorious, but did not care to complete the victory by pursuing an enemy who had abandoned the field. Reports of French columns marching on us were circulated among the volunteers, and there was no time to investigate their origin; for which, of course, our enemies—priests or devils—were responsible. It was known that the Italian army was against us, arresting our men at the frontier, and intercepting all supplies and communications intended for us. In short, the Italian Government, the priests, and the Mazzinian party combined had succeeded in spreading discouragement in our ranks. And it is not every man who is of a temper to resist discouragement, and march resolutely through good and ill to the fulfilment of his duty.

About 4 p.m., the report, which after all proved to be false, that a column of 2000 French soldiers was attacking us in the rear, gave the last blow to the failing endurance of the volunteers. It was, however, true that the expeditionary corps of De Failly was then arriving on the battle-field to reinforce the Pope's shattered ranks.

The positions regained with such efforts were again

yielded, and a crowd of fugitives massed together on the high-road. In vain did I and many of my brave officers raise our voices to arrest their flight. I shouted myself hoarse; in vain. All of them took the way to Monterotondo, leaving a gun behind, which did not fall into the enemy's hands till the following day, and deserting a few gallant fellows, who kept up a hot fire on the Papalini from the houses of Mentana.

Any one can be brave with the enemy in retreat; and this, of course, was the case with our adversaries. Those of the Papal troops who had escaped us, now that they were supported by the French columns, came on with the greatest confidence. They pressed closely on our retreating ranks, and, with their superior weapons, caused us many losses both in killed and wounded.

The French, whom at first we took for Papal troops, came on with their terrible chassepots, pouring on us a perfect hail of projectiles, but fortunately caused more alarm than injury. Ah! if our men had only listened to my voice, and, acting purely on the defensive, held— as we might have done without much danger—the re-conquered positions of Mentana, November 3 would perhaps have been numbered among the glorious anniversaries of the Italian democracy, in spite of our many wants and the great inferiority of our force.

In many of the preceding battles, the tide of fortune had gone against us till nearly the end of the day, when a favourable turn brought back the victory to our side. At Mentana we were masters of the field at four in the afternoon, and if we could have held out another hour, night would have come on, and perhaps induced the enemy to retreat towards Rome, their position outside the walls not being very tenable against men who would have left them no rest by night.

About 5 p.m., all our column, except the few defenders of Mentana posted inside the houses, were retreating in disorder on Monterotondo. We were scarcely able to occupy the strong position of the Capuchin convent with a few hundred men. We had no more ammunition for the cannon, and very little for the muskets. It was the general opinion that we ought to retreat to Passo di Corese.

From the tower of the castle at Monterotondo I had convinced myself that the report of the 2000 French on the Roman road, who were to attack us in the rear, during the fight (as I myself had been assured by many men) was quite baseless. It seems impossible that such things should happen, yet they do happen. Several among my own officers, of undoubted trustworthiness, assured me that they had heard it, and it was certain that the rumour had been in circulation amid the vicissitudes of the fight. In such a confusion as that, who is to find the originator of a report implying the blackest treason? Yet this rumour, circulating among the soldiers, discouraged them, and spread from one to another with lightning speed. The depth of human depravity is unfathomable. Of how many depraved characters will it not be necessary to purge Italian society, so corrupted by the priests and their friends!

A system of *field police* is indispensable in every body of troops ; but such is the repugnance of the volunteers to police of any kind, that it seems difficult or impossible to institute it.

At dusk on November 3 we retreated on Passo di Corese,* and passed the rest of the night on Roman territory, within or near the inn. Some of the officers informed me that part of the soldiers were still willing to keep their arms and try their luck again, but in the morning I was convinced that, if such dispositions had ever existed, they existed no longer.

On the morning of November 4 we laid down our weapons on the bridge, and the disarmed soldiers passed out of papal territory.

Here I owe a word of commendation to General Fabrizi, my chief of staff, whom I left in charge of all further arrangements for the disarming. This gallant veteran of Italian independence behaved with his usual valour on the battle-field of Mentana, and, worn out with fatigue and years, was, after having animated our men by his words and presence to do their duty, carried into Monterotondo, accompanied by the soldiers.

Colonel Caravà, commanding an Italian regiment at Corese, who had been an officer under my orders in former campaigns, treated us on all occasions with praiseworthy kindness. He received me in a very friendly manner, did all he could for me and the volunteers, and placed a train at my disposal to take

* The bridge at Corese at that time divided the Roman from the Italian territory.

me to Florence. But not such was the disposition of the Government. The Deputy Crispi, who was in the train with me, was of opinion that there was no fear of an arrest. I was compelled to disagree with him, knowing with whom I had to deal. However, as there was nothing else to be done, I followed my friend's advice, and let the train go on towards the capital.

On the journey, the usual Government precautions— carbineers, bersaglieri, etc. After travelling at full speed, I was at last lodged in my old abode at Varignano; whence, after a time, I was allowed to return home to Caprera.

FIFTH PERIOD.

CHAPTER I.

THE FRENCH CAMPAIGN.

To those who have the patience to read me, I should like to point out a circumstance which seems strange, but which is perfectly true, and on which I offer no comment, preferring to leave that task to the reader.

It was quite natural that I should not have gained the favour of the Savoyard monarchy, on my arrival from America in 1848. That I should have excited universal antipathy among its servants, from the prime minister to the generals of the army, and from these to the ushers of the court, whose existence was bound up with that of the royal Government, follows quite logically from the nature of the men and things in question. What I cannot so clearly understand, is the unfavourable reception I met with from those men who may justly be called the luminaries of the modern period of national resurrection, and who deserved so nobly of that cause —Mazzini, Manin, Guerrazzi, and some of their friends.

I met the same fate in France in 1870 and 1871. Yet in France, as in Italy, I have found among the common people an enthusiastic sympathy certainly far above my deserts.

The Government of National Defence, consisting of three honest men fully deserving of public confidence, received me, because forced to do so by the course of events, but coldly enough, and with the manifest intention (as had sometimes been the case in Italy) making use of my poor name, but nothing more; in short, depriving me of the means which were absolutely necessary, if my co-operation was to be of any use.

Gambetta, Crémieux, Glais-Bizoin, were each personally kind to me, but—especially the first, from whom I had expected, if not personal sympathy, at least active and energetic co-operation—left me to myself during a time which might have been most valuable.

In the first days of September, 1870, the Provisional Government was proclaimed in France, and on the 6th of that month I offered my services to that Government, which was always ashamed of calling itself republican. The French Government waited a month before replying—a priceless interval in which much could have been done, but which was almost entirely wasted.

Here I think it well to repeat that it is a great mistake for those nations which remain their own masters (as happened, within a short space of time, to both France and Spain) not to decide on the government of a single honest man; under the name of dictator or any other, but one only. It is no use to have recourse to complex governments, generally composed of theorists, who pass the greater part of their time in deliberating instead of acting promptly, as required by pressing circumstances.

In France they did still worse—instead of *one* government, they had two; and every one knows the result of this defective system. If they had, on the other hand, elected one man, he would probably have identified the seat of government with his head-quarters, which was virtually the case with the Prussians, and was what gave them such an immense advantage over their opponents. Instead of a Babel, France would have had a strong government.

It was only at the beginning of October that I knew I should be received in France, and General Bordone, to whom alone I owe the acceptance of my offer, came to fetch me at Caprera with the steamer *Ville de Paris* (Captain Condray), which conveyed me to Marseilles on October 7, 1870.

Esquiros, *préfet* of that illustrious city, and the people, welcomed me with great enthusiasm; and a telegram from the Governor of Tours immediately summoned me to come to him.

When I reached Tours, I found Crémieux and Glas-Bizoin there, both sympathetic and, I think, thoroughly honest men, but not equal to the task of raising France out of the terrible catastrophe into which Bonaparte had hurried her. Besides, they belonged to a vicious system of government, in which, even with a capacity for understanding what was right, they could not do it.

Gambetta, arriving the day after in a balloon, gave some sort of impulse to the inert machine of government

—he galvanized it, improvised enormous resources; but for him likewise circumstances were too strong, whether because the system of government was a wrong one, through the mistaken arrangement of entrusting what remained of the army to the same men of the empire who had lost the first part, or for want of the experience necessary in so terrible a crisis.

At Tours I lost several days through the indecision of the Government, and found myself on the point of returning home, having understood, as I said before, that they wished to make use of my poor name—nothing else.

The task they wished to entrust to me was that of organizing a few hundred Italian volunteers, then at Chambéry and Marseilles. After several discussions with these gentlemen, I at last repaired to Dôle, in order to collect those elements of every nationality which were to serve as a nucleus to the future army of the Vosges.

The Prussians, marching on Paris after Sédan, were, of course, obliged to keep scouts on their left flank, where the new recruits of France were being massed. These same scouts several times appeared in the neighbourhood of Dôle, where the few men I had been able to collect were being organized. badly provided and armed as they were for a long time.

Our attitude, however, was energetic enough, as we took up our position, first at Mont Rolland, and afterwards in the Forêt de la Serre, so that Dôle remained untouched by the enemy during the whole time we remained there.

As the hostile army was marching on Paris, it was naturally necessary for us at least to threaten their line of operation from the Rhine to the capital. This necessity was fully felt by the Government of Defence, who sent into the Vosges the greater number of the franc-tireur corps, and General Cambriels with 30,000 men of the new levy of Gardes Mobiles, some battalions of the old army, and a few cannon.

All these forces were driven back from the Vosges on Besançon by the superior weight of the enemy, while we were still at Dôle; and M. Ordinaire, prefect of Besançon, twice telegraphed to me to come to him, in order to devise means for preventing the disbanding of the troops above mentioned.

M. Ordinaire had had the idea of collecting together and placing under my command the fractional corps scattered throughout the department, and I had been welcomed by all these troops, and by the population of Besançon, with the same enthusiasm as if I had been in Italy. But M. Gambetta, who arrived soon after, thought best to smooth over matters, and replace all the united forces of the east under the orders of General Cambriels. It should be remembered that General Cambriels himself asserted that he needed rest, in order to recover from a wound in the head, which greatly inconvenienced him.

In November, I had orders to march with my men from Dôle to Morvan, which, with the important foundry of Creuzot, was threatened by the enemy. I chose Autun for my head-quarters. Here we found the population somewhat alarmed at the approach of the Prussians—so much so that they had thrown into the little river Arroux the only two small guns they had.

The arrival of Tanara's and Ravelli's Italians, a few Spaniards, Greeks, and Poles, and a few battalions of the Garde Mobile, began to raise the efficiency of our nucleus of an army. We even began to form an artillery corps with a few mountain-guns, followed by two field-batteries of four rifled cannon apiece; and also had a certain number of guides on horseback, for the most part Italians, who became two complete squadrons towards the end of the campaign.

The same thing took place with the French line cavalry, which, beginning with a detachment of thirty mounted chasseurs, had, by the end of the war, increased to a complete regiment.

Three brigades were organized, the first commanded by General Bossack, the second by Colonel Delpeck (it was afterwards under the orders of Colonel Lobbia), and the third by Menotti.

Several companies of francs-tireurs, one of which was commanded by Lieut.-Colonel Odoline, a second by Lieut.-Colonel Braun, a third by Lieut.-Colonel Grouchy, a fourth by Lieut.-Colonel Lhost, a fifth by Major Ordinaire, were all, except Braun's, acting under Menotti's orders, and formed part of his third brigade. All these companies, while being organized, carried on skirmishing operations between the enemy's columns, and caused the latter great annoyance.

The fourth brigade, under Ricciotti, was, at the beginning, composed of franc-tireur companies only, acting, like the others, in flying columns; but towards the end of the campaign, some battalions of mobilized Gardes Nationales were added to it.

The chief of staff of the army was General Bordone. This man—who, more than any one else, was the cause of my going to France, and who met with so much opposition—I am very far from considering perfect; and, indeed, I know little of his antecedents, except that he came to the south of Italy with the brave Deflotte, and served with great credit in the campaign of 1860. But in any case, for truth's sake, I must confess that he was of the greatest service in organizing the army, and procuring every kind of supplies, and that he behaved like a brave man on the battle-field. He took my place, moreover, whenever my infirm state of health rendered it necessary.

As second chief of staff, Colonel Lobbia was also very useful to me. Colonel Canzio was chief of. my head-quarters, till he took the command of the fifth brigade, to which, after General Bossack's death, the first was added. Canzio was replaced in the command of head-quarters by Major Fontana. Colonel Olivier was in command of the artillery. Commandant Bondet, who, afterwards summoned to the army of the Loire, was killed there, commanded our first cavalry detachment of thirty men. The cavalry regiment at the end of the campaign was commanded by the major of a hussar squadron, whose name I do not remember. Our two squadrons of guides were organized by Commandant Farlatti. Dr. Timoteo Riboli was head of the ambulance.

The sous-intendant Beaumès served as intendant, till the arrival of an officer to act in that capacity, whose name I do not remember. Our paymaster was Colonel Martinet; the head of the telegraph department, Colonel Loir; the head of the engineering department Colonel Gauklair.

Lieut.-Colonel Demay was *commandant de place* at head-quarters; I do not recollect the name of the president of court-martial.

With this extempore organization, we started, about the middle of November, for Arnay-le-Duc, and the valley of the Ouche, which descends to· Dijon. At that time, Werder's Prussian army was there, threatening the Rhone valley, and keeping its outposts towards Dôle, Nuits, Soubernon, etc., scouring all the surrounding district with foraging-parties.

The self-styled army of the Vosges, from 6000 to 8000 strong, all told, was therefore marching against Werder's victorious force of about 20,000 men, with a strong body of cavalry and artillery.

Our francs-tireurs engaged in a few skirmishes of slight importance, with the exception of Ricciotti's brilliant enterprise at Châtillon-sur-Seine, and that of Ordinaire. In the first, the francs-tireurs of the fourth brigade executed a magnificent surprise, described in the following order of the day:—

" Order of the day.

" The francs-tireurs of the Vosges, the chasseurs of the Isère, the (Savoyard) chasseurs of the Alps, the battalion of the Doubs, and the Hâvre chasseurs, all of whom, under the direction of Ricciotti Garibaldi, have taken part in the affair at Châtillon, have deserved well of the Republic.

" Being only 400 strong, they attacked about 1000 men, defeated them, made 167 prisoners (including thirteen officers), and took eighty-two saddled horses, four *fourgons* of arms and ammunition, and the mail-waggon. On our side there were six men killed, and twelve wounded; the enemy had more.

" I commend the prisoners to the generosity of the French nation.

" G. GARIBALDI.

" Arnay-le-Duc, November 21, 1870."

It may be said that, as a general rule, our francs-tireurs became more formidable to the enemy every day.

During the first Prussian occupation of Dijon, while we were still between Dôle and the Forêt de la Serre, we attempted a night-attack on the enemy in that city, being of opinion that, as was said, the people of Dijon were prepared to defend themselves.

Considering the state of the men I commanded, our resolution to try our strength against an enemy so superior in numbers, and victorious in so many battles, and therefore well accustomed to fighting, was truly a rash one.   But, hearing that the Dijonnais were already fighting, we willingly went to share their peril.

We were already within a few miles of the capital of Burgundy, when a messenger from the city brought us word that Dijon had surrendered, and that the municipal authorities had forbidden all resistance. We then marched back to our positions.

We had now reached the middle of November, without as yet effecting anything, except the exploit already mentioned on the part of the francs-tireurs.   Our men were growing impatient, being, as usual, desirous of measuring their strength against that of the enemy; and, moreover, complaints of our inaction were raised in those very quarters where we had been refused the means for energetic action.   It therefore became necessary to do something.

It would have been folly to try our strength with Werder's army—then in occupation of Dijon—in an attack by day; and we might have found it impossible to return.   It seemed feasible to attack by night, when the difference of weapons was equalized; the usual bits of old iron, which had been supplied to us even in France, were, in the dark, as good as the needle-guns with which our enemies were armed.   Besides, it is my conviction that there ought to be no firing in a night-attack, especially with raw recruits.   While the small army of the Vosges was marching towards Dijon along the Ouche valley, nearly all our franc-tireur corps were on our left with the first brigade, all converging towards us, to take part in the enterprise.

On the morning of November 26, having ridden up to Lantenay, in order to reconnoitre that plateau, I found myself on those heights with the staff and the officers of my head-quarters, when a column of several thousand Prussians, horse, foot, and artillery, coming from Dijon, was seen advancing towards us along the high-road.

The position of Lantenay is a strong one towards the river Ouche. On the side of the platform, however, towards Pâques and Prenois, it is completely commanded, and cannot be held against a superior force. Consequently, I made all the forces we had in the village of Lantenay ascend thence to the plateau, and arranged them there, as they arrived, in their places for the battle, to right and left of the road by which they came, leaving on this road some battalions in column as reserves, and for a decisive charge, in case the enemy should advance into our lines. The greater part of the third brigade, which formed the sinews of our force, occupied the left, drawn up on the edge of the wood, with its lines of sharpshooters in front, on the crest of the hill overlooking this same wood. The reserves on the high-road also belonged to the third brigade.

The Genoese carbineers were posted on the extreme left, and our artillery—consisting of one field-battery of four rifled pieces, and two mountain-batteries—on the left of the Genoese, as this position commanded all the rest.

On our right were Lhost's francs-tireurs, afterwards reinforced by Ricciotti's and others. The small body of cavalry, composed of thirty chasseurs and a few guides, had been posted in front of our centre, in a depression of the ground. It will therefore be seen that our principal force consisted of the third brigade, which by itself alone formed centre, left, and reserve, in all about 3000 men. The so-called fourth brigade, entirely composed of francs-tireurs, did not, on that day, count more than 400 or 500 men, the total number of all the different bodies of francs-tireurs amounting to about 2000. In all, therefore, we had not more than 5000 men.

Neither the first nor the second brigade took part in the fighting at Lantenay, November 26, 1870. The first, having been the day before engaged in the direction of Fleury, had, in consequence of that defeat, retired towards Pont de Pany. The second was on the march, and only arrived at Lantenay on the 27th.

Ravelli's regiment of the third brigade, composed of Italians, was also absent in the neighbourhood of the Ouche.

CHAPTER II.

FIGHTS AT LANTENAY AND AUTUN.

OUR line of battle at the edge of the wood, on the plateau of Lantenay, was almost entirely concealed from the enemy, who could only distinguish Lhost's francs-tireurs on our extreme right. This was perhaps the reason why they sent a battalion to occupy the village of Pâques, near our left, while their main body occupied Prenois, and could be seen in order of battle on the heights of that village. The battalion sent to Pâques would have been taken prisoners, had we only had a hundred horse. Pâques being occupied by the enemy, I sent forward two of our cannon, supported by some lines of sharpshooters, who, with a few shots, drove the enemy from the village.

The Prussians, while this was happening, had made a great display of their force, drawing it up ostentatiously on the commanding heights of Prenois. Their battalion, however, precipitately retired, and they gave it the scant support of a few guns, without advancing the splendid line which they kept in reserve.

"Then they are not in great force!"—so I reasoned with myself. "Are they not coming?" I said again. "Well, we must go to find them."

I resolved, therefore, to attack, and we marched resolutely on the enemy in the same order in which we had been awaiting them in our positions.

Our francs-tireurs on the right bravely charged the enemy's left, and threatened to throw it into confusion. The third brigade advanced in perfect order, with its lines of riflemen in front, followed by columns of battalions, in close enough order to arouse the envy of veterans.

I was proud of commanding such men, and felt no small pleasure in contemplating so fine an army on an unobstructed field, and such courage on the part of my young comrades.

The enemy's artillery, stationed on the heights of Prenois, poured such a hail upon our advancing lines as only Prussian guns can, yet I did not perceive the slightest hesitation—the lines never wavered for a moment; in short, our men behaved admirably.

The energy, firmness, and cool bravery of the republicans shook the impassive intrepidity of the proud victors of Sédan, and when they saw that we did not fear their shells, but advanced steadfastly and swiftly to the charge, they began their retreat on Dijon.

The road leading up to Prenois on the side where we attacked it, which turns to the left on entering the village, has a zigzag course, as the place is situated on a hill. Our men, in charging the village, where there still remained a battalion of the enemy, did not perceive this winding of the road, or else did not pay any attention to it, and, marching quickly in a direct line on the houses, were brought up short by the high wall of an orchard close to the village, which they only passed with much difficulty and loss of time.

A single company flanked the village on the right, to protect our few horsemen, and together they charged a Prussian reserve battalion which had remained behind with two guns to protect their retreat. Colonel Canzio and Commander Bondet, both of whom had their horses killed—indeed, we lost the greater part of our horses—distinguished themselves in this charge. I am sorry I cannot remember the name of the captain of the infantry company who took part in it, and also behaved splendidly.

The high wall met with by our men charging in front, which caused them such loss of time, and another, not so high, which stood in the way of our flank attack on the right, saved the enemy. But for these walls, a Prussian battalion and two guns would assuredly have fallen into our hands.

The fight of November 26, on the plateau of Lantenay, was nothing much so far as results are concerned, but as regards the behaviour of our soldiers when face to face with the trained warriors of Prussia, it was brilliant.

After the engagement on the plateau, the enemy offered no further resistance, continuing their retreat towards Dijon; and we pursued them as far as that city.

It was, I confess, a rash act to attack Werder's corps, entrenched as it was in the capital of Burgundy, with about 5000 men, and very little artillery; and certainly I would not have attempted so formidable an enterprise by day. But such was the plan that had been conceived—a *coup de main.* And we had been so fortunate during the day; while, on the other hand, only a desperate *coup de main* could restore the fortunes of the unhappy Republic in that part of France, and perhaps oblige the enemy to raise the siege of Paris, by threatening his chief line of communication. But what sort of means had the Defensive Government put into my hands? I shudder to think of it.

The spirit of my poor soldiers was unbounded, and all marched to the attack on the city with admirable pluck. It was great presumption to hope for victory, yet, on a rainy November night, there is time enough to retire in case of failure. I have already seen numerous and well-trained troops seized with panic, and, judging by what I afterwards heard from the inhabitants of Dijon themselves, there was on that night a good deal of confusion among the conquerors of Bonaparte. The numerous artillery hurried aimlessly hither and thither over the country, and ended by not being posted anywhere.

The baggage department of Werder's army corps, though much better regulated than the French, did not fail to enter on a hurried retreat, some to save the military chest, others the ammunition, others on other pretexts. The fact is, there was great confusion. However, to the honour of the Germans be it said, the numerous infantry corps stationed at Dijon, écheloned themselves in the strong positions of Talant, Fontaine, Hauteville, and Daix, and received us with such a hail of bullets as I have never seen equalled; something more than intrepidity was wanted to face such a tempest.

My young soldiers did their duty as well as any men could under such circumstances. The Prussian outposts were assailed one after another, and destroyed in spite of an obstinate defence. In the morning, the corpses of our men were found piled up on those of the enemy, the greater part of the latter pierced with bayonets, as I had issued orders not to fire.

In the thick of the hornets' nest, just under Talant, the Prussian fire became too heavy for us, and we began to fall back to right and left of the high-road, to escape the direct shots which ploughed it up in a horrible way.

Our assault on the Dijon positions began about 7 p.m. It was very dark and rainy, and the circumstances, therefore, favourable to this kind of undertaking; and till two o'clock I had great confidence in our success. Our men marched briskly, and as close as possible one behind the other—a system which I think is always preferable in night-attacks, unless it is possible to send skirmishing-parties to other points in order to divert the enemy's attention. This was impossible to me, considering the small number of our forces and the nature of the ground.

About 10 p.m., the leaders of the vanguard sent me word that it was useless to persist in the attack, as the enemy's resistance was something frightful, and it was impossible to make our men—who were gaining the country on either side of the road—advance any further. I reluctantly yielded to the representations of my faithful friends, and at once began to think of the unfavourable and repugnant circumstances of defeat. Fortunately it was night, and November. The enemy did not move from their position, and we were able to execute our retreat undisturbed.

A retreat after a victorious conflict and an unsuccessful attack—that is, after having been on one's feet from morning till 10 p.m.—could not, by untrained troops such as those under my command, be executed in good order, especially as they had been all day without food. Hence the order to retreat on Lantenay, which was immediately carried out. Some took the road by Soubernon and Arnay-le-Duc, never stopping till they reached Autun; but the greater number remained at Lantenay, and, a regiment of Gardes Mobiles, with Ravelli's and the greater part of the second brigade, having already reached that point, we found ourselves still numerous enough to do something.

On the afternoon of November 27, the Prussians reached the heights of Lantenay, in more considerable numbers than on the preceding day, which proves that they were very numerous at Dijon, and that Werder, having repulsed us from that capital, naturally wished to follow up his advantage. The first shock of the enemy's charge was sustained by the new corps, those who had fought through the preceding day being tired out.

The Prussian forces, however, being strong, and the retreat through the woods easy, no serious engagement took place, and we continued our retreat towards Autun, where we hoped to collect our scattered troops.

Among our losses in the affair of the 27th was one very deeply felt, that of Commandant Chapeau, of Marseilles, a gallant and excellent officer.

In certain cases, one must treat men as one would treat bullocks. If they break loose, one must let them run at their own sweet will. Woe to the man who commits the imprudence of crossing their path ; he will be overthrown, horse and rider, as happened to me at Velletri in 1849, where it was only a miracle that I escaped with my life, and black and blue at that. Break loose ? Let them break loose, run away, dash themselves headlong—don't trouble your head about them ; content yourself with taking your place on one side or in the rear. They will find some obstacle ; they will be stopped by a river, a mountain, by hunger, by thirst, or by a new terror, nearer or greater than the first. Then is your time. Get your human animals into order again as best you can ; try to give them food, drink, and repose ; and when they are refreshed, rested, and their spirits raised once more, they will remember a shameful flight, duty trampled underfoot, and glory ! The worst of all human follies !

The same thing happens with bullocks, except that those brutes, fortunately for us, do not think of glory. Guided by several horsemen, bullocks are easily frightened by anything and everything—a thunderclap,

a flash of lightning, a gust of wind—and begin to run
as only wild beasts can. The leader, if he is a sensible
man, is not such a fool as to tell his men to stop them
by getting in their way, which would be certain death.
But he follows them, in flank or rear, without losing
sight of them, till some obstacle or other comes in the
way of the fugitives—a river, a wood, a mountain; then
the front ranks stop and turn, and all the rest stop and
turn also. At this point the skilled leader orders his
horsemen to surround the herd, once more quiet as
lambs, and thus the brutes are once more brought under
the dominion of their tyrant, Man—though I do not
know whether, after all, he is really much better than
they.

Nearly all the retreating corps of the so-called army
of the Vosges concentrated themselves at Autun, with
the exception of a few which, for various reasons,
retired to a greater distance. Some of these were entire
corps, some isolated individuals—scattered, most certainly, because they had no desire to fight. Among
these last was a Colonel Chenet, commander of the
eastern guerrillas, whom the priests have placed among
the holy martyrs, like St. Domenico Arbuès, and similar
scoundrels; and they would have made a still greater
martyr of him, if I had allowed the sentence of death
pronounced by the Autun court-martial to be executed.
Chenet had been guilty of a military crime—cowardice
—which deserves death a hundred times over. At
midday, he was to have been shot, and I reprieved him
about 11 a.m., at the intercession of some officers—on

condition, however, of public degradation, which I should consider worse than death.

At Autun, my favourite head-quarters—where the prefect, Marnis, had received us with right goodwill, and helped us in our organization—we reformed the army of the Vosges, and were reinforced with additional cannon, of which we stood so much in need.

On December 1, however, the enemy, emboldened by our retreat, sought us in our positions at Autun, and came in sight unexpectedly. I say unexpectedly, and I may even say, without exaggeration, that they surprised us. It was about noon, and I had gone out to reconnoitre as usual. Every morning, mounted scouts were sent out in all directions, and all our posts on the side nearest the enemy occupied by strong detachments. I had already visited these advanced posts early in the morning, had assured myself of their existence, and had advised the officers in charge of them to keep watch with the most scrupulous care. They were occupied by the eastern guerrillas, commanded by Chenet; the Marseillais guerrillas—who reached the convent of St. Martin, the centre of our outposts, just as I was leaving it—commanded, after Chapeau's death, by a brave officer whose name I do not remember; and, lastly, the battalion of the Basses-Pyrénées, on the left, in the convent of St. Jean. The outposts on the right were stationed in another convent, St. Pierre (save the mark!). During my midday drive, though I thought all our outposts well guarded, I did not fail to direct my telescope, from the ruins of a Roman temple which commands Autun; and to which I had climbed, to the surrounding plains. But it would seem that my observations were made at too great a distance, for I saw nothing. Not discovering anything from the site to which I had descended to make further observations, I returned to the carriage, and my staff were, as usual, kindly assisting me to get into it—indeed, I had one foot on the step—when, casting my eyes on Autun, I perceived, in the lower part of the city, in the Bourg St. Martin, the head of a Prussian column slowly advancing. Had it continued to advance, the city of Autun would assuredly have fallen an easy prey to the Prussians; and the army of the Vosges—I blush to remember it—would have sustained one of the most tremendous defeats ever known.

"Ride," I said to the mounted officers of my staff—"ride as fast as you can to Bordone, to Menotti, to every one; tell them to take their arms and fight!" I was more upset by shame and vexation than by alarm. My orders being issued, the carriage ascended with all haste to Autun, traversed the city, and made as swiftly as possible for the small seminary where our artillery was stationed, on the platform of this clerical establishment—in a position, fortunately, to command the enemy's column.

Our artillery was at that time composed of two field-batteries, of four rifled guns each, and one mountain-battery—in all eighteen pieces; but no gunners were on the spot. Canzio and Basso mounted the first gun; these gallant aides of mine, one at each wheel, had soon pointed it. They were presently helped by the rest of my staff, who came up in succession, and, at last, by the respective gunners, who came rushing out of their quarters, and behaved admirably.

It was our good luck that the enemy did not discover the state of surprise we were in, and probably—on account of the silent and deserted condition of the place—suspected some ambuscade. If, instead of the head of the column stopping at St. Martin, they had at once entered Autun, they would assuredly have met with no resistance, and would have surprised our men in their quarters. Instead of this, they planted their artillery on the heights of St. Martin, and began to shell our position.

This arrangement of theirs was our safety. Our eighteen guns, concentrated in a position which commanded that of the enemy, and enthusiastically served by our young gunners, full of mortification at having been surprised, overwhelmed the enemy with projectiles, and obliged them. after several hours' fighting, to withdraw their artillery.

Several companies of francs-tireurs, and some battalions of mobiles, thrown out against the Prussian left flank, completed the success of the day, and the enemy were forced to retreat.

The losses we felt most were those among the artillery, both officers and privates, and the greatest of all I can remember was that of Major Guido Vizzardo, who was wounded in the thigh, and had to have it amputated.

The francs-tireurs behaved with their usual gallantry.

The two Italian regiments were kept in reserve inside the city, and few men belonging to them took part in the action, except the Genoese carbineers, who marched in the centre, and had a great share in causing the enemy's retreat.

The three advanced positions which were to cover our small army, but did not succeed in doing so at Autun, were St. Martin in the centre, St. Jean on the left, and St. Pierre on the right. (In France, too, the number of saints is no joke; they seem, as with us in Italy, of little use for purposes of national defence.) St. Jean was garrisoned with a battalion of mobiles from the Basses-Pyrénées belonging to the third brigade a body of men who had all Menotti's sympathy and mine, and, though always worthy of it, were especially so on this occasion, when they behaved most gallantly, and inspired the enemy with some respect.

Several detachments of Mobiles were also posted at St. Pierre. In the centre, however, the strong position of St. Martin was abandoned by the eastern and Marseilles guerrillas, about 700 men, through a cowardly order from Colonel Chenet. This desertion, it seems, took place before the arrival of the enemy, so that the latter could occupy this important post quite at their leisure. If this was not treason on the part of the colonel above mentioned, I do not know what else to call it. However that may be, and whatever excuses he may find for himself, with the assistance of the French clerical party, the conduct of this officer, who without orders abandoned our most important position, thus exposing the army to the risk of destruction, and the city to that of plunder, dragged along with him the corps which he commanded, and another which yielded to his insinuations through the inexperience of the officers, and fled to a distance of forty or fifty kilomètres,—his conduct, I repeat, is something for which no name will serve, something which I never remember even to have heard of in all my military life—a kind of guilt for which there is no adequate punishment. And this Colonel Chenet, whom I was sufficiently weak to save from the death to which the court-martial had doomed him—this dastard became the chief hero of the priesthood and the *chauvinerie*, among whom he only just fell short of being canonized ; while the reactionary journals issued laudatory biographies of him, and indulged in the most exaggerated panegyrics of the basest action in the world. Such is the civilization of this age, whose foundation rests on corruption and falsehood.

I do not wish to end this chapter without mentioning young Vizetelly, the brave and sympathetic correspondent of the *Daily News*. He was not fighting the Prussians, his mission was entirely different, yet he rendered me the greatest services as staff-officer during the time I was fortunate enough to have him in my company. At the fight of Lantenay, I was several hours on horseback, and, having no charger of my own, took the first that was offered me. This poor animal, at the very beginning of the battle—from what cause I do not know—slipped with all four feet, and fell with me, lying across my right leg in a way to cause me great pain. Thanks to the exertions of the friends who surrounded me, I was soon extricated, and Vizetelly, who was beside me, kindly offered me an excellent white horse of his own, which I accepted, and rode for the rest of the day.

Marais, sous-préfet of Autun, is another man whose name the Italians of the Vosges army will remember with love and gratitude. That honest republican welcomed us on our arrival at Autun with the greatest kindness and sympathy, which never failed during our stay in that city. On December 1, when we were attacked by the Prussians, Sous-Préfet Marais laid aside his office, and presented himself, with his rifle, in the front rank of the combatants, firing away like any private soldier.

CHAPTER III.

JANUARY 21–23, 1871.

THE victory of Autun raised the courage of our young soldiers, which had been somewhat shaken, and those Prussians who had repulsed us at Dijon were in their turn repulsed by us and driven back in disorder.

One fresh corps, and that not a large one, would have sufficed to hasten the enemy's retreat, and force them, at least, to leave behind the guns and a large number of prisoners. I sought them in vain. But what we could not do was accomplished by General Cremer, who, being in the neighbourhood of Beaune, with some thousands of good troops, crossed the mountains from Beaune to Bligny, and, attacking the enemy in flank near Vendenesse, completely routed them.

The greatest part of December was passed at Autun in organizing new corps, with a little more artillery and a few squadrons of cavalry; always in expectation of the cloaks which the rigour of the season rendered indispensable, not to speak of other articles of clothing, and better rifles to replace the wretched worn-out ones we were armed with.

The affair at Autun also increased the prestige of

our small corps; we were overwhelmed with the bless-
ings of the inhabitants, saved by that victory, who vied
with each other in sending warm woollen garments for
the soldiers, and sums of money for our wounded.

At Autun, we served to cover two flank movements—
that of General Crousat, from Chagny to Orleans; and
that of the great army of the Loire towards the east,
commanded by General Bourbaky. The country, being
covered with snow and ice, made these movements not
only difficult, but murderous for men and horses.
In consequence of Bourbaky's movement, the Prussians
evacuated Dijon, which we occupied with some companies of francs-tireurs; indeed, we should have done so
with our whole force at once, if all the trains on the
railway had not been engaged in the service of that
general.

About the end of December and the beginning of
January, the weather had become exceedingly cold;
the snow had hardened into ice, and transport was
very difficult, especially for cannon and cavalry. The
enemy, with well-trained troops, equipped at all points,
with the prestige of victory, and the insolence of the
victorious soldier in a foreign country, who thought
nothing, not only of despoiling the poor inhabitants of
all their provisions and furniture, but of driving them
out of their beds in order to take possession themselves,
had great advantages over the inexperienced French
soldiers, newly recruited, and in want of the most
absolute necessaries.

General Bourbaky's movement, however good in idea,

was, for the above-named reasons and many others, difficult to execute, particularly in the miserably disorganized state of the intelligence department.

A cavalry general of Bourbaky's army, who visited me while passing through Autun with his division, assured me that the army was in a very deplorable state. He said to me, " I can get my horses to march a few kilomètres, but they are certainly not fit for fighting, and are getting worse every day." The same was the case with the horses of the artillery and baggage train, and with the men in every branch of the service, so that, even then, disaster might have been confidently predicted for the army of the Loire.

That fresh and numerous army, with another fortnight of organization and rest, having once got over the terrible time of the January frosts, might have revived the hopes of exhausted and prostrate France. Instead of this, it was literally thrown away, and wasted in the most atrocious way.

I was aware of Manteuffel's movement, parallel with that of Bourbaky, in order to reinforce Werder and the besiegers of Belfort; and I would certainly have done my best, in accordance with the desire of the Government, to arrest his march by a flank movement. Heaven knows what grief it was to me to be unable to carry out this operation, which would so greatly have assisted the army of the East.

I made the attempt once, and marched out of Dijon, with the main strength of my troops, to attack the enemy at Is-sur-Till, leaving General Pellissier with

15,000 mobilized Gardes Nationales in command of the city; but I was induced, by the strong Prussian columns which I found confronting me, to resume my first position. Notwithstanding this, two of my four brigades, the second and the fourth, operated on the enemy's communications, conjointly with all the franc-tireur companies.

Having resolved to defend Dijon, my first care was to continue the defensive works already begun by the Prussians and by General Pellissier.

The positions of Talant and Fontaine, two kilomètres west of the city, which overlook the main road to Paris, and are, at the same time, the most conspicuous and important, were the first to have some flying works placed on the top of them, two field-batteries of twelve guns and two of four being stationed at Talant, and at Fontaine, one field-battery of four rifled guns and one mountain-battery of the same calibre.

Several batteries of twelve guns, which the Government had successively sent to General Pellissier, were placed in other works thrown up at Montmuzard, Montchappé, Bellair, and in all the most conspicuous positions in the neighbourhood of Dijon, in order to keep the enemy's fire at a distance from the city in case of an attack, which was expected from day to day.

Dame Fortune is paramount in war, and we were truly favoured by her, the enemy having, on January 21, attacked us in the west—or, one may say, taken the bull by the horns.

As we had carefully studied the ground on that side

which had strong positions, protected by walls and banks for lines of sharpshooters to right and left of the high-road, with thirty-six guns stationed on the commanding heights of Talant and Fontaine, the success of our defence was brilliant. And a vigorous defence was needed, for the formidable column marching on us from Paris might well be called a column of steel. Our thirty-six pieces enfilading the road, and several thousands of our bravest men spread out behind shelter, were scarcely enough to check it. The attack on the west being ascertained, we concentrated a strong force on that side, without having to lay bare the northern and eastern sides of the circuit of defence, where I always expected the principal attack to take place, with only a feigned attack on the west. My expectations were not fulfilled ; the attack, fortunately for us, was made on the west, and on that side only, though with simultaneous attacks of flanking corps on the enemy's left, towards Hauteville and Daix, and on his right, towards Plombières, in the valley of the Ouche. The attack was a formidable one. I had never faced better soldiers than I saw before me that day. The column marching on our central position showed admirable valour and coolness. They came up, compact as a rain-cloud, not quickly, but with a uniformity, an order, and a calmness, which were perfectly terrible.

This column, raked by all our enfilading artillery, and by all the lines of infantry in advance of Talant and Fontaine parallel to the road, left the field covered with corpses, and, re-forming several times in depressions of the ground, resumed their forward march in the same calm and orderly way as before. They were famous soldiers.

Our men also showed great valour that day, and were quite worthy of their assailants. For one moment only they were disconcerted by a terrible flank attack on our right in the direction of Daix, which cost us a good many gallant fellows. The enemy being driven back into the cemetery of the village, our men were seen climbing over the wall, and clinging to the Prussian bayonets, to drag them out of the men's hands. On our left, on the other hand, the enemy was hemmed in by strong lines of sharpshooters posted at right angles to our main line, so that their right was nearly cut off from Plombières.

The Prussian right was also attacked with musketry-fire by the forces of Colonel Pelletier and Braun's francs-tireurs, who, descending from Bellair into the valley of the Ouche, compelled them to make a hasty retreat.

Thus the battle raged from morning till sunset, with the greatest possible fury on both sides, and without a marked advantage on either. On the north, we still kept the positions we had held during the day, and the Prussians still retained theirs.

But here a thing happened which I have often noticed on similar occasions, where new troops have been in conflict with a veteran army. The latter remain under arms; the former, under pretext of hunger and thirst, of fetching ammunition, or anything else, try to leave their posts and go to refresh themselves, or talk over the glories of the day. And this is apt to occur more especially in the vicinity of a town. I therefore take this opportunity of pointing out to my young countrymen—as I shall never cease to do— the necessity for the greatest endurance and perseverance in fighting.*

With nightfall, our soldiers, who could very well have held the positions so valiantly defended during the day, retired towards the city under one pretext and another, and crowded together on the road beneath Talant, forming such a confusion that orders could neither be given nor received, and no man could hear another speak. Descending from Talant, where I had been during the whole time of the fight, I found myself involved in a throng so dense that I could not control my horse, and was pushed about so brutally as to be very nearly thrown head over heels, horse and all.

The enemy, on the other hand, more astute, and better inured to warfare, having reconnoitred our advanced posts and found them vacant, marched forward, and poured a tremendous volley into us while we were in the confusion above described. Fortunately, as we were in a depression of the ground, there was a distinct rise between the enemy and us, so that their bullets nearly all passed over our heads.

* Two armies in America had fought bravely all day; with nightfall both of them left the battle-field. One of the two generals found this out, returned to the field, and proclaimed himself the victor.

The retreat of our outposts, and the enemy's advance, made the night a wretched one for me, and it was not improved by subsequent occurrences.

At 11 p.m., I was stretched out, dead tired, on my bed in the Dijon préfecture, when a committee, consisting of General Pellissier and the mayor of the city, with part of the municipal council and the magistracy, waited on me to tell me the enemy were within our lines, in possession of Talant, and perhaps of Fontaine; and that a Prussian colonel had signified, on behalf of the commander-in-chief, to a magistrate there present, that if Dijon did not capitulate at dawn, the city would be bombarded.

At sixty-four, when one has seen a little of the world, one is not so easily made a fool of, and I perceived at once that this was merely an idle boast on the part of the hostile general, tempted to rodomontade by the astonishing victories of the Prussian arms. Yet this intelligence, communicated to me by men able to speak with authority, was not to be despised—especially as the magistrate who brought me the information had gone in search of his son—who, he feared, was wounded—to the battle-field, and thus met the Prussian colonel. My rest was therefore at an end, and, giving orders to have the horses put to at once, I made all possible arrangements for sending out scouts and verifying the truth of the report.

The roads were frozen hard, and it was snowing; for an invalid like myself, it was no light undertaking to go the round of the outposts. But it was the only thing to be done. How could we remain indoors after receiving such news, with the men tired out, and in presence of so brave and enterprising an enemy?

After having spent several hours in arranging a detachment of our best troops to form a nucleus, and given orders for every one to be ready for battle before daylight, I started in the early hours of the morning for Montchappé, the first of our positions in the direction of the enemy, where were two twelve-pounders, protected by a battalion of mobilized National Guards. I found nothing new at that point, but all in good order.

I then went on to Fontaine, and finally to Talant, where we found no trace of the enemy. The threat of bombardment had been sheer bravado on the part of the enemy; and not only were we *not* bombarded by them on the 22nd, but towards evening we were fortunate enough, after once more fighting all day, to drive them from the positions occupied on the previous evening, and put them to flight.

Perseverance and endurance to the end in battle— this is one of the keys of victory! But the men are weary and cry, "We are worn out and starving!" Very well, go to seek food and rest; the enemy will advance, eat the food you have prepared, and give you the rest you want with the butt-end of their rifles. Perseverance, endurance, and, above all, watchfulness— of this last you can never have enough. How many generals one knows at the present day, who think that their rank will excuse them from being present in the immediate neighbourhood of a battle; who content

themselves with receiving information, and giving orders
to their subordinate officers, at a distance !   A mistake !
The supreme commander ought, without needlessly exposing himself, to remain as near as he can to the centre
or objective point of the battle-field, and if possible
on a height, so as to overlook a larger extent
of country, and more effectually hasten the despatch
of orders and receipt of information.   Moreover, the
view of operations obtained in person by the man who
is to direct them, is worth far more than any information.

The 22nd of January, 1871, proved that, if we were
tired out by the fight on the previous day, the Prussians
were still more tired and unhinged than we.   Brave and
intrepid as they had been on the first day, so also they
were on the second ; but they did not hold out so well,
which made me hope that on the 23rd we should have
time to rest from the fatigues of the two preceding days.

On January 22nd, we lost, among others, an officer of
great merit—Lhost, commander of the united francs-
tireurs, a corps composed of over 800 men, who had
greatly contributed to the enemy's discomfiture on the
preceding day by a vigorous attack on their right flank,
and had a great share in the victory of the 22nd.   His
place as commander of that gallant corps was supplied
by Lieut.-Colonel Baghino, an officer of great promise.

The avalanche of Prussians—to use the expression of
an excellent officer of mine—was so great that it
threatened to bury us, even on the 23rd.

About the middle of the day, they threatened an
attack on Fontaine, and sent some battalions thither to

make a feint of attacking, but almost immediately afterwards appeared in dense columns on the Langres road, with other columns flanking them to the east, at St. Apollinaire, towards Montmuzard.

The attack on the Langres road was formidable, and worthy of the terrible army confronting us. Nearly all our corps wavered, except the fourth brigade, which maintained itself in a manufactory of artificial manure—fortunately surrounded by a wall, in which they had made loopholes—to the left of the road. Several hundred men of the third brigade, which was in course of formation, and had been decimated in the fight of the 21st, after sustaining the shock of the Prussian onset in an adjacent building further back from the road, also joined the fourth.

Through the retreat of our right wing, these corps were for a time hemmed in by the enemy, who had placed their artillery on a hill overlooking Pouilly and Dijon, to the north. Firing with the skill and precision to which they had already accustomed us, they in a short time silenced all the guns of our centre, both on the road and on either side of it. We could reply only with a few shots from our two guns at Montmuzard, the two at Montchappé, and two others. These last, when we saw the impossibility of keeping them in their first position under the fire of the Prussian artillery, were placed on a road to the right of the main one, and forming an acute angle with it.

Towards the north our situation was critical, and the Prussians, being masters of the field, threatened an attack on the city. We tried to post our retreating corps in the rear, near the enclosure already mentioned, which had several serviceable walls, some of them pierced with loopholes. Certain cowards, who had deserted their posts in fear, or wished to place their money in safety, had already raised the alarm in the town, and spread panic everywhere by demanding trains at the railway station, to take them to a place of safety.

Our extreme left, consisting principally of the third brigade, and posted at Talant and Fontaine, in view of the retreat of the centre, had pushed forward its francs-tireurs on the enemy's right, and was resolutely march-ing to their support. About dusk, a few corps of mobilisés on our right, throwing themselves energetic-ally forward on Pouilly (the principal objective of the battle-field), repulsed the enemy from the ground they had gained, and drove them back a long way beyond the castle.* In this way, the fourth brigade, to whom the chief credit of the battle is due, were freed from the storm-cloud of foes which had for a time enveloped them, and even succeeded—in a hand-to-hand fight, while repulsing the repeated attacks of the sixty-first Prussian regiment—in taking their colours, which had been left buried under a heap of slain.

I have seen more than one murderous fight in my time, but certainly not often looked on so great a number of corpses piled up in a small space, as I saw in the position to the north of the building I spoke of

---

* The Castle of Pouilly, within cannon-shot of Dijon, had been abandoned by our men at the beginning of the battle.

before, occupied by the fourth brigade and part of the
fifth. When I speak of the fourth and fifth brigades being
opposed to a Prussian regiment, it must not be opposed
that they were complete brigades, but nuclei of brigades
in course of formation, containing, the fourth about 1000
men, the fifth less than 300.

During the early hours of the night, the enemy were
in full retreat, and for several days left us quiet at
Dijon, evacuating also the surrounding villages, which
we immediately occupied.

The greater number of our francs-tireurs, after bearing
a worthy part in the three days' battle, were again
thrown out in all directions, towards the enemy's
communications, between Soubernon, Dôle, and other
places. The second brigade, separated several days
before from the main body, was fighting splendidly to
northward, in the environs of Langres.

I cannot bring my narrative of the glorious battle of
Dijon to a close without making mention of my dear
friend and valiant comrade, General Bossack. This
Polish hero sent me word on the morning of January
21 that, as there was a report that the Prussians were
approaching from Val Suzon, he was himself going to
reconnoitre. He advanced, at the head of a few men,
to make his observations and ascertain the number of
the enemy. But, urged on by his indomitable courage,
and wishing to assure himself with his own eyes of all
that was necessary, so as to give me an exact account,
he ventured so near the Prussian vanguard that he was
involved in a skirmish, and, disdaining to fly, fell a

victim to his bravery. I heard nothing of him for many days, and it was thought that he had been left wounded in some peasant's house.

The loss we had sustained, however, was known among the staff, who kept it from me, with a delicate consideration, as long as they could.

I trust—nay, I am certain—that when France shall have a better government, the State will adopt the orphans of the gallant Bossack, who died for her.

CHAPTER IV.

RETREAT—BORDEAUX—CAPRERA, 1871.

THE news of the armistice, and afterwards that of the capitulation of Paris, and finally of Bourbaky's emigration to Switzerland, completely changed the aspect of affairs, and a kind of panic and uncertainty seized upon the people, who had hoped for an improvement in the condition of France consequent upon the advantages we had gained. With the majority the effect was a favourable one, looking, as they did, for the approaching end of that terrible war.

As I had always found it the case in Italy when once the war was drawing to a close, the Defensive Government became very liberal as regards supplies of every kind, and reinforcements to every branch of the service.

Our little army, by the addition of some 15,000 men of Pellissier's mobilisés, now amounted to about 40,000. However, the enemy, now that Paris was off their hands, and the army of the east had passed into Switzerland, began to collect an imposing force to act against us, and, in spite of all the defensive works thrown up by us, and the late increase in our numbers, would have ended by scattering or surrounding us, as they had surrounded the French armies at Metz, Sédan, and Paris.

The Prussians, with the prestige gained by victory, were naturally expected to act in a high-handed manner; and accordingly, while the armistice was being kept in Paris, and all over France, it was not valid for us.

Besides, in a delimitation which was said to traverse Burgundy, the neutral ground between the enemy's lines and our own, was very ill-defined, and, in any case, we were driven out of Dijon and all the positions we had hitherto occupied, and thrown back towards the the south.

Flushed with success, the enemy grew more and more insolent, as they received fresh reinforcements—which they did every day. Under different pretexts, they several times tried to surround our men on out-post duty and make them prisoners, but without success, as they had to deal with men who did not trust them. By order of the Bordeaux Government, we were to make our own arrangements with the Prussians, as to the armistice and delimitations; and General Bordone, my chief of staff, paid several visits to the enemy's camp on this errand. But, as I have already stated, the result of his mission was, that there was to be no armistice for us.

From January 23 to February 1, we held out as best we could, in the capital of Burgundy, and in all our positions, against the encroachments of the enemy. After the lessons received in the three days' fight, they certainly understood that a small force was not enough to produce any effect on us, and quietly collected a very large one, so that towards the end of January, their columns occupied our front in force, and were beginning to extend far enough to surround our flanks. Manteuffel's army, now that it was free of ours of the east, was descending towards the Rhone valley and threatening our line of retreat.

On January 31, the fighting began on our left in the early morning, and went on till late at night. The enemy tried us on various points, taking up positions outside Dijon for a general attack. Some Prussian corps showed themselves in the valley of the Saône, threatening to take our right in the rear.

There was no time to be lost. We were the last mouthful that tempted the greed of the great army which had conquered France, and no doubt wished to make us pay for the temerity of having for one moment contested its victory.

The retreat was ordered in three columns. The fourth brigade (commanded, after Bossack's death, by Canzio), to which the fifth was added, was to descend in a direction parallel with the Lyons railway, guarding the heavy artillery and all our supplies, which were being transported in waggons. The third brigade, under Menotti, set out along the Ouche valley towards Autun. The fourth marched for Verdun, by St. Jean de Losne, along the right bank of the Saône.

The staff left by rail, and the head-quarters were fixed at Chagny, a central point for collecting the army, while several other corps and companies of francs-tireurs detached from the brigades repaired likewise to the new base of operations. All was executed in the best possible order, thanks to the activity of the chief of staff, of Colonel Olivier, commander-general of artillery, and of all the leaders of the corps, without our being molested by the enemy, and with less confusion than one might have expected from raw troops on a night-retreat.

The retreat took place during the night of January 31, and the enemy occupied Dijon about 8 a.m. on February 1.

From Chagny, our head-quarters were transferred to Châlons-sur-Saône, and thence to Courcelles, where a castle in the neighbourhood of the town was utilized for the purpose.

The capitulation of Paris being an accomplished fact, and the armistice transformed into preliminaries of peace, I decided, as they had elected me deputy to the Bordeaux Assembly, to repair to that city on February 8, with the sole object of giving my vote in the service of the unhappy Republic. I left Menotti provisionally in command of the army.

Every one knows how I was received by the majority of deputies to the Assembly. Certain that I could do no more for the unhappy country I had come to serve, I resolved to go to Marseilles, and thence to Caprera, where I arrived on February 16, 1871.

The army of the Vosgés, composed of elements too republican for the taste of Thiers' government, naturally came in for the antipathy of the latter, and was disbanded.

APPENDIX.

Civita Vecchia, July 15, 1875.

THE battle of Custoza, the plan of which is now before me, resembles all other ancient and modern battles won by genius being on one side. From Epaminondas, at Leuctra and Mantineia, to the Prussian generals in 1870, it has always been incontestable that the oblique order is the proper one; and when employed, it has always resulted in victory.

At Rosbach, Frederick II., by massing his forces, and by the swiftness of his manœuvring, took the French army in flank and utterly routed it.

At Mantua, Napoleon I., hearing that the Austrians were marching down, one column on either shore of Lake Garda, in order to defeat the two hostile corps separately, left his heavy artillery behind, marched with his entire army, and threw its full weight against one wing.

In America, Paz, knowing that Echague had his men drawn up in battle array behind a *cappão* (clump of trees), presented a parallel line to the enemy, with orders, however to withdraw the rear ranks from the right, and reinforce the left. In this way, Echague's left found on the enemy's right only a few cavalry squadrons, who retreated at a gallop. Meanwhile Paz's left, reinforced by the best troops, defeated Echague's right, and thus obtained a splendid victory.

It grieves me to have to utter a panegyric on an

Austrian general, yet nevertheless, for the edification of our young men, who will perhaps have once more to engage in combat with foreign soldiers, I must relate the truth.

The Archduke Albert was the true and only general at the battle of Custoza. Taking advantage of the blunder we had been guilty of, in crossing the Mincio on our most extended line, between Mantua and Peschiera, he made a feint of attacking our right and centre, and, massing his three army-corps on our left, routed Durando's corps (which stood alone there) with the 80,000 men under his command.

Our centre and right, drawn off by some feigned cavalry charges, did not hear of the defeat of our left till too late; and, in consequence of the mistakes made from the very beginning of the campaign, six or seven splendid divisions had to retire, biting their lips with vexation because they could not fight.

I say, "mistakes made from the very beginning of the campaign;" and, indeed, such was the case. Why was the army divided into two—a blunder condemned in all ages? Perhaps to please the brilliant General Cialdini, to whom it was a matter of repugnance to obey General Lamarmora, the chief of staff? Why was not one division enough to threaten the passage of the Po, without employing on that service 90,000 of the best troops, who were of no use except to give a shameful appearance of retreat to the action of our gallant army?

I speak of our gallant army with pride. It is a real pain and grief to me that we should have lost those splendid generals — Govone, Bixio, Cugia, Sirtori, who achieved so much that day, at the head of our brave soldiers. Through them, if they had been decently supported, that battle-field would have been made glorious with hymns of triumph.

Young Officers—you who may yet perhaps have to face

powerful enemies on the battle-field. These are the blunders committed on our side : Cucchiari's whole corps, consisting of three divisions, and Bixio's division, with Prince Humbert's, Pianell's, and Cosenz's—seven divisions in all—took no part in the battle, while the enemy's three army-corps were fighting with our left, and shattering it to pieces. All this was owing to the Austrian general's sagacity. Besides the seven divisions which took no part in the engagement, more than thirty batteries of the reserve remained inactive, and withdrew from the field without firing a shot.

If employed in time, all these untouched forces would have been quite enough by themselves completely to disperse an enemy necessarily shaken and demoralized by a day's fighting.

END OF VOL. II.